USA TODAY BEST SELLING AUTHOR
KRISTEN PAINTER

BOOK FIVE

HER FIRST TASTE OF FIRE

To anyone who ever wished they could fly. Or eat unlimited amounts of chocolate.

HER FIRST TASTE OF FIRE
Shadowvale, Book Five

Copyright © 2021 Kristen Painter

All rights reserved. No part of this book may be reproduced in any form or by any electronic or mechanical means, including information storage and retrieval systems—except in the case of brief quotations embodied in critical articles or reviews—without permission in writing from the author.

This book is a work of fiction. The characters, events, and places portrayed in this book are products of the author's imagination and are either fictitious or are used fictitiously. Any similarity to real person, living or dead, is purely coincidental and not intended by the author.
ISBN: 978-1-941695-69-2

Published in the United States of America

Shadowvale isn't typical small town America. The sun never shines, the gates decide who enters, magic abounds, and every resident bears some kind of curse.

Most people think Nasha Black lives in Shadowvale because that's where her father, one of the Four Horsemen of the Apocalypse, lives. But Nasha has another reason for staying in Shadowvale and it's not just the bakery she owns and operates. She has a devastating curse of her own. One she's never told a soul about.

Shadowvale has given chocolatier and dragon-shifter Charlie Ashborne a refuge from the reality of his cursed life. Until now. He's been summoned to the dragon census, where all unmated dragons will be paired off. If he doesn't show, the dragon council will come to him. His desire to protect Shadowvale means not only will he end up with a wife he doesn't want, but the curse he's kept hidden for so long will be exposed.

Facing certain humiliation, Charlie is about to leave for the census when an attractive woman shows up at his house, desperate for more of the chocolates Charlie sells in his shop. Nasha needs to know what magic he puts in his chocolate. She's never tasted anything like it, literally, and it's changed her life. Discovering he's headed out of town pushes her to make a crazy offer. She'll pretend to be his wife in exchange for his recipe. Seems fair enough.

Making a pact with a chocolate addict might not be the right move, but Charlie will do anything to avoid the dragon census mating games, so he jumps at the chance to claim Nasha as his wife for a week.

It seems like the perfect plan, until they find out the rules have changed, leaving them no choice but to compete in the games. Unexpectedly, they begin to fall for each other, amazed by what a good team they make. But as competitors try to tear them apart Charlie and Nasha wonder if they will ever taste sweet victory, or just the bitter dregs of defeat?

CHAPTER ONE

Nasha Black flipped on the lights in her bakery at exactly four A.M., just like she did every morning. The faint but familiar scents of flour, sugar, vanilla, chocolate, and coffee greeted her with the warmth of old friends.

Those scents were all that kept her going sometimes. They encouraged her. Told her she was working with wonderful ingredients. Reminded her that these were the flavors that made people happy.

Sure, she followed her recipes, too. That was a given. An ironclad rule, actually. In fact, she clung to those tried and tested equations, never deviating, never straying by a pinch or a dash or a dollop. Doing anything else would be foolish.

She went to a rack on the far wall, took down a clean apron, and slipped it on over her black T-shirt and black-and-white checkered print leggings. Then she began to gather her supplies and ingredients for the morning's work.

Bread was first. Loaves of white, wheat topped with oats, and a real customer favorite, pumpernickel raisin.

Then she'd move on to muffins, three kinds today. Lemon crumb, apple streusel, and cranberry white chocolate chip. Once those were in the oven, she'd start on the pies. Blueberry, chocolate silk, apple, pumpkin, and blackberry.

Hmm. Blackberry sounded particularly good today. She'd make that the pie of the day. Even if it had been the pie of the day yesterday.

Cakes would be next. Today, she'd keep it simple. Vanilla buttercream, chocolate buttercream, and carrot. Or maybe a spice cake. She hadn't quite decided that yet. She'd do enough batter to make both nine-inch cakes and several dozen cupcakes with each flavor.

Finally, she'd finish up with a few trays of brownies and some cookies. M&M, sugar, and molasses. Although, she'd been thinking about making some fruit and custard tarts, lately, too.

As she dug into the work, she glanced over at the notice board by the entrance to the retail part of the shop.

There were no special-order forms tacked up there, but that didn't mean someone might not come in having just remembered they needed a cake for an occasion. It happened sometimes. And when it did, she made sure to do everything she could to fulfill their order in the time allotted. She was able to work with supernatural speed, so it was very rare that she had to turn down a request.

She hated having to say no to a customer. Black Horse Bakery was her life, and baking was her outlet.

It was also her way of giving back to the world, a way of balancing out the damage her father did because of his work.

Her First Taste Of Fire

Wasn't his fault. It was just his job as one of the Four Horsemen of the Apocalypse. He was Famine. And if he didn't do the job, someone else would take his place. Someone who might not be as prudent.

Another Horseman might spread hurt and hunger like wildflowers, without the care and compassion and utter heartbreak she saw in her father. He was a good man, regardless of what some people thought.

Sometimes, she liked to think of herself as Abundance, feeding people delicious things to counteract the work he had no choice but to do.

Because everything at her bakery was free. All people had to do was come in and ask for what they wanted.

To be completely honest, the delicious part was based on what she was told. She knew her creations looked good – she worked hard at making them as appealing as they could be. She also knew how wonderful they smelled.

But despite all of Nasha's work, the actual flavors she produced remained a mystery. To her, buttercream was smooth, but nothing else. Cookies were soft and crumbly, but that was it. Fruit pies? Flaky and sticky. Bread? Chewy and dense. Cake? Light and spongy.

Even the premium coffee she served in her shop only came off as wet and hot, although she adored the aroma and the kick of caffeine.

The truth of all that was her deepest, darkest secret and no one, except for her father, knew what that secret was.

She was sure other citizens wondered what kept her in Shadowvale. After all, nearly everyone in this town was cursed in some way. But as far as anyone knew, she was here because of her father. She'd never told another soul that she was just as troubled as they were. Never hinted that she suffered on a daily basis, too. Never implied that she belonged here just as much as anyone else in this hidden-away, perpetually overcast town.

Because she did. But if the truth got out, she feared it would make her a laughingstock. Or worse, mean the end of her bakery.

The awful truth was that she, Nasha Black, owner of the most popular bakery in town, had never tasted *anything* in her life.

Neither had her father or her grandfather or her great-great grandmother. The curse had been passed down, apparently, straight through the line of those who'd served as Famine. Was it a sign that she was destined to take her father's place? It certainly seemed that way.

Would that be such a bad thing? She really wasn't sure.

Elbows deep in dough, she glanced at the time. She'd been working for almost two hours. Her two bakery employees, Clara and Brighton, would be in soon. Then things would really fly.

Emeranth Greer, Nasha's most recent hire, would arrive at eight. Em was the new barista and mostly handled the coffee side of things. No baking for her, just coffee and serving customers.

Coffee was the only thing in the shop that cost money, but no one had yet to complain about that. She'd done it because there was another coffee shop in town, Deja Brew, and giving away free coffee wouldn't be fair to them. Nasha was a big fan of fairness. There wasn't enough of it in the world, if you asked her.

The vampires in town, who were primarily from Louisiana, favored the flavor of chicory in their coffee, so she'd made sure to offer that variety as well.

So far, coffee sales were doing well, and the bakery continued to do a brisk business.

For the sake of her employees, Em included, she'd recently added a tip jar. Nasha paid her people well, but there was no reason they couldn't earn a little more if customers were so inclined.

Nasha put a tray of pies into the oven and started cracking eggs for the cakes she was making next. Money wasn't a driving factor for her, obviously. Her father's position came with more than the two of them could spend.

Granted, he had few expenses, outside of Domino, his horse. That creature lived like a prince.

Nasha smiled. She loved Domino, his fearsome appearance and ability to snort flames aside. He was really just a fluffy ball of horsey goo inside. Maybe she'd go visit him when she got home.

She lived on her father's estate, but not in his house.

Her place had once been the guest house, but she'd lived there so long neither of them thought of it as anything *but* her place. She'd added a lot of her own touches, including a garage.

She got the cakes into another oven, then started whipping up a few batches of buttercream. As she worked, some of the vanilla icing splattered on her hand.

She stared at it. Just once, she'd like to know exactly what it tasted like. She knew in theory, of course. Sweet and rich with the high-grade vanilla paste she used.

But what did that mean? What did vanilla taste like? She imagined it would be similar to its scent. Sort of balmy and floral and lightly caramel, because of its color, but maybe that wasn't what it was like at all.

Vanilla sold better than any other flavor, but chocolate was a close second. Chocolate was something she wondered about even more. After all, there were movies about the stuff. It was *Willy Wonka and the Chocolate Factory*, wasn't it?

Chocolate had to be magical. No one made movies about vanilla.

She wiped her hands on her apron and went back to mixing.

Clara and Brighton came in not long after.

Clara, short for Claraphina, was a tall, statuesque brunette with the kind of hair that belonged in shampoo commercials, even with the strands of silver that were starting to show. She was an Amazonian warrior, but had been injured in battle and moved to Shadowvale to heal and start over. She'd never spoken of that injury in detail, and Nasha had never asked, but she assumed Clara's injury was essentially her curse.

Not talking about curses was an unwritten rule in Shadowvale, and everyone respected it.

Brighton was tall, too, but reed-thin and much younger. He had a shock of dark red hair and a smattering of freckles that spoke to his pixie blood. He'd been born with malformed wings, unable to fly, and had been ostracized from his clan.

Nasha thought that was a crime. She adored his wide smile and eager attitude. And he adored Clara, although she pretended not to notice. He was always coming up with new recipe ideas, but Nasha had never given him the go-ahead on any of them. How could she? Wasn't like she could taste them and see if they were good.

She hated that.

Clara was first in. She stashed her things on the shelf by the door, then put her apron on. "Morning, Nasha. Where would you like me to start?" She always asked that when she arrived. That was the soldier in her, wanting to make sure she was exactly on task.

"Morning. Bread's about ready to come out." That was always Nasha's answer, but she appreciated that Clara never deviated from the routine. Something about it gave Nasha comfort.

Brighton showed up next, parking his bike at the back of the shop. He hung his jacket on a peg, then slipped into his apron. "Morning, ladies. How are you both today?"

Clara gave him a nod. "Fine."

"I'm good," Nasha responded. "How are you?"

"Just grand," Brighton answered. "I've been thinking about chocolate macadamia nut bars with toffee bits. How does that combo sound?"

Nasha smiled. She wished she knew. "Sounds interesting. Do you think you could check on those cupcakes? They should be just about done and ready to go in the fridge."

He nodded, although his eyes followed Clara. "On it."

By the time Em arrived, the display cases were full of the morning's efforts and Nasha was about to unlock the front door.

Em had a funny look in her eyes, though. And she was holding her hands oddly behind her back. "Hey, there."

"Hey," Nasha said. "What's going on with you this morning? You're up to something, I can just sense it."

Em laughed. "Maybe just a little." She pulled a tall box from behind her and thrust it at Nasha. "For you."

Nasha took the box. It was heavy pressed stock in a deep dusky blue with cranberry trim and, on one side, a gold foil emblem in the shape of a stylized dragon. "What is this?"

"Open it and see," Em said.

Nasha could already smell something sweet, but she hoped it was perfume. The box was weighty enough. She wriggled the top off and saw crinkled cellophane and a bit of cranberry ribbon. She knew instantly it wasn't perfume. Taking hold of the cellophane, she lifted the item out.

Her mouth came open at the sight of what was inside. "A chocolate egg. This has to be from that shop, The Chocolate Dragon."

About the size of an elongated softball, the egg was molded to look like it had scales, delicately colored in shades of red and gold with decorator's luster dust. It shimmered, changing color as she turned it. On the front, a small, embossed heart sat in the middle of the scales.

Inside the box, tucked into the corners, were a small wooden mallet and chisel. Presumably for cracking into the egg.

"Yep." Em nodded, eyes bright, smile wide. "Deacon got me one a couple weeks ago and it was so amazing, I wanted to get you one, too. I've never had better chocolate in my life. And I've been trying to find a way to say thank you for all that you've done for me. This job has been everything to me, you know?"

Nasha was touched. It was rare that anyone gave her a gift. And while it was true that she'd begun selling coffee in her shop just so Emeranth could have a job, the move had benefitted the bakery as well. "You didn't have to do that. I know you appreciate the job."

Em shrugged. "I just wanted to really show you how thankful I am. And how much I love this job. That's why I got the Ruby egg with the heart. There are more chocolates inside, too."

"That was very kind of you. Thank you."

"You're welcome." Then Em leaned in. "Now close that box up and take it home where you don't have to share."

Nasha laughed. "All right." She was happy to close up the box and put the amazing confection away so she could stop thinking about how she wasn't going to be able to enjoy Em's touching gift. "I can't wait to try it after dinner."

What was one more lie on top of the one she was already living?

Chapter Two

Charlie Ashborne frowned at the sealed scroll he'd received. It was the third one in three months. He hadn't opened any of them, but he also knew he could no longer ignore them, even if he knew what message was inside. He'd already started to prepare, even though all he wanted was to be left alone. Unfortunately, the official stamp embossing the wax seal might as well have been a neon warning sign.

One that had no Off switch.

With a long, frustrated sigh, he cracked the seal on the latest message and unfurled the scroll. Of course, he already knew what it said.

The annual census was about to take place. Attendance for any unmated dragon of a certain age was mandatory.

That was him. He was of a certain age. And unmated. A status he was perfectly intent on keeping.

He read farther. And frowned deeper.

Maintaining his bachelorhood was about to become impossible. The census had always been one of the main ways dragons found mates. Not only was it required that the unmatched attend, but with the games they participated in at the census, connections were made and partners were found.

As he read, he saw that the games would be used differently this year. As a means of matching more dragons up. There would be no avoiding being paired up at the census. There was mention of the preservation of their species.

Utter nonsense. The dragon race was in no danger of dying out.

He tossed the scroll aside. It skittered across his work bench as it rolled in on itself. He ignored it and went back to his chocolate work. He was carving a new mold for a new egg. One he planned to pour in white chocolate and accent with touches of silver dust and deep blue. He just didn't have a name for it yet.

That would come in time.

Except now he was being called away, which meant he'd have to put his project on hold until he returned. And he wouldn't be coming home alone.

His new mate had better like chocolate.

He frowned again. Blasted census. If he was anyone else, skipping the event would only earn him a mild reprimand. Maybe a slight fine.

But he'd be dealt with much more severely. He was expected to behave a certain way. And had been all his life. That deferential treatment was a big part of the reason why he'd separated himself away from his people in Shadowvale.

That and his curse.

He rolled his eyes and went back to his work. He really wanted to finish this mold before he left in the morning. Because he had no choice. He *had* to go to the census.

As much as he'd hoped to escape his life and his destiny by moving to Shadowvale, the truth was, if he didn't go, the council would eventually come to him.

And having a thunder of angry dragons descend on Shadowvale would cause all kinds of problems for this town that had sheltered him for so many years. No one here deserved that. Not when many of them had come here to be left alone, too.

Better that he go. The exposure of his curse was inevitable. He'd accept whatever fate that brought him, deal with the fallout as best he could, then return to Shadowvale and live out his life hidden away from the scorn and ridicule that most certainly awaited him.

Even if that meant returning with a wife who didn't necessarily want to move here. Maybe she would warm to the idea of a life of seclusion after she realized her new husband was damaged goods, despite his status.

Whoever they paired him with was going to be miserable, which meant his life would probably be miserable, too. Might as well be miserable in a place he liked.

A place where he actually had some friends who weren't dragon-shifters and didn't care that he was about to embarrass his entire race when the truth came out.

He glanced over at a pot of chocolate he was tempering, checking the temperature readout. It needed to be warmed up a bit. Then, once it was tempered, he'd pour it into a large block mold for future use.

First, he had to raise that readout by a few degrees. He went into a half-shift, feeling the bones of his face change and the movement of muscles and sinew within his body. His senses adjusted, sharpening with great precision. Here and there, patches of skin hardened into scales. But most importantly, heat built in his chest and throat. Heat that would become fire.

A moment later, he locked onto his target — the base of the copper pot holding the chocolate — and breathed a narrow stream of fire across the room.

The briefest thought went through his brain that maybe the curse would be gone this time. It was the same thought he had every time he used his powers. It had never come true.

He directed the swathe of heat across the pot, careful not to scorch the delicate substance within. Eyes on the thermometer, he extinguished the fire as soon as the temp began to rise, knowing just how much carryover there would be.

The jingle of the bell over his shop door told him he had a customer. He quickly shifted back to his full human form and got up. As he did, the soft clink of something hitting the floor sounded on his right side.

He glanced down to see proof of his curse lying there in plain view. Blue-violet and glistening with iridescence, the scale was beautiful against the pristine white tile of the back room. But the scale shouldn't have come off.

That wasn't something that was supposed to happen. It *didn't* happen to any other dragon that he knew of.

Just him. Because that was the curse he lived under. Breathe fire, lose a scale.

Be vulnerable until that scale grew back.

He sighed and scooped up the leaf-sized shell of dragonskin, depositing it in the drawer of his workbench with the rest of them, then went out to greet the customer.

He didn't have time to think about his curse more than he already had. There was no reason to. There was no answer in any book he'd ever read about why it happened or how to fix it or what was causing it. Not even a mention that it had ever occurred to any other dragon in history.

He smiled at the man in his shop. Not someone he recognized, although his circle of friends was small. A newcomer? The town didn't get that many of those. "Welcome to The Chocolate Dragon. Anything I can help you with?"

The man pulled his gaze from the display cases to answer. "Everything looks amazing. Do you make all of these?"

"I do." Charlie was proud of his work. He might not be curing cancer or working on world peace, but chocolate made people happy. And he liked to think his was especially good. Beautiful, too.

The man shook his head as he gazed at all the selections. "I'm not sure where to start. But I'd like to get a present for the woman in my life. I love surprising her with little gifts."

"Very nice." Since the man had said "little", Charlie gestured toward the smallest eggs at the front of the case. There were only a few eggs in each size, since he'd stopped making new ones in anticipation of being away at the census. "Are there any flavor combinations that she likes? All of the eggs you see are filled with a selection of handmade chocolates, but I can fill them with a custom assortment if you like."

"Theo loves sweets. I don't think she'd be unhappy with any of these." The man stuck his hand out. "I'm Robin Gallow, by the way."

The Goblin King. Charlie knew of him, but had never met or seen the man. Rumor was he never left his castle. Clearly wrong. That's what came of believing rumors. "Nice to meet you, Robin. I'm Charlie."

Robin grinned. "I know who you are. I've heard a lot about your shop and these incredible eggs."

Charlie laughed softly. "Then I must confess, I know who you are, too."

Robin's expression turned slightly melancholy. "You're probably surprised to see me."

That caught Charlie off guard. "I…"

"It's okay, I know the rumors. That I never left my house. That I was a recluse. They were true, too. Although I did leave my house a little, but not in a way that allowed me to be truly social. All because of a curse I was under. Thankfully, that was broken by a remarkable woman. A woman I fell in love with." He smiled brightly again. "That's why I'm here. Because I can't thank her enough for what she did for me."

"I can imagine," Charlie said. He really could. But there was no one, male or female, human or dragon or otherwise, who could break his curse. He shut all that unpleasantness away and focused on Robin, gesturing to the green and gold egg that was first in the case. It shimmered with purple iridescence. "How about the Emerald? The chocolates inside are a mix of creams and jellies, all berry flavors."

"That sounds good. And she'll love the look of it." Robin pointed. "I'll take the biggest one. How do you open it, by the way? Just smash it? Seems a shame to do that to something that looks more like art than food."

"Well, in case cracking it against something hard doesn't seem like enough of a ceremony, each egg comes with a wooden mallet and chisel to help with the process."

"Outstanding." Robin pulled out his wallet. "She's going to get a kick out of this."

Charlie packaged the egg in a wooden crate, standard for the large sizes, then rung Robin up and put the crate into a large shopping bag. "If anything isn't to your satisfaction, just let me know when I get back. I am about to be out of town for almost a week. That's why the cases look a little bare. I haven't been adding any new stock."

Robin laughed. "I can't imagine how it won't be to

Theo's satisfaction. It's chocolate filled with more chocolate."

Charlie shrugged good-naturedly. "You never know. Thanks for coming in. Please stop by again sometime."

Robin lifted the bag as he backed out the door. "I have a feeling we might become regular customers. Have a good evening."

"You, too." Charlie watched Robin head off down the street. The Goblin King, right here in Shadowvale.

Not that surprising, he thought. He wasn't exactly Joe Average Dragon himself. Of course, no one knew who he really was.

Just like no one in the dragon community knew what an embarrassment he was about to become.

Chapter Three

One of the great things about owning a bakery, besides how happy Nasha's products made people, was how early the shop closed.

Since she started work at 4 A.M., no one expected her to be open late. In fact, Nasha had recently started leaving around two instead of staying until the end of the day, letting her employees close up. That usually happened a few hours after she left. Sometimes she left sooner, depending on how depleted the day's stock was. No point in hanging around if the shelves were nearly bare.

It wasn't unusual to be completely sold out by two in the afternoon, especially with the lunch rush that often came in. Lots of people stopped in for dessert, or to get something to take home to their families for after dinner. The blackberry pies were especially popular.

There was always a little prep and cleaning to do for the next day, so that gave them another hour of work or so.

Today, however, Nasha was feeling particularly sorry for herself. The darker-than-usual clouds didn't help.

With her mood being what it was, she'd left as the lunch crowd started to peter out.

She drove straight home, put her purse and Em's egg on the steps into her house where they'd be protected if the rain started, then went directly to the stables and Domino. Even though he wasn't her horse, she'd grown up with the supernatural creature and thought of him as hers as much as her father's. She was the only person, outside of her dad, who was allowed to ride Domino. That lifetime relationship was the reason she wasn't afraid of him, either.

Even Falstaff, her father's groom, kept a safe distance from the creature when he could.

To Nasha, the enormous animal with the sleek black hide, eyes that sometimes glowed red, and the ability to snort fire and smoke from his nostrils was the same giant goofball that rolled around on his back when spring was in the air and liked to headbutt her for sugar cubes. She found it completely endearing that he never acted that way for anyone else.

For all that was dark and dangerous about him, she found comfort in his company.

He whiffled at her as she approached, bringing a smile to her face. "Hiya, Domino. Yes, I have treats for you. Would I come see you and not bring you something sweet?"

She fished a couple of sugar cubes out of her pocket and offered them to him on her palm.

He found them immediately, his velvety lips soft on

her skin. She patted his nose, then stroked her hand down his face. "How are you, big boy? Did you have a nice day?"

Done with his sugar, he blew air out of his nostrils with a soft whinny that sounded like an affirmative answer to her.

"Did Falstaff brush you?"

He nodded, then tipped his head to see her better.

With one hand on the side of his muzzle, she kissed his face, inhaling the smell of him, a combination of horse and smoke. "I'm glad you had a good day. Mine wasn't so hot."

She leaned her forehead into him. "Just feeling sorry for myself today, that's all. You know how it is."

He snorted again, as if confirming he did.

Domino's gentleness almost made her feel worse. She sucked in a ragged breath, realizing she was on the verge of a big cry, something she hadn't done in ages. Something she honestly never wanted to do again.

It was silly being that pathetic. It made her feel weak. She didn't like that. She was, in layman's terms, heir to the throne of Famine. Granted, not exactly the kind of throne most people aspired to succeed to, but there was no denying it was her destiny. She ought to live up to it with the right kind of attitude.

Her father didn't sit around and cry and feel sorry for himself.

She dug out a few more sugar cubes and put them on her palm. Domino took them without a fuss, gobbling them down. She stared up at the fearsome steed. "Don't tell anyone how pathetic I am, okay?"

He snorted. She took that as his agreement.

"Maybe later we'll go for a ride. If Dad doesn't need you."

She loved to ride at night through the Enchanted Forest. It wasn't really that dark at night due to all the phosphorescent mosses that grew on the trees, but it was a place most avoided, herself included. Unless she was on Domino's back. He was built from that kind of dark, sinister magic and when she was with him, she had nothing to fear.

To be honest, the Four Horsemen had been born from that same brand of menacing magic, which meant she had it in her veins, too. She could probably walk through the Enchanted Forest at night by herself and have nothing to worry about.

Why had that never occurred to her until now? Funny how life made sense in bits and pieces instead of all at once.

Something about having a kinship with the Enchanted Forest made her feel a little tougher. Less like she needed to curl up into a ball and cry. She needed to own that tough feeling more often. Maybe not when customers were around. Nor should she mention she found the Enchanted Forest to be her safe space.

In general, the citizens of Shadowvale didn't regard the Enchanted Forest as an empowering kind of place, which she understood.

Maybe if she could remember who she was more often, she wouldn't feel sorry for herself the way she had been lately.

Domino shook his head, snuffling at her and nudging her with his nose.

"That's enough sugar for now, you big goof." She patted his side as she smiled up at him. "Thanks for listening. See you later."

She walked back to her house, picked up her purse and the dragon's egg off the steps, and went in. Her stomach growled, a sure sign that she needed to eat, but she never really felt hungry. Hard to when nothing had any taste.

Wasn't like she ever got cravings, either. How could she? How could she crave a certain food when it was just as bland and boring as the next thing?

She tossed her purse on the table in the foyer, then went through to the kitchen. Her standard meal, as boring as it might appear to an outsider, was a nutrient-dense, high-calorie, high-protein shake.

She added ice cream to boost the calories and make it cold. Her twice-daily milkshake could have been well-chilled wallpaper paste for all it appealed to her. It was merely meant to keep her body fueled.

Before she made her shake, however, she took the chocolate egg out of its box and set it on the side table next to the couch where she sat to watch TV. She left the cellophane on it, to protect the egg. It was a beautiful object and she wanted to be able to see it, even if she had no intention of eating it.

At least that way she could enjoy it in her own way.

She took a shower, rinsing off the day, put on her favorite cashmere lounge pants and long-sleeve top, and went back to the kitchen to make her shake.

The house seemed quiet once she turned off the blender. It wasn't often that silence bothered her, but tonight it did. Tonight, the quiet only made the nonsense in her head louder.

She ought to get a pet. She'd thought about it before. She certainly had time for one. But that wasn't going to do her any good tonight.

She took her shake into the living room, turned on the television, and looked for a show to distract herself with. She found a new series on one of the streaming services, *My Five-Star Life*, a show about a woman who'd grown up poor, made a name for herself as a social media influencer, and was now using her fame and fortune to expand her horizons.

Twenty minutes into the show, Nasha realized the whole thing was just meant to bring this incredibly shallow woman more fame and fortune.

She started surfing around again, looking for something less annoying. She found a season of a baking contest show she hadn't seen yet and settled in to watch that. If nothing else, she might learn a new recipe.

Although if she did, she knew very well she'd never try it. There was too much potential for an untested recipe to go wrong, and then people would question why she'd thought such a thing worthy of being sold in the shop.

Still, the show was interesting enough. Nasha sipped her shake, trying to get it down before it became lukewarm.

Despite her interest in the baking competition, her gaze kept shifting back to the egg. There was no question that it was beautiful. As someone who knew the intricacies of decorating edible things, she appreciated the time and effort that had gone into all of that work.

But the longer she looked at it while drinking her tasteless, pasty shake, the more her feelings of resentment and self-pity returned.

How unfair was it that she couldn't taste that egg? She knew she ought to count her blessings that she had such an amazing life. In the grand scheme of things, not being able to taste anything was pretty minimal.

But in the moment, that was cold comfort.

She downed the last of her shake and grabbed the egg, untying the ribbon that held the cellophane closed.

As soon as she opened the bag, the incredible aroma of chocolate rose up to greet her. Dark and rich, it made her mouth water as she took the egg out of the cellophane. The egg was weighty and as she turned it in her hands, she could feel the movement of the smaller chocolates inside. She inhaled again. Was that gorgeous smell what chocolate tasted like? It was something she'd wondered about all her life.

At every Christmas when chocolate goodies seemed to fill all of her schoolmates' lunch boxes. At every Halloween when her friends would boast about their hauls. She had one, too, but found no joy in treats that had no flavor. At birthday parties and other special events, she was always left wondering about the decadent cake or brownies or cookies or ice cream that she just couldn't enjoy like everyone else.

Even in her own bakery, she faced the stuff on a daily basis.

She breathed in more of the dark, luscious scent, eyes closed. The past was a hard thing to fight. All those years of feeling left out tore at her soul like hungry little demons determined to leave their scars on her. She sniffed and a tear slipped down her cheek.

She was truly pathetic. And she no longer cared. If she wanted to be sad and miserable in the privacy of her own home, then why not? She'd never carry on like this where anyone could see her.

She didn't even want her father to know, because he'd only blame himself and he had enough to deal with as a Horseman.

Taking Domino out for a ride was sounding better and better. A deep, shuddering breath left her as she pushed to her feet, setting the egg back on the table as she did so.

But she misjudged the distance and the egg landed on the edge, toppled over, and fell to the hardwood, shattering into large and small fragments and sending the

Her First Taste Of Fire

contents across the floor. The chocolates inside were just as beautiful as the egg had been.

What a waste.

"Blast it," she muttered. She bent to pick up the pieces, feeling impossibly worse than she had just a second ago. She sniffed as she collected the shards and the whole chocolates, trying to stack them in her hand.

The more she worked, the more of a mess it became. The chocolate was melting against the warmth of her skin.

She carried the first handful into the kitchen and dumped it onto the counter. The loss of the gorgeous egg only added to her miserable state. Another tear slipped out, running down her cheek to the edge of her mouth.

Tears were supposed to be salty. All she tasted was wet.

She wiped it away with her chocolate-smudged hands, then licked her lips.

She hesitated as something *new* filled her mouth. *What was that?*

But she knew exactly what it was. Flavor. She'd *tasted* something. The breath stuck in her throat. How was that possible? No idea. But there it was, something faintly sweet and smoky and dark and delicious and creamy and so many things she didn't have words for.

It had to be chocolate.

She ran to the mirror in the living room

A dark smudge crossed the corner of her mouth and extended to her cheek. She felt faint as she stared at her own face. Her tongue darted out to find the smudge again. More sweet and dark and smoky and creamy and—

She spun around, looking at the remaining shards of egg on the floor. She scooped up a piece and shoved it into her mouth, desperate to understand what was happening.

The flavors exploded over her tongue in full force as the chocolate melted.

New tears came, tears that had nothing to do with feeling pathetic and everything to do with joy.

She didn't know how this was possible, but she didn't care. She could *taste*. She knelt beside the bits of egg and individual chocolates and began to try each one. Dark chocolate and milk chocolate. Both so very different.

She couldn't get enough even when her teeth began to ache with the sweetness.

Abruptly, she stopped and ran back to the kitchen, her fingers sticky. She hauled the tub of ice cream out of the freezer and stuck a spoon into it, scooping up a big chunk. She'd bought blackberry for no particular reason other than she liked to vary the flavors she chose just for appearance's sake.

She took a bite of the purple-streaked stuff and frowned. Nothing but cold. She waited a moment, but that didn't change.

She glanced at the pile of chocolate on her counter. Was that all she could taste? If that was true, then the remains of the egg weren't enough.

Her First Taste Of Fire

She stuck a piece in her mouth. The flavors of chocolate returned. With sudden desperation, she realized she had to have more. She wiped her hands on a towel, then grabbed her purse.

Her only thought was that she needed to go back to town and visit this chocolate shop herself. Although would that raise suspicions? The bakery and the chocolate shop weren't exactly rivals. They sold very different things.

Would people think she was there for nefarious reasons? She shook her head in exasperation and sighed. She was making herself crazy over what was probably nothing, she knew that.

But she'd been judged before because of who her father was. When she'd opened her bakery, she couldn't get anyone to step foot inside, thinking her goods were somehow tainted with bad magic. As if eating something Famine's daughter had baked might bring darkness upon themselves.

Best if she went as incognito as possible to the chocolate shop, bought a few samples to try, and got out.

Best for whoever owned the chocolate shop, because they didn't deserve to be tainted by her family's curse.

Chapter Four

Charlie spent some time reorganizing the display cases so the lack of product wasn't as obvious, then went back to work on his new egg mold. Half an hour into it, he wondered if he should close up early. There wasn't much product left to sell.

Besides that, he needed to pack and get himself mentally prepared for what awaited him at the census. Was there really a way to prepare yourself for what could only be the biggest embarrassment of your life? He thought not.

The bell above his shop door jangled, causing him to glance up as a woman entered his shop. He was happy for the customer's arrival. Anything he could sell would mean fewer chocolates that would sit in the cases while he was gone.

He put his tools down and went to greet her.

Oddly, she didn't exactly look like she wanted to be greeted. She seemed tentative about being in the shop, like she might bolt at any moment. She wore a big, oversized jacket and she'd covered most of her face with a ball cap and large, dark sunglasses. Not that unusual, he supposed, except they lived in a town that was perpetually overcast and today was darker than usual with the threat of rain.

It didn't matter. He honestly didn't care if a customer came in wearing a Batman mask. Shadowvale was supposed to be a safe haven for all. Some felt the safest when they were isolated. If this was what she needed to do, then so be it.

That was her right. And he wasn't about to make life harder for anyone. Especially not a customer. And especially not when he'd come here to be left alone, too.

He gave her a brief greeting. "Afternoon. If there's anything I can help you with, just let me know."

She glanced at him, quickly, like she didn't want to make eye contact. Nothing she needed to worry about wearing those dark glasses. He couldn't see her eyes anyway. "Just some chocolates, please."

"Sure. Do you know how much you'd like? A half pound? A pound? Or just a couple?" He gestured to the display boxes on top of the main case to show her what sizes were available.

She pointed at the very last one. "That one, I think."

Two pounds. That would deplete his stock pretty well. He took a box from under the counter. "Good choice. What flavors would you like?"

She went back to staring at the chocolates in the case. "Can you just make up an assortment?"

"Absolutely. Happy to." He started filling the box.

While he did that, she wandered over to where the chocolate eggs were. "I'd like one of these small gold eggs, a small blue one, and one of the small green. Unless you have a small red one?"

"No, sorry, I'm out of the small Rubys at the moment."

"Is there a better choice? Which one is the best one?"

He laughed. "That's like asking a father to select his favorite child. I think they're all the best one. It really comes down to what flavors you like the most."

She frowned and muttered something under her breath that sounded very much like, "If only I knew."

That didn't make a lot of sense to him, but he didn't question it. Maybe these weren't for her, and she was buying them for someone else. He put the last chocolate into the box, then closed the lid and set it on the counter. "Three small eggs, then? The Gold, the Sapphire, and the Emerald?"

She nodded, giving him a quick look. "Yes, thank you."

"Would you like them gift-wrapped?"

"No, that's not necessary."

Maybe they *were* for her. That was a lot of chocolate for one person. He wasn't judging, only curious. And impressed. He knew there were chocolate addicts in town. He'd just thought he'd met them all. He packaged everything up as beautifully as if it was all being given as gifts anyway, then filled a large shopping bag with her items.

She was still looking at the chocolate eggs, so he hesitated before ringing up the total. "Anything else for you?"

"No, that will be it. You make all of this chocolate yourself?"

"I do. The chocolate is my own blend, I create all the molds I use, and I decorate everything myself."

"That's a lot of work. Beautiful work, too. That takes time."

It did, but not a lot of people recognized that. He smiled even as he shrugged. "I enjoy it. That makes it a lot less work."

She nodded, and for the first time since she'd come in, her mouth bent in a hint of a smile. He couldn't see much of her face, but the angles of it were captivating. "I understand that."

He rang up her purchases and gave her the total. Not a small bill, either. She'd purchased quite a lot.

She gave him cash, which disappointed him. He'd been looking forward to finding out her name on a credit card. There was something about her that intrigued him, and not just because she seemed to be trying to hide.

From her slender build to the graceful slope of her neck and the curve of her cheekbones, there was an elegance about her. Some might say she was too thin, but to him all of her angles made her look lean and strong. Like a dancer, maybe.

And now that she was closer, he could smell the faintest hint of smoke about her. To a dragon-shifter, that was nearly an aphrodisiac.

He handed her change back, his fingertips brushing

the palm of her hand. "I hope you find everything to your satisfaction."

She stuffed the change into the pocket of her loose jacket, then grabbed the handles of the shopping bag as she stepped away from the counter. Her long black ponytail swung free as she turned. "I'm sure it'll be fine."

He was about to tell that if it wasn't, she was welcome to return anything she didn't like, but she was halfway to the door and seemed intent on getting out as fast as she could.

He let her go without another word, just watched her and wondered what darkness drove her. Because in that brief moment that they'd connected, he had definitely sensed a grimness within her. Whatever curse possessed her soul, it weighed heavy on her.

Such an odd thing to think. Everyone's curse weighed heavy on them. That's why so many of the cursed were here. But she seemed to be in the throes of a battle.

Whatever it was, he hoped she won.

~

Nasha thought she'd bought too much, but as she spread out the chocolates on her kitchen table, it seemed like barely enough. One box of chocolates, granted a good-sized one, but still only one box. And three eggs, roughly each the size of a child's football. Thankfully, they also held chocolates.

Even so, this wasn't going to last her very long. Not

Her First Taste Of Fire

that it would be such a hardship to visit The Chocolate Dragon again. Or the handsome man who'd waited on her.

Of course, making a second visit hinged on her being able to taste this chocolate. If that first time had been a fluke, then she'd just bought herself a lifetime supply of chocolate, because she wouldn't be eating any of this.

It smelled just as wonderful as the egg she'd gotten from Em, so Nasha's hopes were high. Not too high, though. She'd known more than her share of disappointment in life and that had taught her to keep her expectations low when it came to most things.

Still, she'd tasted this chocolate once. It had to happen again, didn't it?

She opened the box of chocolates. They were so pretty. Not only was the man who'd waited on her handsome, he also had a very artistic eye. She definitely appreciated food that looked good.

The blackberry creams were speckled with purple and gold. The strawberry jellies had streaks of red dotted with tiny black spots. The mint bombs had tiny swirls of green and white decorating their smooth tops.

They were all beautiful. But looking at them was getting her nowhere. She picked up what could be a cappuccino cream, based on how the very pale milk chocolate was sprinkled with what looked like instant coffee granules.

She sniffed it. The chocolate smell was strong. So was

the aroma of coffee. Would she be able taste the coffee, too? That would be something.

There was no point in putting it off anymore. She bit the cappuccino cream in half. Instantly, the taste of chocolate spread over her tongue, this time accompanied by another strong flavor that had to be coffee.

Coffee *and* chocolate. She almost wept. How was this possible? She cared, but not enough to stop eating the bounty before her.

She devoured the chocolates, trying to savor them but losing that battle as the joy of finally tasting her food overwhelmed her. She cracked the eggs against the tabletop, eager to get to the chocolates inside them.

She ate until her teeth ached from the sugar and her stomach protested, but the flavors on her tongue were impossible to ignore. She was helpless to stop stuffing herself, until at last, delirious with sugar and happiness, she wandered out to the couch, a large piece of chocolate egg in hand, and passed out.

She dreamed that everything had turned into chocolate. The town, the streets, her house, her bakery, even Domino. All of it decorated in edible colors and metallic flecks like the chocolates from the shop. It was a glorious dream, much better than her recurring nightmare of being at a buffet that only served glasses of her standard protein shake.

She woke up and squinted at the time on the wall clock. Almost 3 A.M., which was a few minutes earlier than when she normally woke up. Close enough.

Her First Taste Of Fire

She also didn't normally sleep on the couch, but last night hadn't been a normal night by any stretch of the imagination. It had been far better.

She got up and went into the kitchen. Brown paper chocolate cups and little shards of chocolate eggs covered the kitchen table.

She picked up a small piece and popped it into her mouth, immediately smiled at the taste. She gathered up the empty chocolate cups to throw them away. As she did, she knew two things for certain.

She had to have more chocolate. A lot more. An endless supply of the stuff.

And the only way to do that was to get her hands on the recipe.

CHAPTER FIVE

Charlie tired of tossing and turning, finally getting up to make himself some breakfast and face the reality that his life would soon never be the same. In a matter of hours, he'd be headed to the census.

Once there, his curse would end up being revealed and after that…he really didn't know what would happen after that. Would he be ostracized? Shunned? Or simply made the butt of every joke from here on out?

Hard to say. Maybe all three. And none of it was something he wanted to face. Not even a little bit. But keeping the council from seeking him out here in Shadowvale was more important. Protecting this place, which would soon be all he had left, was paramount.

He started a pot of coffee. After that began to brew, he cracked half a dozen eggs into a bowl. He didn't have much of an appetite, but he'd need energy for the journey ahead. Arriving weak wouldn't do. In another pan, he fried up some bacon. He spooned some of the bacon fat into a third pan, then shredded a large potato into it. The good smells helped him feel hungry. Didn't matter. He'd get the food down regardless.

Next, he filled the slots of his four-slice toaster with

Her First Taste Of Fire

whole grain wheat bread before pressing both levers down. From the fridge, he got a pot of raspberry preserves, bought at the farmer's market, and set it on the table while the rest of his breakfast cooked.

It was still dark out and would be for a few more hours, but he could leave early. He'd packed last night after he'd gotten home.

His only regret, besides the fact that he had to go to this stupid census, was that he had to close his shop for the days he'd be gone. He hated leaving a project unfinished, but most of all he enjoyed talking to the folks that came in.

Loved seeing how happy his creations made them.

He also really loved making the chocolates. Losing himself in the creation process was his way of escaping. He'd probably need that more than ever when he returned. He closed his eyes, trying to imagine what it would be like to live this life with a mate. He hoped whoever he was paired with was kind and understanding, but he'd grown up with dragon females. That wasn't generally their way.

Most of them wanted strong warriors who cared only about building their hoards and defending their homesteads.

He was all for those things, but his curse would make a lot of females see him as weak and vulnerable. And therefore...less than.

His doorbell rang, happily derailing that wretched train of thought.

He turned the heat down on the bacon before going to answer it. Shadowvale was a highly nocturnal town, thanks to the wide variety of supernaturals who called the place home, but he couldn't imagine who would be at his door this early.

He still wasn't sure when he opened it. "Can I help you?"

"Hi," the woman said. "You don't know me, but—"

"The woman in the sunglasses. From the shop earlier." He recognized her not by her looks, but by the scent of smoke that clung to her like a haunting refrain. He couldn't imagine why she was on his doorstep.

Or how she knew where he lived.

"Yes, that's me. Nasha Black."

The name was familiar, but he couldn't think of why. Then again, Shadowvale was a small town. If you lived here long enough, every name would be familiar soon enough.

"Yes, I was in your shop yesterday. I, uh, went by this morning. I knew you wouldn't be open, but I guess I don't know what I thought. Anyway, I saw the sign in your window that said you were going to be closed for almost a week."

He nodded. "That's right. Maybe longer." She seemed upset by that news. So much so that he felt compelled to add, "You know they sell chocolate at a lot of different places in town. Including the Green Grocer. I think they even have some of those fancy organic bars."

Her arms were tight at her sides, her hands clenched.

Her First Taste Of Fire

"It's not *your* chocolate, though."

He smiled. "It's very flattering that you enjoy my chocolates that much."

The worried bend of her brows had yet to change. "Do you think maybe you could...sell me your recipe?"

"My chocolate recipe?" He laughed. "No, sorry, that's a proprietary secret." Couldn't be duplicated anyway, unless she could breathe fire.

"I was afraid of that." She sighed. "Then maybe you could open your shop for a few minutes so I can get some more before you leave? Also, when do you think you'll be back exactly?"

They were verging into weird territory here. On one hand, he wouldn't mind selling her more chocolate before he left; on the other, she was asking questions he wasn't prepared to answer. "I don't know. That's why I didn't put a date on the sign. Maybe as long as a week. Possibly longer." Especially if he had to take a trip to his new wife's place first.

"Longer than a week?" She shifted uncomfortably and chewed her bottom lip. "That's a long time."

"Can't be helped." Speaking of help, she might need a twelve-step program for her sweet tooth. He'd never encountered someone with a chocolate addiction this intense.

Her breathing had picked up. She stepped toward him slightly. "Please. I need that chocolate. You don't understand. I have money. And I'd be willing to sign something promising I'd never share your recipe with anyone else, if that's what you're worried about. I have my own chocolate supplier. I only want yours for my own personal use."

Her own supplier? Then it clicked. She was Nasha Black of Black Horse Bakery. But that only raised more questions. And not just about why she wanted his chocolate recipe. His eyes narrowed. "How did you find out where I lived?"

She frowned. "I asked a friend. Will you at least open your shop? How about if I promise to buy everything? All of the chocolate you have left."

His brows shot up. "Really?"

"I swear. I'll take it all."

"Okay. I'll meet you there in half an hour." That should give him time to finish cooking his breakfast and eat it.

"Half an hour. You promise?"

Boy, she sure was worried about that chocolate. "I promise."

She exhaled. "Thank you. See you there."

~

NASHA PACED OUTSIDE of The Chocolate Dragon ten minutes before Charlie was due to arrive. She couldn't help herself. She was a desperate woman. She couldn't go without tasting again after the sudden revelation of what she'd been missing out on all these years.

Thankfully, Deacon Evermore had been understanding enough to give her Charlie's address. Granted, she'd fibbed and said it was a birthday cake emergency, but Deacon had been too tired to ask questions.

She had to try again to talk Charlie into parting with his recipe. There had to be something in there that would explain why she was able to taste his chocolate. Maybe it was magic. So what? She was fine with that.

She'd tried magic before. Custom made spells designed to heighten the taste of her food to the point that a normal person's tastebuds would be blown out.

Hadn't worked. She'd tried having herself spelled, too. That hadn't gotten her anywhere, either.

Of course, she'd had those spells built blindly because she refused to tell anyone what her curse was. Maybe if she'd had the spells built specifically for her, that might have made a difference.

Emeranth was a witch. So was her aunt. Maybe if Nasha confessed the truth to them, they could do something for her.

She stopped pacing to look through the shop windows.

Then again, she'd already found an answer. It was right there, behind that glass. She just had to figure out what the trick was. What was he putting in his chocolate?

And if he didn't give her the secret, how on earth was she going to survive a whole week without being able to taste again?

The very idea set her nerves on edge. She did *not* want to go back to the bland, flavorless life she'd been living. Not after experiencing the joy of taste. The joy of chocolate.

The jangle of keys behind her made her turn.

Charlie walked toward her. He'd parked at the curb and she hadn't noticed. He gave her a look. "You really like my chocolate, huh?"

"Yes."

He stopped at the door, making no effort to unlock it. "You own the bakery on Main Street."

She nodded. "That's right."

"What's wrong with the chocolate you use in your shop?"

"Nothing. It's great. But for personal consumption, I like yours better. A lot better."

"Mm-hmm."

She could tell he wasn't convinced that was the whole truth. Just saying it out loud seemed to underline how thin of a reason it was to show up at his house and offer to buy out his whole shop before the sun was even up. "I know this is an inconvenience for you. I'm sorry. I really appreciate it."

He shrugged and finally put the key in the lock. "It's fine. You get what you want, and I don't have any product sitting around going stale while I'm away."

He pushed the door open. "Come on in."

As soon as she stepped through, the delicious, mouth-watering, life-changing aroma hit her. She closed her eyes and stood in the center of the shop, inhaling it. She needed a piece right now.

She opened her eyes and scanned the display cases for the piece she wanted first. Which was when she realized there was hardly any chocolate left at all. "This won't do," she muttered.

"What won't do?"

"There's hardly any chocolate left."

His brow bent. "There's still a good bit."

She shook her head. The panic she'd felt earlier was rising up again. "Not enough. I need the recipe. Please. Name your price."

He snorted. "It's not for sale. I told you that. Look, I'm sorry, but all I can offer you is the chocolate left in the shop. If you want it, great. If not, I need to get back home."

She was on the verge of losing it. She had to make him understand. "There has to be *something* you want. Something you'd trade in exchange for the recipe. Please."

"Ma'am, the only thing I want isn't something anyone can give me so—"

"Name it. I can get you anything you want. My father is a very powerful man. He has resources."

Charlie crossed his arms, eyes suddenly fiery with interest. "Can he provide me with a wife for the next week or so?"

Nasha had no idea what this man might need a wife for, but at this point, she didn't care. She refused to let her curse win. She gave Charlie a haughty gaze. "No. But I can."

CHAPTER SIX

Charlie hadn't been expecting that. He uncrossed his arms. "You mean...*you*?"

"Sure," Nasha said. "I'm a woman. I'm the right age to be your wife. Why not?"

Well, for one thing, she wasn't a dragon-shifter. "You don't even know what I need a wife for."

She shrugged. "You said you're going away for a week and now you say you need a wife, so I'm guessing you need to make some people believe that you're married. How hard can that be? I took theater in college. I'm sure I can handle a little play-acting."

For a moment, she had him convinced. For a moment. Then he shook his head. "No. I'm sorry, it would never work."

"Why? Aren't I pretty enough for your friends?" There was a challenge in her voice that sounded like it came from a place of hurt.

"They're not my friends." He studied her just like he'd done when she'd first come into his shop. "And your looks are not the issue. If anything, you're too pretty. Too...elegant and interesting. That's not what I'm worried about."

Her First Taste Of Fire

She seemed surprised by his assessment of her. "You think I'm too elegant and interesting? I'm not sure I've ever been described like that before. In fact, some of my friends would probably laugh at that. I know my father would."

"It's how you appear to me. And how you'd appear to my people, too." Dragon females were not delicate flowers. To keep the plant metaphor going, they were more like invasive weeds intent on taking over everything they touched.

"Your people?" Her eyes narrowed. "What are you exactly?"

"Dragon-shifter. I thought the name of the shop was a dead giveaway."

"In this town? I never assume anything."

"Good point. What are you?"

She lifted one shoulder. "Just a run-of-the-mill supernatural. Nothing special."

He almost rolled his eyes. "Nothing special" really instilled confidence. But that scent of smoke around her made him question just how run-of-the-mill she really was. And why she wasn't telling him more, but that was her business. "Listen, I should get to work packaging up all this chocolate." He started to go around the counter.

She stepped into his path. "Does that mean you're not taking me up on my offer?"

"That's right. I'm not."

"Let me get this straight. Whatever this thing is you're

going to where you'd really like to have a wife, I'm not good enough."

More of the same challenging tone. "It's not that you're not good enough." How was he going to explain this? "It's just that I don't think you're...up to the job required. I'm sure you're a lovely woman with a great personality, but—"

"I'm not enough, is that it?" She glared up at him.

Blazes, she was pretty. Even more so with fire in her eyes. He began to second-guess his decision. He sighed. "Look, I have to attend the dragon census. They're going to count all of us up and any of us who aren't mated will be by the time the event is over. That's why I want a wife. So I don't have to participate in the mating games and end up with a mate I don't want." She didn't need to know about how the games would inevitably expose his curse.

She frowned. "So the married couples just get counted? What part of that do you think I wouldn't be able to deal with?"

"We'd still have to interact with others. We'd be expected to watch the games. Go to meals. That kind of stuff. All while selling the pretense that we're a real couple. For at least five days. Maybe longer. That's a pretty good stretch of time to carry off a ruse of that magnitude."

Her eyes softened suddenly, and she put her hand on his cheek. Her palm was warm and soft and he realized it had been a long time since a woman had touched him like that.

She gazed into his eyes. "Oh, Charlie, you wound me to the heart saying I couldn't convince people that I am madly, deeply," she moved closer until she was practically pressed against him, "*passionately* in love with you."

He swallowed. The heat from her hand radiated down into his bones. He opened his mouth to get more air into his lungs. "I, uh..."

She closed his stammering mouth with a soft kiss that lit sparks all through him. Her mouth was just as warm as her hand. Warmer. *Hot.* His head went funny. Like he'd suddenly lost altitude. He reached out for the counter next to him just as she backed away.

He stared at her, mouth open. His brain slightly scrambled. His temperature rising. For a moment, he wasn't sure what they'd been talking about. "I, uh, have to leave today."

"I can be ready in an hour. Meet you at your house?"

"Sure." He nodded, unable to stop himself. Barely controlling the urge to grab her and kiss her back. What had he just agreed to? It was utter foolishness. They were bound to get caught.

Then again, she wasn't a dragon. That might play in their favor.

"I told you I was a good actor." She smiled at him, gesturing over her shoulder at the display case. "And I still want all of this chocolate."

〜

Nasha packed quickly and simply. She realized she should have asked where this dragon census was being held, but she knew dragons liked the mountains. With that in mind, she went for layers. Tights, leggings, tall boots, T-shirts in short- and long-sleeve lengths, a couple of sweaters, one basic stretchy mini-skirt, a good vest, a long T-shirt-style dress, and two thin cashmere scarves in purple and scarlet. Everything else was black or gray or black-and-white patterned, which was almost all she wore. None of it fancy, but all mixable and cute and a little Goth.

She was who she was. That wasn't going to change because she was someone's fake wife.

On a whim, she added a swimsuit. Mountain resorts often had hot tubs, and she did not want to miss out on that.

She also packed a toiletries bag, a small bag of essential makeup, and a few pieces of jewelry. She changed out of her work outfit of leggings and a T-shirt, and into black jeans, a black-and-white patterned vee-neck sweater with a gray tank top underneath, short boots, and her charcoal wool coat. She tucked her gloves in one pocket, her beanie hat in the other. Wearing the bulkiest stuff seemed like the best way to go.

She couldn't believe she was actually about to embark on this trip but getting his chocolate recipe meant she could have flavor in her life for the rest of her days. That was worth a week of her time with a man she barely knew.

Her First Taste Of Fire

Charlie seemed like a good guy. A little too concerned with what other people thought, but maybe dragons were just like that. She'd never really known one, so it was hard to say.

It wouldn't be a hardship to pretend to be his wife. Or to kiss him again. She paused her packing, a pair of socks in her hand, to think about their kiss. Much like Charlie's chocolate, she'd been able to *taste* him.

Sweet and smoky.

Nothing at all like the last man she'd kissed. Shepherd Evermore. That had been ages ago, and they'd parted amicably, but she'd known almost instantly that they'd never work out. It wasn't Shepherd's fault. How could she be with someone when kissing them was as bland and boring as the rest of her life?

Not so with Charlie. She exhaled. She needed to keep her head about her and remember that this was just a ruse. Just a way to keep him from getting hitched against his will and to provide her with the recipe she needed to make her life truly interesting.

She tucked the last pair of socks into her duffel, added a last-minute pair of sneakers, zipped it up, then sent a quick group text to her employees. Clara and Brighton would probably be up. Em, she wasn't so sure about.

Sorry for the short notice, but I'm going out of town for about a week and leaving immediately. The bakery is in your hands. If you can go in early to bake since I won't be there, that would be great. If not, I understand. I trust you to run it in whatever way you see fit. Same goes for the recipes you use. Keep track of your hours. Bonuses if you haven't burned the place down by the time I get back.

She added a smiley face emoji for good measure. She knew Brighton and Em would have questions. Clara would probably just carry on, business as usual.

They answered her not long after, confirming that they would take care of everything, including going in early to get the baking started. Things might not hit the shelves at their usual times, but it would be fine for a day.

Then she shut the lights off, locked up her house, threw the duffel in the passenger seat of her car, and walked across the vast yard to her father's house.

She couldn't just leave without telling him she was going. She let herself in. "Dad? You up?"

He would be. He rarely slept. Besides that, she smelled coffee.

"In the kitchen," he called out.

She went straight there. Her father was sitting at the breakfast bar, reading the news on his tablet like he did a lot of mornings, a steaming cup of black coffee beside him. He was a lean man, slender to the point of skeletal. It came with the job. He glanced up at her, smiling. "Hello, sweetheart. Playing hooky from the bakery this morning?"

"Sort of." Hooky was the right word. A pang of guilt about leaving the bakery struck her as she helped herself to coffee. She felt bad about leaving on such short notice, even if Clara and Brighton were taking care of things. She was going to miss the bakery, but Charlie clearly needed her help.

She took the mug of black coffee to the bar to sit with him. There was no point in adding anything. Just like her father, she wouldn't be able to taste sugar or cream. They basically drank it for the caffeine kick. "I'm going out of town for about a week, and I just wanted you to know so you wouldn't worry."

He put his tablet down, giving her a glimpse of the screen. World news. Crop reports. Weather patterns. "Rather spur of the moment, don't you think? Or have you been planning this?"

"Nope, just happened." She sat next to him. "I'll explain, but don't freak out, okay?"

His eyes narrowed. "You know I'm your father, right? A small amount of freaking out is probably to be expected."

"Try."

He sipped his coffee, his Horseman's ring glinting in the overhead lights. "I'll do my best."

She explained everything, from being able to taste the chocolate to agreeing to be Charlie's wife in exchange for the recipe.

He didn't say a word until she was done talking. Then he just nodded. "You're an adult, capable of making your own decisions, and I can certainly understand why you'd make this one. But the dragons are a wild people. Rough. Ready to fight at a moment's notice. A true warrior race.

Promise me you'll keep your wits about you and think before you speak."

She sighed. "That's a big ask."

He smiled. "I know." He pulled the ring off his finger and held it out to her. "Take this. For protection. And in case you need the power boost. Or backup."

She recoiled. "Dad, that's your ring. I can't take that." Each of the Horsemen had one. It not only helped them focus their power, it enabled them to find each other, should such a need arise. Legend said that if the four rings were ever combined, they formed the key that would unlock the chains that bound the Great Apocalypse and unleash it upon the world. Her father refused to confirm that.

"You can if I give it to you."

"But Dad—"

"You want me to be okay with this? Then do this for me. This way you'll have greater power if you need it."

"I'm not going to use that kind of power. You know that." She'd seen what he was capable of. She didn't want that kind of responsibility.

"Be that as it may, I can find that ring wherever it is. If you're not back in a week, I will come looking for you. If you need me sooner, you have only to take the ring off. Trust me, I'll know."

There was no point in arguing. She took the intricate silver ring and slipped it onto her index finger, the only one it would fit on. "I'll call you if I need to be gone for longer than a week."

Her First Taste Of Fire

"Fine, but if I don't hear from you on day seven, that's it. If this dragon can't accomplish what he needs to in that amount of time, he's just going to have to deal with me showing up."

"I'll do my best to get us back here in a week. Mostly because the sight of you riding in on Domino might even make dragons pee their pants."

"Good." He smiled. "Because I miss you already."

CHAPTER SEVEN

Charlie stood at the sink, washing the frying pan he'd used to cook the bacon and questioning his life choices.

Namely the one in which he'd suddenly decided trying to fool the dragon council was a smart thing to do.

He was an idiot, obviously. Because there was no way this was going to go well. But...could it? Maybe? Was there a chance they might pull this deception off?

If he could avoid the mating games, he could also very well avoid using his fire and revealing his curse. It *was* possible.

They'd have to really sell the married thing.

Which Nasha seemed fully prepared to do, based on the way she'd kissed him in his shop.

He was surprised the remaining chocolates in the shop hadn't melted. He was sure he'd been radiating heat after what she'd done to him. That kiss had been a scorcher. Or maybe he just hadn't been kissed in a long time, which was true. Either way, she'd certainly thrown him for a loop with that unexpected smooch, making her point very distinctly. She was a good actor. Possibly even a great one.

He rinsed the pan and set it aside to dry. She'd have to

Her First Taste Of Fire

be. The dragon community would be harder on her because she wasn't one of them.

He needed to make sure she understood that. And then give her a chance to back out of this deal.

He didn't think she would. For some reason, she was determined to get his chocolate recipe. Part of him felt bad. The recipe wouldn't do her any good. It was his dragon's fire that really made the chocolate so special.

If she was hoping to reproduce his chocolate for some concoction in her bakery, she'd pretty soon find out it wouldn't work.

He dried his hands on a towel. Not his problem. This had all been her idea. He glanced at the time. She should be here soon. Her hour was almost up.

He'd barely finished thinking that when he heard a car pulling into his driveway. That had to be her.

He went out to the front porch. She was getting out of her car, a large duffel in one hand.

She smiled at him. "I'm all ready."

He pointed at her bag. "Really? Is that all you're bringing?"

She glanced at it. "Why? Do you think it's not enough? You didn't tell me where we were going but I assumed mountains and cooler weather, so I packed layers."

She was a smart woman. Maybe she'd be able to hold her own after all. "No, that's good. I didn't expect you to be such a light packer. But good assumption on the mountains. That's right where we're headed, so you're dressed well, too."

"Great." She looked around. "Where's your car? In the garage?"

"Yes, but we're not driving." He probably should have mentioned the travel details sooner. "You're not afraid of heights, are you?"

Her eyes narrowed slightly. "I'm not afraid of anything. Why? Are we flying?"

"In a manner of speaking." He backed up and held the front door open. "Come on in."

She walked toward him, came up the steps, but hesitated before entering. A moment later, she stepped inside. Had she been rethinking her decision?

He walked in after her. "You still okay to do this? Because if you want to change your mind—"

"No, I'm good." She checked out his living room. "Nice house."

"Thanks. What part of town do you live in?"

"Dark Acres."

His brows shot up before he could stop them. "Interesting neighborhood." It said a lot about her that she lived out there. Explained the scent of smoke about her. Certain kinds of magic carried that kind of dark, sooty smell. Usually the kinds that were just as murky and gray.

She nodded. "Filled with interesting people."

"Robin Gallow lives out there, doesn't he?"

"Yep. You know him?"

"Not really. He came into my shop yesterday. Nice

Her First Taste Of Fire

guy." The small talk was getting them nowhere. "We should go."

"Right." She took a breath. "Listen, when you say we're flying, you mean...actually flying, don't you?"

"Yes."

"Am I going to...ride you? Because that's not going to be weird at all."

He laughed, seeing the absurdity of it. "Hey, it's not going to be any weirder than the rest of this week."

"I suppose you're right."

She was such a petite thing. He hoped she did all right with his kind. "You really think you can do this?"

She lifted her chin in clear defiance. "Don't underestimate me."

He held his hands up. "I won't. Come on. The backyard is where I usually shift." He locked the front door, then started toward the rear of the house. "More room. Especially for takeoff. I just need to grab my coat."

She didn't move. "When you shift, where do your clothes go?"

"I guess they just become part of my new form. I've never really looked into the magic of that."

"Interesting. And convenient. Question. When you're in your dragon form, are we still going to be able to communicate?"

"Yes. I can still speak as a dragon. My voice changes a little, but you should be able to understand me."

"Okay, one last question. You're still going to know

who I am, right? Like, you're not going to suddenly think I'm a snack or something, right?"

He grinned. "Dragons don't eat people. Anymore. I mean, maybe once upon a time, but—"

"Let's just not put those images in my head, okay?"

"Agreed. Any other questions?" She was highly amusing. The way her brain worked was something else.

She held her hand up, knuckles towards him, fingers splayed. "Wouldn't rings make the whole married thing more believable?"

He stared at her hand and sighed. "Yes, it would. I completely forgot about that. But I can fix it."

Her expression turned doubtful. "You have wedding rings lying around, do you?"

"Not wedding rings, exactly, but I'm pretty sure I can come up with an engagement ring."

"Really?"

He nodded. "You know dragons have hoards, right?"

She made a face. "Hordes of what? Soldiers? You're losing me."

"Not hordes as in armies, hoards as in stashes of treasure."

"Oh. Nope, didn't know that. That's pretty cool. You have one?"

"Yes. We all do. We can stop by mine and see if we can find a ring. And while my real wife would probably know the location of my hoard, they are considered private and sacred." He couldn't believe he was about to reveal his to a woman who was essentially a stranger, but she was right about the need for a ring. It would make things seem much more legitimate.

"I'll keep my eyes closed."

"I just meant that you shouldn't talk about it or the location to anyone you meet at the census."

"I promise I won't say a word."

"Thanks." He trusted her, so far. He didn't have a reason not to. And she was willing to put herself out to help. That bought her some instant trust with him, even if she was getting something out of this deal. "Any other questions?

"Tons. I can't think of them right now, but I'm sure I will."

"Then let's go."

Together, they walked outside. His bags were on the back deck. He locked the French doors, then picked up his two bags and took hers from her hand. "Give me a moment in the yard to change, then come on down."

"Okay."

She stayed on the deck, watching with a great deal of interest.

He put the bags on the grass, then moved a few feet away. He'd never shifted forms in front of anyone who wasn't also a dragon. He'd never pretended to be married to anyone before, either. They were breaking all kinds of new ground.

Seeing him shift was something she was going to have to be comfortable with. Might as well start now. If she couldn't handle that, there wasn't much hope for pulling off the rest of their deception.

He positioned himself in the middle of the yard, making sure he wouldn't knock anything down with his tail when he changed. Then he opened up to his true self and let the dragon loose.

CHAPTER EIGHT

Nasha blinked.

One second, Charlie was standing in the middle of his yard, the sky above the trees going pale as the sun crept closer to the horizon; the next, he was gone.

And the biggest creature she'd ever seen was in his place.

As the daughter of a Horseman, she'd seen a lot of interesting, frightening, curious things in her days. A *lot*. But none of them compared to the glorious beast before her. She didn't even care that her mouth was hanging open as she stared.

Charlie in his human form was a very handsome man. In his dragon form, he was epic. The sort of creature that made her feel incredibly small and insignificant, and proud, because although it might be just pretend, she was about to be his wife for a week.

The world was going to believe that this extraordinary being had chosen her for his mate. It was impossible not to get a thrill out of that.

She took one step down off the deck, itching to get closer, yet feeling like she ought to be cautious in her approach.

He had to be thirty feet long from the tip of his spiked tail to his snout, but his size, while impressive, wasn't the most jaw-dropping thing about him.

His color was. As he moved, his scales reflected the most magnificent gleaming blues, greens, and purples. Shades of some fantastical night sky.

His throat and chest were slightly lighter than the dark tones of his head, back and tail, but together the colors were breathtaking. Were all dragons so beautiful? He looked bejeweled, although she imagined he might not like to be described that way.

Her fingers burned to touch those scales, to see if they were hard or soft, maybe leathery, warm or cold, slick or rough.

His wings definitely looked leathery. But soft at the same time. She was fascinated by every inch of him. Even the massive, hooked talons that adorned his feet. Each one looked as long as her forearm and about as thick.

She realized she'd come all the way down off the deck and stood about a yard from him.

He turned his head to look at her. "Are you ready to fly?"

His voice was low and gravely. Exactly what a dragon should sound like.

She nodded, not trusting her own voice.

"Climb aboard."

"Okay," she whispered. Not such an easy task, however. She wasn't sure where to start or what to take

Her First Taste Of Fire

hold of. She didn't want to hurt him. If that was even possible.

As if understanding her thoughts, he stuck his front leg out, making a sort of step with his elbow.

She put a hand on his side – his scales were smooth, leathery, and warm – then stepped up onto his elbow and, after balancing herself, began to climb toward his neck. It wasn't hard. His scales were easy to grip.

It was just…odd. She was climbing up a dragon who was actually the man she was about to pretend to be married to for a week.

Life in Shadowvale certainly had taken an interesting turn.

Spiney plates ran down his neck, along his back, and all the way to the tip of his tail. They were larger at the base of his long neck and on his back, just large enough that she could sit between two of them with the one behind her serving as a back rest, although they were flexible in that they could also lay flat against his body. His wings attached just slightly ahead of where she was, at the joint of his shoulders.

She settled in, using the hard boney plate in front of her as something to hang on to. "Is this okay?"

He nodded. "Perfect. Hold on. You can't hurt me."

"Good to know. Will do."

He stood up, only jostling her slightly. Her time on Domino was proving useful, enabling her to respond to Charlie's movements with those same instincts. She gripped his body with her legs for stability, just like she did Domino. Granted, Domino would have looked like a toy beside Charlie.

He picked up the bags with his talons, then looked back at her. "About to lift off. Hold on."

"Holding on."

He spread his wings. The one on the right side almost reached the house; the one on the left brushed the tree line. He took several steps forward, pumping his wings. They rose into the air slowly at first, but gained momentum fast. His wings moved a tremendous amount of air with each thrust.

Before long, they were sailing over Shadowvale. She stared down, fascinated as she tried to pick out landmarks. As they continued to ascend, they broke through the town's permanent cloud cover and the town below disappeared.

The sun rising on the horizon of clouds made up for the lost view.

The clouds beneath them were on fire with pink and orange, the sky as bright as could be. She closed her eyes and let the sun hit her face. It wasn't something that ever happened in Shadowvale and she wanted to soak it in.

"You all right?" Charlie asked, his gravelly voice whipping past her on the wind.

"Yes!" She shouted back, not sure if he'd hear her otherwise. She held on with one hand, sticking her other arm straight out into the air rushing past them, just to feel the sensation of it. The air was cold, but she didn't care.

She'd never imagined she'd someday ride a dragon. If nothing else good came out of this adventure, this one experience might be enough.

She felt like she was in a fairy tale. Not exactly a feeling she was familiar with as the daughter of a Horseman. Usually her experiences were more akin to nightmares.

Grabbing hold of the spiney plate in front of her again, she glanced at her father's ring on her finger. "If you could see me now, Dad."

Then, almost as quickly as they'd risen, they began to descend, cutting down through the cloud layer.

Below was mountainous countryside as far as the eye could see. No signs of civilization at all. She had no idea where they were.

Charlie slowed, his wings tilting as he changed course. She hung on. The ground rose up to meet them, and small details became more distinct.

Finally, he landed on a craggy patch of ground partially covered in snow. The landing was surprisingly gentle. He glanced at her.

"Off?" she asked.

He nodded. In the light of day, she could see his dragon eyes more clearly. They looked like they held a galaxy. She climbed down. The three bags were still clutched in his talons.

As soon as she was on the ground, he shifted back to his human form, leaving the duffels a few feet away. "You doing all right?"

She nodded, smiling. Impossible not to. "I'm doing great. That was amazing. A little breezy, but amazing."

"I can control the wind once we get back on course."

She looked around. "So this isn't where the census is? I did think it would be further away."

"No, this is where my hoard is. Do you know where we are?"

"You mean like what state? Not a clue. We could be in Canada for all I know. Although I don't think we were flying long enough to make it that far."

He crouched down and got a small camping lantern out of the big, zippered pocket at the end of his duffel. "We weren't, but I'm glad you don't know. It'll be safer for you that way. You can't let slip what you don't know."

"Hey," she said. "I'm not the kind of person who lets secrets slip. Of course, you wouldn't know that. But I'm not."

"Always good to hear." He stood and tipped his head toward the sheer rock wall behind them. "Ready to go find a ring?"

"Sure, but where?"

"Right here." He walked over to the rocks, grabbed hold of the largest one, and rolled it aside, revealing the entrance to a cave.

"Impressive." She was pretty strong, but she'd never imagined that rock could have been moved by anything less than heavy machinery.

He smiled. "Wait until you see inside." He turned on the lantern and walked in.

Her First Taste Of Fire

She followed, her eyes adjusting with the help of the light. At first, there was nothing. Just a narrow passage of scorched earth and rock.

Then the space opened up into a small cavern. The floor and natural rock shelves were covered with treasures. Gold and silver coins, cut gems, crates of jewelry, statues carved from precious stones, objects made of gold, silver, and bronze. There were several barrels of pearls, hunks of geodes with sparkling crystals exposed, even a few bejeweled swords and daggers.

She tried to take it all in. "This is crazy. It's like a pirate's treasure."

"Or a dragon's hoard," he said.

She laughed. "Right, or that."

"Look through the jewelry. There has to be something we can use as an engagement ring in here."

In several of the crevices in the rocks sat large candles that had clearly been lit before, based on the wax pooled at their bases. She gestured to them. "Can't you light a couple of these? My eyes are good, but a little more light would be helpful."

"I didn't bring a lighter." He held out the lantern. "Here, take this. I don't need it."

She hooked her fingers under the handle. "Do you really need a lighter? I thought dragons could breathe fire."

"We can." He shifted uncomfortably. "But in a small space like this, I'd melt everything in here. It's not practical."

"Oh." She wasn't totally convinced that was true, but if he didn't want to show off that particular skill in front of her, she wasn't going to hound him about it.

She took the lantern and went over to the first crate of jewelry. It was a mix of things. Bracelets, necklaces, earrings, brooches, rings, all sorts of things in all sorts of styles. She glanced over her shoulder. "This might take a minute. Do you want me to find wedding rings, too?"

"Yes. Whatever you can come up with to sell the illusion."

"Okay."

He hooked a thumb over his shoulder. "I'll be outside if you need me."

"Got it." She went back to the search, pulling out larger pieces and setting them aside so it was easier to see the smaller things.

By the time she'd gotten to the bottom of the crate, she'd found three pieces that could work as engagement rings, mostly because they were the only three that fit her small fingers.

One was a large, pear-shaped ruby surrounded by smaller diamonds set in yellow gold. The second was a fat silver pearl surrounded by sapphires in white gold. The third was a chunky square diamond solitaire accent with a single baguette diamond on each side. That one was in platinum and the stone was large enough that it could have been the headlight on a small European sports car.

Talk about a knockout.

No plain wedding bands, though. A couple of diamond ones, but they were too large for her. Nothing that would do for him.

She took the three rings out to show him. "I found a few. Which one do you want me to wear?"

"Whichever one you like. Or whatever fits the best." He took her hand in his, turning it like he was imagining the rings on her. "You have delicate fingers. Will any of those work?"

"They all fit. The diamond probably fits best."

"Then wear it. Diamonds are the most traditional anyway."

She hesitated. "It's probably also worth the most. What if something happens to it?"

He shrugged. "If something happens to it, then it does." He took the ring from her and held it out. "Nasha Black, will you be my pretend wife this week?"

She grinned. "I will."

He slipped the ring on her finger. "It's a done deal now."

She'd never worn anything quite so sparkly. Or expensive. It was hard to stop staring at it. "I guess it is."

"Any wedding bands?"

"None that would work. And no men's bands. A couple of big men's rings, but they looked more like they belonged on a riverboat gambler than a newly married man."

He laughed. "Then we'll just have to be engaged. Same thing as being married. No big deal."

"Okay. But that means we'll have to really play up how in love we are. To the point of being in people's faces about it."

His smile flattened a bit. "Are you saying you don't want to do this?"

"Nope. Just saying we're going to have to be on our game. Pooky."

He snorted. "Pooky?"

"Yeah, I was trying out a pet name. Scratching that one. Or all of them. Maybe pet names aren't our thing." She could feel her cheeks heating up. Pooky? What was she thinking? That was no kind of nickname for a man who could turn into a dragon the size of a yacht.

"Are you blushing?"

"*No.*" She bent her head, letting her hair fall forward to hide her face.

This was starting to feel like a bad idea.

"By the way, that third duffel has all the chocolates in it."

Her eyes went right to it. Maybe not *that* bad of an idea...

CHAPTER NINE

Charlie found a comfortable altitude and settled in, then adjusted his magical shielding to protect Nasha from the worst of the wind and cold.

The census was being held at a remote mountainous location completely protected by more dragon magic, but an innate sense served as his GPS. The gathering of dragons would help as well.

The more dragons gathered together, the stronger the energy they gave off. Almost like a magical beacon. It was how they'd survived over the centuries, by being able to locate each other with a kind of mystical radar.

So far, that hadn't kicked in, which meant they still had a ways to go. He knew the magic pull he felt was true, so he glided along, letting it be his guide.

"Hey, Charlie? I just thought of something."

He turned his head enough to see Nasha. She stared back at him, a concerned look on her face. "What's that?"

"We have no story. About how we met, I mean. And how you proposed. That really feels like something we should work out, you know? Won't people ask?"

Of course they would. And he'd been an idiot not to think of that sooner. He began to descend. This was the kind of conversation they needed to have on solid ground. "Yes. You're right, we do need to work that out. Just a moment."

He found an open field that seemed a reasonable distance from any residential area and landed. Then he turned his head toward her again. "Do you have any ideas?"

"Well, the meeting part is easy. We live in the same town. We could just say we met...in the grocery store." She dismounted like she was getting off a horse, swinging one leg up and over, and then sliding down his side until her feet hit the ground. She looked up at him again. "Or something like that."

"No, that's good." He lay down so he wasn't so much taller than she was. "Maybe we were reaching for the same flavor of ice cream. What's your favorite flavor?"

She frowned into the distance like she was thinking. Who didn't know their favorite flavor? "Vanilla? No, chocolate."

"You don't know?"

She squinted at him. "What's your favorite flavor?"

"At the moment, I like the Creamatorium's Wake-Up Call." The ice cream shop was one of his favorite places in town. "It's coffee ice cream with chocolate-covered espresso beans, chunks of brownie, and a swirl of hot fudge. Honestly, that place just inspires me to get more inventive with my own flavors. I'm sure you can relate to that, seeing as how you're a baker."

Her expression went slightly blank. "Right."

Her First Taste Of Fire

"Don't you like the Creamatorium?"

She shrugged. "I've never been there."

"Really? I always thought it was pretty special to have a shop like that in town. But then, I think my shop's pretty special, too. Yours as well. I've never seen or heard of a bakery where everything's free."

It struck him that he really knew nothing about her. And that he ought to, considering the week that lay before them. "Why do you do that, if you don't mind me asking? Are you just independently wealthy or what?"

"It's just my way of giving back. And helping to balance some of the injustices of the world. I'm not any wealthier than the next person, but my needs are taken care of."

It was a good answer. Also a vague one. What wasn't she telling him? He decided to call her on it in the nicest way possible. "If this charade is going to work, we should be as honest with each other as possible. So I have to tell you, it feels like you're holding back details I should know."

She stared at him like she was looking for words. "You know, it's not the easiest thing in the world to have a conversation with a dragon."

It hadn't occurred to him that she'd be more comfortable talking to him in his human form. He shifted immediately. "Sorry. I just wasn't thinking about it. Better?"

She smiled. "Yes. You're incredible to look at in your dragon form, but also a little intimidating."

"Not to mention if anyone saw me..." He shook his

head at his own stupidity, but her compliment wasn't lost on him. "You don't have to be shy about being straight up with me about that kind of stuff. Or anything, really."

She crossed her arms and stayed silent for a long moment. So long he thought she was going to drop her walls and tell him something personal. "So...how would you have proposed to me?"

So much for thinking he was about to get to know her better. "Dragons tend to make grand gestures. I might have flown you to the top of the Seattle Space Needle to see the stars. Or taken you on a midnight flyover of the Grand Canyon. Something like that."

"Well, it's your proposal. Whatever you want to say you did, we'll go with it."

She didn't seem impressed with either of those things, so he gave it some thought. For as little as he knew about her, he was well aware of one thing she liked. "What if I made you a special chocolate egg and when you broke it open, the ring was inside it? Then I got down on one knee and asked you to marry me?"

She uncrossed her arms to press her hands together in front of her chest. "I like that. That's my kind of grand gesture."

He laughed, feeling pleased with himself. "I thought you might. That's our story then."

"Perfect." She pulled up a tall piece of dried grass and wound it around her finger. "What other stories should we have?"

"I don't know. Maybe we should go with something as

Her First Taste Of Fire

close to the truth as possible. That we've only known each other a short while but we just fell in love and knew it was right and are getting married as soon as possible."

"Do we have a wedding date?"

"Spring of next year."

She nodded. "Okay."

"Are you Goth? Or do you just like black?"

She snorted. "Black is my favorite color. Are there any dragon courtship rituals I need to know about?"

"Seeing as how you're not dragon, none of that would apply to you. I guess we should talk about our families, too." It was bound to come up sooner or later. Better to get it over with now. "I have two younger sisters. They live in Belarus with my parents. How about you?"

"Only child. My father lives in Shadowvale."

"My mother is a pretty famous sculptor of metal art. My father is a history professor at the state university." Maybe that would keep her from asking much more about them. "What do your parents do for a living? Do they live in the States?"

Her expression turned dark. "Are you teasing me? Or do you really not know who my father is?"

Charlie was taken back. "I'm not teasing you. I have no idea who your father is or what he does. Why? Should I?"

She stared off into the distance. "I thought everyone knew."

"I guess I'm not everyone."

"Sorry." She glanced at him quickly before looking away again. "I get judged a lot because of who he is."

"It's not going to change what I think of you."

She huffed out a short breath. "You say that now..."

"And I mean it. Who is he?"

She twisted the large silver ring on her index finger. "He's one of the Four Horseman of the Apocalypse. Specifically, he's Famine."

Her free bakery suddenly made sense, along with her comment about balancing the world's injustices. "Wow. I knew they all lived in town, but I didn't realize... Do you have a good relationship with him?"

She lifted her chin. "Of course. He's my dad. I love him. He's the best."

That was more than Charlie could say about his father. "And your mom?"

"Died a few days after giving birth to me. She was human." Nasha's eyes went steely. "Doctors had no explanation, but apparently carrying the child of Famine drained the life out of her. It was all she could do to bring me to term."

He swallowed down the shock of what she'd just told him. "I'm so sorry."

She shrugged. The gesture was clearly a defense mechanism, because there was no way she really felt so casual about what she'd just confessed. "I'm the reason my mother died. Not much I can do about it."

"I'm still sorry you had to go through that."

"Thanks." But the word was cold and short.

Her First Taste Of Fire

He couldn't stop feeling for her, and what she'd suffered. What she was still suffering, because despite her cavalier attitude, Nasha obviously bore a lot of guilt about her mom. Charlie didn't know how to help her, or how to comfort her.

Those weren't things dragons did. His people were far too stalwart for that. They were brush-it-off-and-move-on kind of people. Sort of who Nasha was pretending to be.

In the light of everything she'd just told him, now didn't seem to be the right time for any more deep, personal confessions. Which was fine with him. Maybe she didn't need to know everything about him.

A lie, of course. Because she did. Otherwise she'd never understand just how desperate he was to keep his secrets.

Now was not the time for that, not when she was so obviously in pain. And so plainly unwilling to deal with it.

Should he hug her? He knew that was probably a standard human response that she might expect. But she wasn't human, either. Not fully.

Before he could decide what to do, she looked directly at him. "We should get going, don't you think?"

He nodded. And just like that, the discussion was over.

CHAPTER TEN

Nasha settled in on Charlie's back again. As long as he stayed at the same altitude and maintained course, there was no need to hang on. That suited her just fine, because she really just wanted to cross her arms and sulk. Maybe stew was a better word, but the bottom line was she was mad. At herself.

Mad that she'd confessed so much of her past to Charlie. She hadn't planned on telling him any of that. Maybe if they were genuinely in a relationship, those things would eventually come out, but this was all pretend! He didn't need to know any of the things she'd told him, although a lot of people in town knew who her father was.

She wasn't sure why she was so mad about telling Charlie, though. He didn't seem to care. He hadn't even reacted to her news about who her dad was. Most people immediately shied away from her. At the very least, they looked at her with some fear in their eyes. Maybe dragons didn't worry about the apocalypse like most people?

He seemed sincerely upset when she'd told him about her mother. But maybe that had just been him

Her First Taste Of Fire

reacting like he thought he should. Of course, she didn't know him well enough to make that determination.

Then again, everyone reacted to the news about Nasha's mother like he did. Not that she'd told very many people. He'd done the standard horrified look accompanied by a long silence, then the obligatory, "I'm sorry."

She knew the drill. Enough that it was part of the reason she'd stopped telling people. Shepherd Evermore was the last person she'd told. Since him, she'd thought about just saying her mother had left them when Nasha was a baby.

Not a lie. Not really.

She uncrossed her arms and dug out the cellophane bag of chocolates she'd stuffed in her coat pocket earlier. A chocolate would really be nice right now. She turned the bag, inspecting them. They all looked so good, but one in particular caught her eye. She fished it out and bit it in half without so much as a second glance.

Mmm. Something new. And not a flavor she recognized. She checked out the remaining half. Just a simple chocolate bonbon with some bronzy flecks on the shiny round surface. She sniffed it. Oh! She knew that scent. Rum.

So that's what rum tasted like. She'd had requests for rum cakes at Christmas, but so far she'd put them off because she just couldn't imagine using an ingredient like that without being able to taste it. Everything she'd read online said there was a fine line between too little and too much and how easy it was to ruin a cake with alcohol.

That wasn't the kind of thing she was cut out to handle. She rarely drank for the same reason. Drinking something that had no taste and could make you lose control wasn't something she was interested in. Maybe the occasional glass of celebratory champagne, but that happened so rarely in Shadowvale it was no big deal.

This rum bonbon was good. Really good. It was making her reconsider. Baking with alcohol, not drinking it.

She stared ahead at the back of Charlie's head as the delicious rum and chocolate filled her with happiness. She *had* to find out his secret ingredient that gave her the ability to taste. If she could just add it to everything she ate, her curse would effectively be ended.

She hoped it *wasn't* a secret ingredient. Instead, she wanted it to be some kind of magic, something she could apply to her life like a balm that covered everything and then, bam! It would all be fixed. A spell, an incantation, a hex, whatever. Her problem would be solved.

Her father's, too. She wondered if gaining the ability to taste would impact his job.

He wasn't just in charge of food famines, but those were one of his primary responsibilities. There were other kinds of famines. Different kinds of deficits that fell under his rule. The loss of common sense, for example, which often led to far greater suffering. The lack of kindness, another thing the world never seemed to solve.

She popped the other half of the bonbon into her mouth, then looked at her father's ring on her finger. She so wanted to give him the gift of taste. He deserved it for all that he bore on his shoulders.

Her father had been a Horseman for longer than she'd been alive. He seemed to manage it all right, but she knew the work took its toll on him. When he thought she wasn't looking, or that she couldn't see him, it was plain to see just how much it wore him down.

He tried to hide it, she guessed, because they both knew the mantle would fall upon her shoulders next. She was next in line. Unless she did something to change that.

What if becoming Famine wasn't her true destiny, despite her lineage? What if there was a way to change what seemed inevitable?

It wasn't that she didn't think she could handle it. It was more that if she took on the job of Horseman, that implied her child would carry it after her. That child might not have been born yet, but did she want to lay that kind of burden on her offspring?

She really didn't.

Would it break her father's heart if she told him as much? That she didn't want to follow in his footsteps or the footsteps of her family before her, even though that's what was expected of her?

She honestly didn't know. But it seemed like something they should talk about when she got back.

They *could* get another Horseman who wasn't born to the job. That did happen every once in a while. At least she thought it had. After all, none of them were eternal.

Long-lived and very powerful, yes. Immortal, no. And the weight of their jobs often left them with such mental anguish that it wasn't uncommon for a Horseman to walk away after just a few short decades.

Had her father stayed in the role so long to protect her? To keep her from having to take over?

It was a sobering thought. And not one she could bear to consider in the immediate future.

She put the bag of chocolates back in her pocket. It was easier to focus on how much of that she had left. Just that small bag and what was in the duffel was all that remained, and the supply needed to last for as long as they were at the census. Maybe she should start rationing the chocolate, because it was making her a little panicky to think about running out.

How crazy was that? In less than a day's time, she'd gotten so used to having flavor in her life that the thought of going without it was giving her cold sweats. Clearly, she was already addicted to taste.

Addicted had to be the right word when she considered that she'd willingly gone away with a strange man for a week, agreeing to be his dearly beloved, all in exchange for whatever secret ingredient he was using in his chocolate.

Regardless of how wild that sounded, it seemed like a small price to pay for breaking her curse.

And Charlie was growing on her. Quite a bit. She smiled. She never thought she'd go for the shifter type again, but there was something deeply moving about him in dragon form.

He wasn't so bad to stare at as a man, either. Especially when he gave her that certain look. As if he was seeing her in a way that no one else ever had.

It was the kind of thing that pinned her and made her focus on him and nothing else. Maybe he was using dragon magic on her?

She should have done a little research on dragons, but it wasn't like she'd had much time to prepare for this.

Although... She pulled her phone out. No time like the present. Except she had no signal. She put the phone away. How high up were they? The air didn't seem thin. And while it was whipping past at a good clip, it wasn't any more bothersome than riding in a convertible.

Had to be magic. Like some kind of forcefield around him that kept the air reasonably calm and temperate. And breathable.

She'd have to ask him when they landed. He'd mentioned something about it, hadn't he?

Another question popped into her head. One she wasn't sure she should even care about. But she did.

How many other women had sat where she was right now?

She pressed her hand to his gorgeous hide, flattening her palm on his glossy scales. He was very warm. She imagined having your own internal furnace would keep you pretty toasty. The muscle beneath her hand was taut and hard, but alive with movement as he made almost imperceptible adjustments during flight.

His hide was so tough and thick he probably couldn't feel much of what she was doing. She traced the scalloped lines of his scales, detailing the intricate way they meshed and overlapped. This was why dragons were so indestructible, wasn't it? This natural body armor they had.

He was a marvel. And for the next week, he was all hers.

Which was the only way she could explain how the thought of another woman sitting where she was made her green with jealousy. Her entire body tensed at the very idea.

Maybe taste wasn't the only thing she was becoming addicted to.

It wasn't a lie that she'd been in a dry spell with men lately. Ever since she and Shepherd Evermore broke up. He was a nice enough guy, handsome, a raven shifter, and the eldest son of one of the oldest families in Shadowvale. Things had just sort of fizzled out between them for no real reason. Except the most obvious one – they just hadn't had the right kind of chemistry.

It happened.

Which was why she'd been fine with the relationship being over between them. It was easier to be alone, anyway. No more going out to dinner and pretending the meal was delicious, for one thing. No more... But that was really all she could think of to explain why being alone was easier.

Didn't matter. She was about to be attached for a week. Just pretend, but still a good way to remind herself that her solitary life wasn't so bad. The fat diamond on her finger winked at her, sparkling in the light as if to say that married life had its perks, too.

Material things had never mattered to her that much. The bakery's free policy was proof of that. She hoped the crew was getting on all right without her. Maybe she'd call them after they landed. Provided there was cell service wherever the census was taking place.

She leaned forward, flattening some of Charlie's spikey plates, and wrapped her arms around him, right where his wings began. She rested her head against the subtle slope of his neck and closed her eyes.

The warmth of him seeped into her, like the best electric blanket ever made. As she began to drift, she patted his side. "Good dragon," she whispered.

She thought she heard a sound like muted laughter, but it might have just been the wind rushing past.

CHAPTER ELEVEN

Charlie didn't know if he should tell Nasha he was aware of her every movement. Even when she fidgeted trying to get more comfortable. Even though she probably didn't weigh a hundred pounds.

Dragon scales were a lot more sensitive than most people understood.

The rest of his senses weren't bad, either. He'd heard the crinkle of cellophane and smelled the dark chocolate she must have taken out of the bag to snack on.

What on earth was it about his chocolates that had her so crazed?

He couldn't figure it out. But he was grateful all the same. Her willingness to accompany him to the census was literally a lifesaver.

In fact, he was beginning to wonder if they couldn't leave early, since once he checked in, his duty to the council would be done.

It was worth looking into.

He flew as smoothly as possible, because she'd gone very still and he was pretty sure she'd fallen asleep. He smiled as best as he could in dragon form, which he'd been told only made him look terrifying.

Her First Taste Of Fire

As slightly odd as Nasha was, he liked her. Some of that was empathy for what she'd been through, losing her mother. Honestly, it was a miracle she wasn't completely bitter at the world for the circumstances of her birth.

But she wasn't even mad at her father. He was really the one to blame, if there was blame to be laid.

Nasha, however, seemed protective of the man. That said two things to Charlie. One, her father must have done an outstanding job of raising her, giving her all the love and attention necessary to keep her from feeling eternally angry.

And two, he must be a good man, despite his role in the world's suffering.

A third thought occurred to Charlie. It was mere speculation, but what if being a Horseman was like being an executioner? Someone had to do the job. The right person could do it with a measure of mercy.

Was Nasha's father that kind of man? Charlie couldn't help but wonder.

He inhaled, trying to detect the traces of smoke that would lead him to the Valley of Fire, the protected location of the census.

The Valley of Fire and Shadowvale weren't so different. Both locations had magic hiding them. Both locations only let in those who were supposed to be there.

And both locations had very distinct dispositions.

The Valley of Fire was never in the same geographical

location twice. It just appeared when the dragon council summoned it.

Once, a century ago, the Valley of Fire had refused to reveal itself. That year, the census had been cancelled.

If only he'd been so lucky this year. He glanced over his shoulder. Actually, he had been lucky.

Nasha might pull off the ruse of being his intended bride. True, she'd get some grief for not being dragon, something he'd worried about until she'd told him who her father was.

He thought if anyone could hold her own against his people, it had to be the daughter of one of the Four Horsemen. He felt a lot more confident knowing that about her. His people might even be a little impressed by her heritage.

All the two of them really had to do was make sure they were convincing in their relationship. He probably had the most work to do in that regard.

He'd avoided dragon women because of his curse. Since moving to Shadowvale, he'd been too busy getting his shop going and working on his chocolates to care about dating. In a way, he'd married himself to his work.

That wasn't so bad, was it? There was a lot of joy in making people happy.

Not the kind of joy a family might bring him, he supposed, but he'd stopped thinking of that kind of future for himself when his curse had manifested.

Naturally, it had shown up when he'd been going through puberty, an especially difficult time for dragon

Her First Taste Of Fire

boys. Learning to use his fire, which had come on so strong he'd had to take ice baths to keep his temperature in check, had been tremendously difficult.

So much so that one night, under the light of a full moon, he'd glimpsed a bright, falling star. As the heavenly body burned its way toward Earth, he'd made a hasty wish.

A promise to the skies, really.

He would sacrifice a piece of himself if only he could master his fire.

He'd lost the first scale a few days later.

Believing that a wish made on a shooting star was the cause of his curse was foolish. Just the very act of making the wish embarrassed him now. However, he could think of no other reason for what had happened to him.

His parents had sent him away to a special school for problem dragon children isolated high in the mountains, where he was drilled relentlessly in the use of his fire.

He'd gained excellent control at Ignis Academy.

And had lost almost half his hide.

Mortified that their firstborn was so afflicted, his parents had encouraged him to live as a human. He'd moved out and made an attempt, but it wasn't an easy thing for a dragon to do. Not when he knew what it meant to soar above the clouds and ride the thermals and see the world from such a rare vantage point. Even breathing fire was a thrill, despite the cost.

They'd begged him to walk away from his dragon

side. Then the begging turned to commands. "For the good of the family," became a regular refrain.

Or "think of your sisters," as if his curse might prevent them from living their lives.

As he grew older, he understood it actually might. Very few dragon males would want to take a wife who might bear him cursed sons.

Charlie was tired of the fighting anyway. Tired of arguing with his father about how he should live his life. Tired of his mother's incessant attempts to cure him with potions and spells and detoxes.

Not long after that, one of the spam emails in his inbox caught his eye. A promise of a better life in a safe place.

He never clicked on spam. Except this one time.

He'd come to visit Shadowvale. He'd only been there for a day when he'd realized that his only happiness might be found in that town.

Five years had passed since he'd returned and made the place his home. Five years of contentment and peace and nearly forgetting he was never going to be the son his parents wanted.

Until the damn census had been declared.

There was comfort in knowing his parents and sisters wouldn't be there. They'd be called to the one on their continent. Would his sisters be paired off with mates?

He supposed that depended on whether they were already married. He had no idea.

There had been no communication with his family

since he'd left. He imagined that worked best for them, to just pretend they didn't have a son.

Heat built in his chest and throat, an attempt to burn away the pain of that truth. He blew out the steam filling his airways.

He had to let all of that go. What was done was done.

No one would know him at this census. There was always a chance, of course, but dragons tended to stay close to their ancestral homes and hoards.

The tantalizing tang of smoke drifted past.

He inhaled, finding more of it. The Valley of Fire was somewhere below. He carefully shifted course and began to descend to have a better look, dropping below the cloud cover.

The land beneath him was as expected. Mountainous. Swathes of pine covered the bases, drifting upwards until bare rocks prevailed. Here and there, patches of snow dotted the mountainsides, increasing until there was nothing but white near the peaks.

Not a single dark plume of smoke was visible, but it was so thick in the air Charlie could taste it. They had to be close.

He tilted his wings to climb over the crest of one of the tallest points, and as he lifted, the Valley of Fire came into view. A lush green basin, it was about a mile long and half a mile wide. Most of that basin was prairie. A large tent had been set up in the tall grass. Much farther away, at the other end, a wide stream bore the meltwater from the mountains down to whatever lay further below.

On the other side of that stream was a thick forest. The trees drifted up the elevation, thinning as the altitude rose.

And all around in the surrounding mountains were caves carved out of the rock.

A few of them had been claimed by other dragons. He did a slow circle, searching for the one that appealed the most.

He found it closer to the forest end of the basin. A wide shelf of rock wrapped around the front of the cave, wide enough that he could land without having to cling to an outcropping. That would make things easier for Nasha, who'd have to rely on him to come and go.

There also seemed to be a natural path from that shelf down toward the forest. Hard to tell from the sky if it was as passable as it looked, but that would give her another option.

He circled back around and landed gently, dropping their bags on the ground. All that remained was to look inside and see if it was roomy enough.

Nasha shifted positions. "Are we there?"

He looked over his shoulder. "Yes. I was about to wake you."

She blinked back at him and rubbed at her eyes. "I can't believe I slept." She swung her leg up and over, and just like the last time, slide down his side until her feet hit the ground.

She stopped suddenly and backed up toward him, away from the edge of the ledge. "Whoa. Where are we?"

"The Valley of Fire. Same place the census takes place every time it occurs."

She stared out at the basin. "Where is that exactly?"

"No one knows. We just show up."

She slanted her eyes at him. "Is that some kind of dragon magic?"

He nodded. "Some kind."

Her gaze went past him. "Is that a cave?"

He shifted into human form before answering. "Yes. It'll be our home for the week."

She tipped her head to one side and her hands went to her hips. "I'm sorry, it sounded like you said we're going to be living in that cave this week."

Was she not an outdoor person? He probably should have mentioned the cave thing sooner, but it hadn't occurred to him. "That is what I said. Pretty much."

"A cave. With spiders and snakes and other creepy things?"

He gave her a once over. "There are bats in the pattern of your sweater. And your necklace has a spider on it."

"Okay, so I'm a little Goth, so what? Doesn't mean I want to actually sleep with those things."

"I'll clean it out, I promise. But maybe we should have a look at it first and see if there's room enough? We may end up picking another one."

She looked around. "Wait. So everyone sleeps in a cave?"

"Yes."

"Is that a dragon thing?"

He nodded.

She sighed. "All right, let's have a look."

He fished out the camping lantern from his duffel and headed in. She followed, getting closer as they went inside. The cavern wasn't really that dark. Somewhere near the back, a naturally occurring skylight let in some sun.

The space widened considerably, and as they went deeper in, opened up so that the ceiling was at least twenty feet above them in some spots.

He knew instantly they hadn't found the best part yet. "Do you hear that?"

She listened. "Sounds like…water?"

He turned on the lantern and held it up.

The cave floor slanted downward about fifty feet in. And went directly to a large pool of clear, blue water. Probably fed by an underground spring. Or maybe by an offshoot of the same stream that ran across the basin.

He smiled. "This is definitely the right cave."

Nasha didn't look convinced. "It's not as bad as I thought it would be inside, I'll give you that. And the private pool is a cool feature. But…" She glanced around. "Where are we supposed to sleep?"

"On the ground. In dragon form." He sighed. "Which doesn't do you much good, does it?"

CHAPTER TWELVE

"Not really." Nasha shrugged like it was no big deal, but she was actually having a moment of regret for agreeing to this charade. "I'm not a diva, I swear I'm not, but sleeping on dirt and rocks is going to be tough for me. I'm not sure I can do it. Maybe if I'd at least brought a sleeping bag—"

"It's my fault," Charlie said. "I wasn't thinking. I'm not letting you sleep on the bare ground. Unfortunately, the only camping gear I brought were these lanterns and a small ax for firewood." He set the lantern down. "Let me get checked in with the council, then I'll solve this. I promise."

"You're leaving?"

"Yes, but I'll be back as quickly as I can."

She didn't want to be left in a dark cave by herself. Especially as the aforementioned spiders and snakes had not been dealt with. "Can't I come with you?"

"You could, but there's a good chance we'd lose this spot to another dragon coming in. Unless you're okay taking our chances with a different cave?" He gestured back toward the entrance. "Part of the reason I picked this site is because there seems to be a reasonably easy path going down the mountainside from here. That will allow you to come and go without relying on me."

"Oh. That probably is a good thing since I can't fly." She took a breath and got herself under control. She was a grown woman. She could handle this. "Makes sense that I should stay here, then. You're going to leave the lantern, though, right?" Even with the shaft of sun coming in, most of the cave was pitch black.

"Absolutely. I have a second one, too." He started walking toward the entrance. "In fact, let me go grab the bags."

"Wait." Actually, a fire wouldn't hurt. Especially with the chill in the air. The cave was like an ice-box. She pulled her coat closer. "Could you start a fire before you go? It's pretty chilly."

"Can you manage until I get back? Then I can gather wood. Otherwise, I can do it now, but the camping supplies will have to wait."

"No, that's fine. When you get back." Camping. Not exactly how she imagined this week away. She wasn't opposed to camping. She'd been several times when she was a Wilderness Girl. She'd been eleven and there had been tents. And sleeping bags. And it had been summer.

There had been s'mores, too, something the other girls seemed to think were reason enough for the whole trip, but Nasha had been more interested in the ghost stories told around the fire while they were eating them.

He came back in carrying all three duffels. "I feel like

Her First Taste Of Fire

an idiot for not mentioning the living quarters sooner. Should I just take you back to Shadowvale?"

She arched her brows and smirked. "Do you really think I'm that much of a delicate flower? Because that's not generally the vibe I give off."

That seemed to amuse him. "I don't think that about you. I also realize you probably weren't expecting this."

"No, I wasn't. But with a few comforts, I can adapt." She hoped. She didn't want to end up regretting those words.

"You're sure?"

She nodded. "I think so. Go do whatever you need to do, then let's work on making this a little more livable for me."

"Done. Thank you." He leaned in and kissed her cheek. "Sorry. Impulse."

She laughed softly, glad to have something else to talk about. "Don't apologize. You're supposed to be kissing me, remember?"

"Right." A new fire lit his eyes. He grabbed the side of her coat, pulled her in close and planted one on her.

The kiss went a long way to warming her up and making her forget she was going to be sleeping rough for the next week. A *long* way.

When he finally broke it off, he held her close a moment longer. "Better?"

She swallowed, pulse racing. The man was definitely skilled at more than just making chocolate. "For sure. But the kissing would probably work better when people can see it."

His eyes narrowed in the kind of mischievous expression that said he was fully aware of that. "It's called practicing."

"You need that, do you?"

"Can't hurt." He was grinning as he let go of her coat to dig out the second lantern. He handed it to her. "I'll be back as soon as possible. Any other dragon tries to claim this cave, tell them Charles Ashborne has already claimed it."

She nodded. "Will do."

With that, he stepped out into the sun again, shifted to his dragon form and took off.

She ran out to watch him go, just to see what he looked like in the air. From the span of his wings to the lines of his powerful body, he was graceful and beautiful and a joy to watch. She kept her eyes on him as he banked and flew straight toward the enormous tent set up in the field below.

That must be where he had to check in. When he touched down, he shifted back to his human form, making him too small to really follow.

She stayed on the outcropping of rock in front of the cave, taking in the land around her. The mountains encompassed the valley, and the staggering heights were cratered with caves. A few had dragons in them.

She looked up again. More were flying in. A lot more. Dragons dotted the sky in every direction.

Her First Taste Of Fire

She wondered if there would be any other non-dragons here. It was a little intimidating to think that she might be the only one. How would they receive her? The way Charlie talked about his people made her think they were a close-knit, insular group, and not a fan of outsiders.

She had to think that was true. Many supernatural races were like that, primarily for survival purposes. Of course, things weren't like that in Shadowvale. You either got along with everyone, or kept to yourself, or you left. Those who caused problems weren't tolerated for very long.

As she continued to stand there, more dragons circled in the skies above her. She thought about going back inside the cave, but thought it was better that she stood out in front and made it obvious that this site was already claimed.

Too bad Charlie didn't have some kind of flag or banner they could have planted outside to make that abundantly clear.

She backed away from the shelf's edge but remained outside. Being in the sun was warmer anyway. And the sun was a rare treat after living in cloudy Shadowvale. Might as well take advantage of it.

The dragons came closer as they descended, slowing to what seemed like a glide. How they stayed afloat at such meager speeds she had no idea. Magic? Probably. After all, without that, dragons wouldn't exist at all.

They were all beautiful. None so much as Charlie, but perhaps she was biased.

A few dragons came closer still. To get a better look at her, no doubt. One in particular, a gorgeous pearl-white creature that gleamed so brightly in the sun it was almost hard to look at, stared directly at her as it flew past.

Hard to read a dragon's expression, but nothing about the beast's face seemed friendly. At least it was half Charlie's size. Nasha took comfort in that. All the same, she was ready for him to return.

"Hurry up, Charlie," she muttered under her breath.

More of them followed. A red and gold one with feathery plumes down its back instead of spiney plates. A few that were fairy tale stereotypes in green scales. A couple in various shades of blue. Then a menacing solid black with a scar along its side.

They kept coming. All shades and sizes, some with double sets of wings, some with long, elegant bodies, some wide and stocky like tanks, some that couldn't stop staring at her. A few blew streams of fire from their mouths and nostrils, like a show of power.

The pearl white one came around a second time, exhaling steam from its nostrils as it passed.

Nasha wasn't sure what effect that was supposed to have on her. Intimidation? By now she'd seen enough dragons that some of the curiosity had worn off. None of them compared to Charlie anyway. Not in looks or size.

The white one was interesting. Charlie was a work of art.

Her First Taste Of Fire

One by one, they each claimed a cave. It was quite a sight to see the valley below surrounded by dragons perched in the mountains.

She pulled her phone out and took some photos, mostly to show her father. She knew she'd never see anything like this again. Her phone signal suddenly returned. She wasn't sure how long it would last, so she sent Clara and Brighton a quick text.

How's it going?

All good, boss, Brighton answered right away. *We got bread and everything made like usual.*

Clara's text came in right after. *All is well.*

Great. Thank you. Text me if you need to. Signal is spotty, but I'll try to answer.

She noticed something as she put her phone away, and listened more closely, like she couldn't be right. There were no birds. None flying. None singing.

Apparently, they weren't interested in competing with the dragons.

Most of which seemed to be settling in. She sat on a rock near the mouth of the cave to wait for Charlie. Time ticked by. Another chocolate disappeared while she sat there. A coconut cream. Easy to identify from the smell and the tiny shreds of coconut mixed into the filling. She liked it a lot. Even if it meant she had one less chocolate to eat.

She closed her eyes and stuck her hands in her pockets as she leaned back against the rocks and let the sun beat down on her. All that warmth was relaxing, lulling her into a new state of calm. She almost got warm enough to take her coat off, but she was too chilled out to move. She started getting sleepy again.

The soft whoosh of wings opened her eyes. "Charlie?"

Not even remotely. A big bronze dragon, chest and belly burnished black, sat on the outcropping, staring at her with amber-gold eyes. "Why are you here, human?"

He had the same gravelly tone as Charlie. She stood up, which didn't do anything to make her look bigger. Being short sucked. "Because I'm here with my fiancé." She decided to name drop right away, to head off any problems. "This cave has been claimed by him, Charles Ashborne."

She didn't bother correcting the dragon's mistake that she was human. Let him figure that out for himself.

The dragon's eyes narrowed. "Charles Ashborne Jr.?"

She could only assume so. Charlie didn't seem old enough to be a senior and he hadn't mentioned any kids. "Yes."

The dragon looked unconvinced as he shook his head. "The heir to the Crimson Treaty Hoard is here? What's he doing in the States?"

She had no idea what the first thing was or how to answer the second question. So she didn't. "If you wish to speak to him, he'll be back in just a few minutes."

The dragon stared at her without saying anything.

She crossed her arms, not about to be seen as a pushover. "Who shall I say was asking about him?"

Her First Taste Of Fire

The dragon lifted one clawed front foot as if about to turn. "Lazarus Stratton. Are you really engaged?"

She held up her hand, showing off the ring Charlie had given her. That should be answer enough.

"Congratulations."

"Thank you."

Then Lazarus, if that was his name, snorted. "This is going to be a more interesting census than I imagined." He shoved off the outcropping and took flight.

Nasha had no idea what that was supposed to mean, but she exhaled, happy to see him go all the same. Happier still to see a familiar shape flying her way. Charlie was back. And he had all kinds of things clutched in his talons. Bags of stuff. She couldn't tell what exactly. One of the bags was an enormous duffel, large enough to hold a body. Maybe two.

The other bags were plastic shopping bags. As he got closer, she could read the name on one. *Wild Woods Sporting Goods*.

He'd gone shopping. For her. Hard not to smile about that. Especially when it looked like he'd bought one of everything. That made up for being left alone at the cave, too.

He landed, the flap of his wings stirring up a little dust. She retreated into the mouth of the cave until he shifted back to human. "Did a little shopping, I see."

He laughed. "You could say that. I hope this stuff helps."

Just the fact that he'd done this had already made a

difference. Whatever happened, she was going to see this through. For him. "I'm sure it will."

"How was it while I was gone?"

"Lots of fly-bys and side eyes. One visitor. A Lazarus Stratton? He seemed surprised to find out you were here."

Charlie squinted. "Lazarus Stratton? A big bronze dragon?"

"That's the one."

"Haven't heard that name in a while. Did he give you any trouble?"

"Not really. Asked what I was doing here. Explained we were engaged and that you had claimed this cave. Said this was going to be a more interesting census than he'd imagined. Seemed surprised you were in the States. You know him?"

Charlie picked up the giant duffel and hoisted it over his shoulder. "Laz and I went to school together in Europe. Only about two years. He was...not a bad guy."

Not a resounding endorsement, but not a defamation, either. Curious that Charlie had gone to school outside the U.S. Made her realize she still knew almost nothing about him. "Why did he think the census was going to be so interesting? Did you find out anything when you went to check in?"

"No, because I didn't get to check in. There was only one councilmember working in the tent when I got there, and they had a line waiting. I figured I'd go back later."

"Oh." As much as she wanted to ask him what being

the heir to the Crimson Treaty hoard meant, she figured that could wait until they had more time. "Well, I guess I should get to work on unpacking this stuff. What all did you get?"

Charlie smiled. "A better question might be what didn't I get." He picked up a bunch of bags and headed for the cave.

She grabbed a few more and followed him in.

CHAPTER THIRTEEN

Maybe Charlie had gone overboard, but the gratitude he felt toward Nasha for accompanying him to the census was easier expressed in gifts than words. At least for him.

Wasn't like he spent money with abandon on a regular basis, and this stuff would come in handy again. Probably. Didn't matter. He had more money than he could spend. Might as well use it.

Nasha shook her head. "This is too much, Charlie."

"Nah. It's fine. You need to be comfortable. Plus it's all pretty practical. For example, that air mattress is specifically made to be blown up without electricity. With that under the sleeping bag, and that travel pillow and the folding cot, you should be in good shape."

"It looks very comfy. But if the mattress doesn't need electricity, then what is that little battery-operated brick thingamajig for?"

"Powering other stuff?" He shrugged. "Honestly, I don't know. I bought so much they threw it in. But this..." He fished around for the one thing that was sure to make her happy. He held it up for her to see. "This is a solar-powered phone charger."

She let out a gasp. "Now that's genius. Won't do you

much good in Shadowvale, but here it's perfect. Even if there isn't cell service."

"You'll find that comes and goes."

She smiled at him, a truly beautiful sight to see. "It's all perfect. The folding chairs, the little folding table, the extra lanterns and candles, the camping stove, the coffee pot, the sleeping gear...I can't thank you enough."

"Considering what you're doing for me, it was the least I could do. Did I forget anything?"

"Not that I can think of."

"To be honest, I can't remember everything I bought and probably won't until the rest of the bags get unpacked."

She kept her smile. "I suppose you'd better go down and get checked in. I can organize all of this and get things squared away."

"Yeah, I should." Then he could help her with whatever else needed doing. Like gathering wood for a small fire, which he'd be starting with the camp lighter he'd bought. If she said something about that, he'd come up with an excuse. Hopefully, she wouldn't even notice. "Back in a bit."

"Okay."

He headed for the outcropping, but glanced back once before leaving. She was opening up the folding chairs and arranging them with the little table between them.

He was looking forward to bringing those chairs out here at night to sit and look at the stars. Not so much because of the stars, but because it sounded like a wonderful way to pass an evening with her.

She was pretty wonderful herself. As soon as he'd realized his mistake in not explaining the whole cave living situation, he'd anticipated she'd end this game they were playing.

The fact that she was still here and not complaining was astonishing to him. It was a lesson learned. She'd told him not to underestimate her, and this experience had proven that to be true.

She'd also apparently interacted with Lazarus Stratton without melting down, so more points for her. Nasha was quite a revelation. Beautiful, quirky, madly addicted to his chocolate, and far more accommodating than he'd dreamed.

His mind returned to Lazarus. Charlie hadn't imagined there'd be other dragons here that he knew, let alone one he'd suffered through Ignis Academy with. Which conjured up new questions. Did Laz know about Charlie's curse? If so, was he willing to keep quiet about it? The school had been careful to help Charlie hide his multitude of missing scales, but that didn't mean they'd gone unnoticed.

Of course, Lazarus had his own problems. He'd barely been able to make fire, let alone control it. He and Charlie hadn't initially been the best of friends, but they'd been more than acquaintances. Both had played on the soccer team. And they'd signed up to be lab partners. No one else had wanted them. As time went on, they hung out more and more.

Then, after two years, Lazarus had just disappeared. Maybe his parents had taken him out of school and moved him to a different program.

Maybe they'd just gotten fed up with his lack of progress and decided enough was enough.

Charlie didn't know. He hoped Laz would agree that they should both keep their mouths shut about their time at the Academy. And as soon as he found Lazarus, they were going to have that discussion.

He shifted and took flight, wheeling once around to see for himself just how many caves were occupied before diving down to the flatlands. He looked for Laz, too, but didn't find him. More dragons here than he expected, but the census wasn't just a way to be counted and find a mate. For a lot of dragons, it was a chance to reconnect with their own kind.

Not something Charlie really cared about.

He landed in the field near the registration tent, changing forms as he walked toward the tables. There was a crowd, but several other councilmembers had shown up, so things were moving along.

He got in line, observing those around him and looking for Lazarus as the queue slowly moved forward.

"Didn't expect to see you here."

Charlie turned and found Lazarus at his shoulder. "Hey. You, either. How are you, Laz? It's been a long time."

Laz nodded. "Yeah, long time. I'm all right. I'd ask

how you're doing but I met your better half, so you're obviously doing pretty well. I'm sure she told you."

Charlie smiled at Laz's description of Nasha as his better half. "She did."

Laz shook his head, grinning. "How did you ever end up with a woman like that?"

"Pure dumb luck." Laz seemed to buy the lie.

They moved closer to the registration tables as they chatted.

"Well, you were smart enough to put a ring on it. A big one, too. Smart man. I would have done the same. You think you'll be able to hold onto her?"

Shocked by the question, Charlie let out a soft growl. "What's that supposed to mean?"

Laz seem taken back. "I just meant because of the census."

"I still don't follow."

Laz tipped his head toward the tables. "Only ones who don't have to compete in the games are the married folks. Engagements don't count. The council wants to be sure all pairings are the best they can be."

"What?" A shot of panic went down Charlie's spine. He looked at the councilmembers checking people in. "They can't do that."

"It's already happening. Birth rates are down, apparently. They say our numbers are shrinking. Why do you think they called this census?"

His stomach soured as dread took hold of him and

Her First Taste Of Fire

heat began to build in his chest. "I don't care what their reasons are. Nasha and I are engaged."

Laz clapped him on the shoulder. "I'm sorry, man. I heard some other people complaining about it, too. Apparently, there are no exceptions being made. Especially if one half is human."

"She's not human. She's a supernatural."

Laz genuinely looked sympathetic. "Doesn't matter. She's not dragon. And they're not about to let a guy with your future get mated to a woman who isn't one of us unless they absolutely have to. Which means you both have to compete."

Charlie knew what Laz meant. His stupid inheritance made him a legacy. The Crimson Treaty Hoard. He wished he could set the whole thing on fire. He shook his head. "We'll just leave."

"You really want the council showing up at your house? Or worse, contacting your parents?"

Charlie exhaled, his temperature scaling ever higher. "No."

"I'm sorry. I didn't mean to be the one to break the bad news. Maybe there's something I can do to help. So long as you're willing to keep our past in the past."

"Absolutely." Charlie glanced at his friend. "You know I'd never say anything."

Laz flashed a quick smile. "Same. And thanks. Look, all you've got to do is place in the top ten. Then you can have your pick. Assuming no other dragon picks her, which they probably won't because she's not dragon. It won't be so bad."

"Unless another dragon does. After all, if she was good enough for me, why wouldn't she be good enough for someone else?" Not to mention how hard it would be to finish that high up in the rankings while trying to hide his curse.

Laz grimaced. "I hadn't considered that."

"Then our only hope is that she lands in the top ten as well, so we can pick each other. And what do you think her odds are of doing that?"

Laz looked doubtful. "Any chance she can breathe fire?"

"None." He might not know that much about Nasha, but that seemed to be a given.

Laz shoved his hands in his pockets. "Then I'd say they aren't so great."

Charlie stared straight ahead, his mind racing for a solution to this unbelievable new problem. The consequences of failing to final in the top ten were too awful to think about, not just for himself but for Nasha.

And she was his number one concern. She had to be. She was here because of him. He couldn't let her become the victim in all of this.

He glanced toward their spot on the mountain as the line shuffled forward. He no longer had a choice but to get her out of here.

"Name, please?"

He turned to see the councilwoman behind the table

waiting for his answer. He shook his head. "I can't stay, I —"

"All dragons are required to register." Her sharp gaze took him in. "Name, please."

"Charles Ashborne Jr."

She wrote in her book before looking up at him with a smile. "Always nice to have a legacy among us. That'll certainly make the games more interesting. Assuming you're not married?"

"No, but I am engaged, so I won't be participating in the games." It was worth a shot.

She smiled indulgently. "I'm sorry, Mr. Ashborne. The rules have changed for this census. I'm sure you've heard about our declining numbers. It's become the council's duty to be certain that all pairings are optimal. You and your fiancée will be required to compete along with all the others."

He stared at her, trying to find the words that would solve all of this, but there weren't any. No nice ones, anyway. "We'll leave, then."

She handed him a packet of information, her eyes filled with stern fire. "Mr. Ashborne, the council prefers willing participants. If you're no longer willing, you may petition the council for a hearing, but you will be required to wait in restraints until that hearing is granted."

"Restraints?"

"Yes. Both of you. Your families will be contacted, as well. Are you sure you want to go that route?"

He couldn't put Nasha – or his sisters – through that. He'd figure out another way. Because there had to be one. "No."

"Good." She went back to smiling. "I'm sure you and your fiancée will have no trouble ending up together. After all, if it was meant to be, a few games won't change that, will they?" She looked past him. "Next?"

He took the packet and moved to the side. He momentarily entertained a fantasy in which he took flight and burned the valley to dust and ashes with no concern for how many scales he'd lose.

But that wouldn't solve anything, either.

Laz grabbed hold of his arm. "You going to be all right, man? Your brain looks like it's steaming."

Charlie looked at him and shook his head. "I have to talk to Nasha. Now."

Chapter Fourteen

The cave hadn't magically become the Four Seasons, but it looked a whole lot better with all the things Charlie had gotten at the outdoors store. Nasha wasn't sure he even knew half the things he'd bought, but she wasn't complaining.

She'd helped herself to the very cool survival knife, tucking it into her boot. Hey, dragons had talons. She ought to have something sharp and pointy, too.

The shiny silver mylar blanket she found in one of the bags had gone up on the flattest part of the wall, held in place by smaller rocks tucked into crevices and laid on little outcroppings. In front of that, she built a firepit of more rocks, three layers high.

It looked pretty good. To her anyway. She'd never built a firepit before. As for the mylar, she figured that would act to reflect heat and light, both of which the cave needed. Charlie could gather wood when he got back, then he could light the fire.

She set up her cot and air mattress, which had been surprisingly easy to blow up, thanks to the honeycomb design that actually took very little air, and then her sleeping bag on top of it, both near the fire. One of the downsides to being thin was often being cold. Even in the summer, she was rarely hot. Just part of who she was.

She lay down on her new bed, testing the mattress and the little travel pillow. Not bad at all. She stared up at the cave's ceiling. What she could see of it. Without a fire it was pretty dark in here. Tonight would be the real test. Sleeping in a cave. With a dragon.

Life had sure taken an interesting turn.

She got up and went back to work. Charlie had been thoughtful enough to grab a rain poncho for her. She hadn't seen a cloud in the sky yet, but maybe he knew something she didn't about the weather.

There were a few items she wasn't sure what to do with. Like the folding shovel. Or the first aid kit. Or the bundle of cording. There was even a camping hammock, which looked very comfy and like a great place to relax, but there wasn't any way to set it up. Nothing to hang it off of.

She put all of those items to one side. Hard to say what could happen in the midst of this very strange gathering, or what might come in handy.

One thing she didn't have to wonder about were the towels. She was grateful for those, and she doubted she would have remembered them, so he got serious points for bringing some back. Now she could use that big natural pool without having to air dry or freeze to death. And if there was one thing she liked, it was a good bath.

That was, after Charlie heated that water up. Because she'd stuck her hand in, just to test it, and the water was like ice. She was surprised there wasn't any floating in it. The temperature made sense, though. That water was snow melt. Expecting it to be anything but cold was just silly.

She'd set a few candles on rocks in front of the mylar blanket and lit them with a lighter she'd found in the shopping bags, just to see how much they'd actually brighten the cave.

More than she'd thought, thanks to the mylar sheet. Between the candles, the lanterns, and the fire, once it got going, they'd be fine.

Maybe they'd even get to use the pack of playing cards she'd found in one of the bags.

The camp stove, coffee pot, cooking utensils, pan, and water-filtering pitcher went by the fire pit. Near that, she set up a little pantry with the food he'd brought back. Coffee, sugar, freeze-dried meals, some canned soups, beef jerky, and lots of chocolate bars.

She smiled. That had been particularly kind of Charlie, all things considered. But the only chocolate she wanted was his. The bag with those remaining chocolates went next to her bed, on the side away from the fire.

She stood back and took a look at her work. Definitely homier than it had been. Sort of the Flintstones meets Bear Grylls.

"Wow, you did a lot of work in here. Looks great."

She turned to see Charlie standing at the cave's entrance. He had a large envelope in one hand. Behind him stood another man, about the same age. "Thanks. I'm pretty happy with how it turned out."

Charlie looked troubled, for lack of a better word. There was a tightness around his eyes that made him seem on edge.

She walked toward him, shooting a glance at the man behind him. "Everything okay?"

Charlie took a deep breath before answering. "Not exactly. I'll explain in a minute. This is my friend, Lazarus Stratton. You met him earlier. In a different form."

Laz stuck his hand out. "Hi. Nice to meet you officially, Nasha."

She smiled and shook his hand. "You, too, Lazarus."

"Call me Laz. If I scared you earlier, I'm sorry. I realize I might have come off a little gruff."

She appreciated the apology. "I'm sure it surprised you to see someone who looks like me staking claim to a cave."

He laughed. "That's for sure. Especially when that person also turned out to be my friend's fiancée." He gestured at Charlie. "We went to school together."

She nodded. "He mentioned that." Small talk was fine, but she needed to know what was bothering Charlie. She shifted her attention back to him. "So what's going on?"

He frowned. "According to the new council rules, there are no exceptions for the engaged, only the married. We're going to have to compete in the games."

"What? How can they do that? Engaged people are

committed to each other just as much as—wait, did you say *we* were going to have to compete? As in, me, too?" That was unexpected. She wasn't exactly the most athletically inclined.

His frown deepened. "Yes. And the only way out of it that I can come up with is to fly you out of here as soon as it gets dark. I'm pretty sure I can take you home and return without them realizing I've left. Without you on my back, I can fly a lot faster, so it shouldn't take that long."

"No."

He blinked. "No? I don't think you're understanding what I'm saying. They're going to make both of us compete. The only way we end up together is if we both finish in the top ten. We'll be up against something like three or four hundred dragons. And you're not necessarily equipped to compete in the kinds of games they're going to have."

She took a moment to process that. Leaving now would mean their deal was off. No chocolate recipe.

More than that, it would mean she'd be breaking her word to Charlie. She hated the very idea of that. Hated the thought of leaving him here to fend for himself and end up with a wife he didn't want. "No."

"Nasha, listen to me. You could end up with a dragon mate."

She gave him a sharp look. Unless he'd explained to Laz what was going on, Charlie was coming dangerously close to spilling the beans. "Um, as you know, I don't have a problem with a dragon mate. Darling."

His eyes rounded in understanding. "Right. I meant one who wasn't me."

"Well, that would suck. I will not marry another man."

"You won't have a choice," Laz said. "It'll be a done deal."

"They can't do that," she said. "I'm not a dragon. They don't get to say what I do. And I don't give my consent."

A muscle in Charlie's jaw twitched. "Entering the games is considered consent. The council is pretty militant like that. If you compete, you're agreeing to abide by their rules."

"Listen," Laz started. "You two have a lot to discuss and I should leave you to it. But I'm here to help in whatever way I can. Just let me know."

Charlie turned toward him. "Thanks. I'm glad you're here."

"Same." Laz lifted his hand to wave at Nasha. "Nice to meet you. I'm just a couple caves away if you need me. You can just yell. I'm sure I'll hear you."

"Thanks." She waved back. "Nice to meet you, too."

He turned and took flight, leaving them alone.

She spoke first. "He doesn't know that we're just pretending, does he?"

"No. And it should probably stay that way. Not that I don't trust him. I do. It's just…easier if he doesn't have to keep the secret, too, you know?"

"Yep. Totally agree." She paced toward the far wall, then turned to look at him. "What kind of games are we talking about? Feats of strength? Obstacle courses? Puzzles? I'm not all that athletic, but I am very competitive." At least she had that going for her.

"It's been almost eight years since the last census, and with this council, I really don't know what to expect. Could be feats of strength and agility. Maybe obstacle courses. But there could be puzzles and mind games just as well. This council has some strange new ideas."

She paced back toward him. "Will I be given any kind of handicap for not being dragon?"

"I don't think there will be any allowances made. You either win or you don't."

That was going to make it harder. Especially if there was anything that involved specific dragon skills. "I'm totally willing to do this. I just don't know how I'll manage if I'm required to fly or breathe fire."

He nodded. "That worries me, too." He went silent for a few heartbeats. "I need to go back and speak to the council. Explain that what they're asking isn't fair."

"Do you think it'll help? Because if it's only going to single me out as different..."

"I understand. But they need to be made aware that you're not dragon. Maybe...maybe they'll exempt you." He didn't look like he really believed that.

She smiled anyway. "Worth a shot then."

He didn't smile back. "I'm really sorry about this." The muscles in his jaw tightened and she could have sworn she saw shimmering waves of heat radiating off him. "What a mess it's turned into."

She grabbed his hand. He was *very* warm. "Hey, it's not your fault. You had no idea. You were just trying to avoid getting hitched to some stranger. Which is how you ended up getting pretend-hitched to a stranger."

He laughed for a second. "You're being very understanding."

She shrugged. "I guess I like you too much not to want this to all work out." She did like him. A lot. And they were absolutely in this together now.

"I like you, too." His eyes narrowed, and there was a soft light in them that made her feel good. "You're the best fake fiancée I've ever had." He squeezed her hand.

"I'd better be." This easiness that was developing between them seemed very much like friendship. They were friends, weren't they? "How many have you had?"

"Just you." He went quiet again. Then tugged her closer, put his arms around her, and held her. "This isn't going to be easy."

She leaned into him, finding comfort in his warmth. "I know. I'm okay with that. Most things worth having or doing take work. My dad taught me that."

He leaned back and smiled at her. "Your dad seems like a pretty smart guy. I'd like to meet him when we get back."

"Yeah?" She'd never had a man say that to her. Not even Shepherd had been that brave. "I'm sure he'd like to meet you."

Her First Taste Of Fire

Charlie let go of her with what seemed like reluctance. "I'm going to talk to the council. Do you want to come with me?"

"I thought we couldn't leave the cave unattended." Going to talk to the council sounded slightly scary, but it might also help if she went with him. Let them see her in person. See how *not* a dragon she was.

"Our stuff is in here. It's fine now that it's obviously occupied."

She nodded. "Then let's go."

CHAPTER FIFTEEN

There would be no exceptions made for Nasha. Charlie knew that before even speaking to the council, but they had to try. He flew them down to the tent and hoped there was a reasonable council member available to speak with.

He landed, let Nasha slide off, then shifted to human form. Together, they walked into the tent. The woman who'd give him his info packet was nowhere in sight, which seemed like a good thing.

He found an older man in conversation with another man, a younger councilmember. He nudged Nasha. "Let's go talk to them."

"Okay."

As they approached, the pair looked at them. The older man spoke first. "Hello. Thank you for attending the census. Do you need to get registered?"

"No, thanks, we've already done that. I'm Charlie Ashborne, by the way, and this is my fiancée, Nasha Black."

"Pleasure to meet you. I'm Xavier Redwing. This is councilman Kreston Whitlock."

"Nice to meet you both. We have some questions.

Maybe you can help us with those?"

Kreston shook his head. "I'm sorry, I have to go. I was supposed to be recording registrations ten minutes ago. Please excuse me."

"Go on, Kreston. I can help these folks." As Kreston left, Xavier glanced at Nasha, then back at Charlie. "What questions do you have?"

"We've been told that engaged couples are required to participate in the games. Is this true?"

Xavier nodded, and his expression darkened. "Yes, that is true."

"That seems rather cruel, don't you think? We can't be the only engaged couple here."

Xavier briefly looked past them. Was he trying to see if anyone else was in earshot? "You aren't. And unofficially, I don't disagree with you. But I'm sure you've heard that our numbers are in jeopardy."

"I have. Still doesn't justify breaking up those who've already decided to spend their lives together."

Xavier sighed. "The new councilmembers had the vote. There isn't anything I can do about it."

Charlie wondered just how true that was. "What about the fact that my fiancée isn't dragon? And yet, she's being made to compete in our games?"

Xavier looked more closely at Nasha and frowned. "So I see." He shook his head, eyes on Charlie again. "No exceptions will be made. I'm sorry. If there was anything I could do…"

Nasha took a step forward, chin lifted, eyes defiant.

"You could stand up to the other councilmembers."

Xavier offered her a weak smile and a shake of his head. "I tried, my dear. But to them, I am an old man with old ideas. And they're too filled with new ones to listen. They think they know best. There are a few of us who disagree with them, but not enough to stop the changes they're implementing. Your best hope is to win. Maybe that's something they'll take notice of."

He touched Charlie's shoulder. "I wish you both the best. I will speak to the council about your fiancée's situation. That much I can do. But don't expect anything to come of it."

Nasha shook her head. "Who can change things if you can't? Which councilmember?"

Xavier sighed and glanced toward the table at the far end of the tent. "Lakshmi Stoneheart. She's the president of the council and the new blood that's behind all of this." He shook his head as he continued to stare at the woman in question. "She's a water dragon, too, which is ironic, since they're supposed to be the most peaceable of our kind."

"Thanks," Nasha said softly.

"You're welcome. For what it was worth." He walked away, looking far older than he had when they'd approached him.

Charlie stared after him, the anger inside him growing. "I refuse to accept this."

Nasha twisted her fingers together. "Okay, but what else can we do?"

Her First Taste Of Fire

"Nothing. But there's something *I* can do." The heat inside him grew to the point that his vision wavered and went red at the edges. He was furious. This new council did not represent him. "As much as I hate to do it, it's time to use my status for good."

Her brows rose. "Your status?"

He hadn't intended on telling her or anyone, but that was no longer an option. He wasn't going to be able to keep it a secret anyway, since some of the councilmembers seemed to know. "I'm a legacy. When my father passes, I will inherit one of the largest hoards in dragon history. It gives me some pull." Pull he'd never wanted to use for a variety of reasons. Namely, it would instantly identify him as a legacy, and it would bring his family into this.

If he was shamed because of this census, they would bear that dishonor as well. He saw no other choice.

"That Crimson Treaty thing?"

"Yes. How did you know?"

"Lazarus mentioned it. So, are you going to talk to that Lakshmi woman?"

"I am." Concern filled Nasha's eyes. Or was it fear? For him? For herself? He wasn't sure. But he didn't want her to be the victim in all this. "Do you want me to take you back to the cave first?"

"Absolutely not. I want to be at your side. Where your fiancée should be."

He smiled. "Thanks." Then he kissed her forehead. "Your support means a lot."

She smiled. "What do you need me to do?"

"Hang back a little. I think it would be better for me to do this alone. At least initially. I'll give you a look when I want you to join me."

"Okay."

With his plan in his head, he walked to the table, and stopped in front of Lakshmi. Her long black hair was plaited in elaborate braids studded with tiny gold and jewel beads. She had more gold and jewels at her ears, her throat, her wrists, and her fingers.

It was fairly common for younger dragons to wear large parts of their hoards as a show of wealth and power. To Charlie, it seemed more like a desperate attempt to appear wealthy and powerful by those who knew they weren't.

He'd have to tread lightly. This woman might not compare to him in real life, but right now, she was the head of the council and held far more power than she should. "Lakshmi Stoneheart?"

She looked up at him. "Yes? How can I help you?"

"I'm Charles Ashborne Jr." He watched her eyes to see if dropping his full name was enough.

The interest that came alive in her gaze said it was. She extended her hand, knuckles up, as if she expected him to brush a kiss across them. "Well, what an honor to have a legacy among us. I didn't know you were attending this census. I didn't even know you were living on this continent."

He shook her hand. That was all she was getting from

Her First Taste Of Fire

him. But he held onto it as well, letting her feel just how warm he was. "I only moved a few years ago."

"It's a pleasure to have you here." She was still smiling, leaning forward with obvious interest. She made no effort to take her hand back. "Say, is the Crimson Treaty Hoard really as large as they say it is."

He shook his head, then smiled broadly and gave her a wink. "No. It's much, much larger."

She laughed, a tinny little twitter that seemed both patronizing and oddly giddy. "Oh, my. Isn't that just marvelous?" She fluttered her lashes. "Are you settling in all right? Did you find a cave to suit you?"

"I am and I did. But I need some help."

She gasped softly, like that was something that must be rectified immediately. "What can I do for you, Charles? Anything. Just name it. I am at your service."

He held onto his smile. "I'm so glad to hear you say that. A great injustice has come to my attention."

Instantly, she looked appropriately distraught. She squeezed his hand as if overcome with the unpleasantness of whatever his problem was. "How terrible. What can I do to make things right?"

"There is someone here who isn't a dragon, but is being forced to compete in the games all the same. There might be more than one, for all I know. As a legacy, I'm deeply concerned by how poorly this reflects on the council. On all of us, really. Treating another race with anything less than respect and fairness makes us seem arrogant. And the council comes off as cold and indifferent by not being willing to make some allowances, don't you think?"

She swallowed and he felt the tiniest twitch in her fingers. Like she was trying to slip her hand free. He held tight. "I suppose it does. I hadn't heard about this, so I wasn't aware of the problem. Surely something can be done."

"A handicap for the others then? Or an advantage of some sort for this non-dragon? That would only be fair, don't you agree?"

Her smile was weakening. "Yes, of course. What kind of advantage do you think would be...fair?"

He almost laughed at how pained she seemed to be just speaking those words. "I'd say a forty percent increase in points. That's not much, is it? But it seems enough to create some sort of balance."

Her eyes widened. "Forty percent? That's too much. I can't approve that."

"Then what can you approve?" He'd never expected to get forty. *Never.* But being in business had taught him to aim higher than he hoped to hit.

She glanced away. Was she expecting her colleagues, who were all listening intently, to step in and save her? None of them seemed interested in doing that. "Twenty?"

"Come now, Lakshmi. I believe the council can afford to be more generous than that, don't you? A non-dragon in our games, who stands little to no chance of placing, let alone winning anything, and the best the council can offer is twenty percent? This is the perfect opportunity to show just how generous the council can be, don't you think?"

She squirmed. "Thirty?"

He smiled serenely. On the inside, he was laughing with joy. "Outstanding, councilwoman. I knew you had it in you. Thirty percent, then." He nodded at the councilmembers seated with her. "Make sure that's recorded so there's no confusion later."

One of them started to write it down.

He lifted Lakshmi's hand to his mouth, and finally kissed her knuckles. "I thank you, councilwoman." Then he released her hand and glanced back at Nasha, giving her a little nod.

She started forward to join him.

The kiss appeared to have placated Lakshmi somewhat. She was smiling at him again. "Well, like you said, what chance does a non-dragon have anyway? Who is this person you spoke of? I'd like to know who they are. So that I can be sure they're treated fairly, of course."

"Of course. And I'd be happy to introduce you."

Nasha stepped next to him just then. He put his arm around her. "This is Nasha Black. My fiancée."

CHAPTER SIXTEEN

Nasha poked at the fire that Charlie and Laz had built. They were all gathered around it now, she and Charlie in camp chairs, Laz on a rock he'd hauled in. Charlie had just finished telling Laz the details about how things had gone with the councilwoman.

"He was unbelievable," Nasha said. "So smooth."

"I bet," Laz said. "I wish I'd been there." He held his tin cup of coffee out to Charlie. "Cheers, my friend. Well done."

Charlie lifted his cup in return. "Thanks. But it remains to be seen if it will actually help."

"It has to," Nasha said. "An extra thirty percent of points? How could it not?

Laz shrugged. "We still don't know what the games are going to be. Knowing that would help. We could at least try to prepare you."

"They could be changing the games right now." Charlie stared into the fire. "Coming up with new ones where the points advantage won't make a difference."

Nasha tried not to think about that. It wasn't something she could change. She wanted to focus on where

Her First Taste Of Fire

she could make a difference. "What's in that packet of stuff you brought back from registration?"

Charlie looked up. "I don't know. I haven't opened it yet."

"A participant number with a lanyard to hold it," Laz answered. "The rules of the games, a hold harmless injury disclaimer, that kind of thing."

"The rules?" Nasha sat up straighter.

Laz nodded. "Yeah. It's about five pages long and in eight-point font. I'm sure no one will actually read them, which is probably their intent."

She looked at Charlie. "Where's the packet?"

"On top of my duffel bag."

She jumped up and grabbed it, then brought it back to the firepit. The light was good there. The mylar sheet was doing its job. Even Laz had commented on the smart setup when he'd come over.

Charlie leaned on one elbow. "Are you really going to read all of that?"

She pulled the papers out of the envelope. "Can't hurt."

Laz picked a small piece of dried bark off the stump and tossed it into the fire. "I suppose not."

Charlie smiled. "I think it's a good idea."

Laz glanced at Nasha. "So do I. Just not sure I have the fortitude to do it myself. Reading was never my favorite thing in school."

"No, that was Miss Sarah Jane Broadmore, our Latin teacher."

Laz laughed. "True. Although I still failed that class. I guess it was a good thing we went to an all-boys school. If there had been girls there, I would have failed all my classes."

"As if the girls would have paid attention to us. You seem to forget we were the outcasts."

Nasha looked up. "Why was that?"

Charlie glanced at Laz, who shrugged, before answering her. "Standard teenage boy awkwardness, I guess."

"Even with you being the heir to that big hoard?"

He sipped his coffee. "Even with that."

He wasn't telling her something, but that was okay. Not everyone liked to talk about their childhood. Besides, she had pages of small print to read.

Laz looked at his watch. "They'll be serving dinner soon."

She glanced up from the pages. "What is it?"

"Chili. Corn bread with butter and honey. Beer. Fruit hand pies. Apple, I think. Or there are box meals of sandwiches, chips, fruit, and a drink."

Charlie's brows shot up. "How do you know all that?"

Laz pointed at the papers in Nasha's hands. "It's all in the packet."

"Which you just said you didn't read."

Laz shrugged, smiling. "I read the food part. I like to know what's to eat."

Charlie laughed. "You really haven't changed."

She liked seeing the two of them interacting like old

friends. It was nice knowing Charlie had someone like that in his life. Her phone buzzed. She took it out of her pocket.

A text had come in from Brighton. *Everything's good here. Hope you're having fun.*

She smiled. *Thanks for the update.*

Good to know they hadn't burned the place down. She put her phone away and glanced at Charlie. "Should we go down to eat?"

"Hungry?" Charlie asked.

She wasn't. She'd had a few more chocolates. But she didn't want to stand in the way of whatever was supposed to happen. "I'm happy to go when you guys are ready."

Charlie got to his feet and stretched. "Might as well go now. Get it out of the way. Then we can come back and make an early night of it. The games start first thing in the morning."

Laz got up, too. "You don't sound like you're looking forward to mingling."

"I hate mingling. Especially now that word has probably spread about who I am." He offered his hand to Nasha.

She set the paperwork aside and took it, letting him help her up. "You think it'll change things?"

Laz answered. "Let's just say he got bumped up a few spots on the most eligible bachelors list."

Nasha thought about that. "I guess being the heir to that hoard is a big deal?"

Laz rolled his eyes. "You have no idea."

Charlie groaned. "I don't want to talk about it."

"Don't worry," Laz ribbed him. "There will be plenty of women down there who do."

"Um, hello?" Nasha held her hands out. "What about the fact that he has a fiancée? I know the council doesn't care, but that has to mean something to some of those women, doesn't it?"

Laz's gaze turned sympathetic. "I'm not sure it will."

She looked at Charlie, her handsome, apparently very rich, pretend husband-to-be. "I guess I'm just going to have to make it clear that I'm not the kind of woman that's going to turn a blind eye to female foolishness."

Charlie gave her a curious glance. "What does that mean, exactly?"

"It means that while the official games start in the morning, the real games start tonight." She headed for the entrance. "Let's go, boys. I have work to do."

They landed a few yards from the tent, which was illuminated with string lights. Tables had been set up around three sides of it, and inside, two serving lines had formed, one on the right and one on the left.

The three of them got into the left one, since it was fractionally shorter. Nasha made sure to hold Charlie's hand.

There were plenty of women looking at him. Some of them whispering to their girlfriends. Some of them just smiling. And a few of them acting like he was the first item on the menu, and they were dying of hunger.

One, a pale, Nordic-looking blonde, stared at Charlie

with such a bold gaze, Nasha half expected her to come over and introduce herself.

Nasha turned her back so the woman couldn't see her speaking, and quietly said to Laz. "Don't look right away, but who's the ice queen in the second line? The one staring at Charlie like he's tonight's blue plate special?"

Laz turned and waved to some imaginary friend. He answered her a second later. "Verochka Lukin. Also a legacy. Russian. She stands to inherit her family's hoard as well as a fortune from her father's shipping company. Currently lives in Los Angeles and is famous for being famous. You know, she's one of those social media influencer people who get paid for being beautiful."

"I know the kind," Nasha said. The woman *was* beautiful. Nasha snuck another look. Verochka was tall, with the kind of Barbie-doll build that had to be surgically enhanced. She had a crowd of men around her, none of whom she seemed to be particularly interested in.

Probably because she was staring at Charlie.

Nasha frowned, disappointed by how short she suddenly felt. "She needs to look at someone else for a while."

Charlie smirked. "Jealous?"

"Isn't that the correct response?" She raised her brows. She could play this game if that's what was required of her.

He nodded. "For a dragon female, definitely. Good for you. That's the kind of reaction that will earn you their respect."

"You haven't seen anything yet." As they moved forward in line, Nasha positioned herself directly in front of Charlie, putting herself in Verochka's line of sight. Then she stared back at the woman.

Laz's smile looked strained and tight, like he was trying not to laugh. "This is getting interesting. And here I thought this census was going to be boring."

"Any chance Russian Barbie turns into a pearl-white dragon?"

Laz nodded. "Yep, that's her. I take it you caught a glimpse of her earlier?"

"Yes. And she made sure I saw her. She flew past the cave twice."

Verochka continued to watch Charlie.

Nasha realized she needed to step things up. She faced Charlie, leaned into him, and smiled. "You really need to kiss me right now."

He smiled back, wrapped his arms around her, and put his mouth on hers. She slipped her arms around his neck, threading her fingers through his hair. For a second, it was all pretend. Then the heat of Charlie's mouth was all she could think about.

It was turning her liquid. Melting away all thoughts of what would look the most convincing and putting her directly in the moment. The kiss *was* real. His hands on her hips were real. The heat building in her own body, absolutely real.

Then the clearing of a throat broke them apart. Laz

nodded at something ahead of them. The line had moved. They were holding things up.

Nasha took Charlie's hand and pulled him forward. He acted dazed, an extra-special touch that really sold it. Although, she felt slightly light-headed herself. Maybe she just needed to eat.

She glanced over. Verochka wasn't watching Charlie anymore.

She wasn't smiling, either. But Nasha was.

They got their food, ate pretty quickly without any major interactions with anyone else, then said goodnight and headed back to their respective caves with the promise to meet up for breakfast on the field in the morning.

Nasha went straight to the firepit. She still had reading to do. She picked up the paperwork, settled into one of the chairs, and flipped through it to the section on game rules.

Charlie came over and stood beside the empty camp chair. "Mind if I sit with you?"

She shook her head. "You don't have to ask. This is your cave, after all." And after that kiss, it felt like things had changed between them in a more intimate way.

Maybe she was reading more into that than was really there. Maybe that was just how good they were at pretending. So good that she was starting to buy it herself.

A half-smile bent his mouth. "It's your cave, too. I just didn't want to bother you." He grabbed a couple more logs from the pile he and Laz had stacked against the wall and placed them carefully on the fire.

"You could never bother me, Charlie. Unless you decided to close your shop and never make chocolate again. Then we'd have a problem."

"I promise not to do that." He snorted as he sat. "You and your chocolate."

"Actually, it's *your* chocolate. But, yes, I am addicted." She could really go for a piece right now.

"Are you nervous about tomorrow?"

She nodded. "Hard not to be. Especially because I don't know what to expect. But no one knows what to expect from me, either. In a way, that kind of gives me an advantage."

"I like that way of thinking. Smart."

"I do think Verochka will be coming for me." Nasha set the papers on her lap. "She wants you. That much is plain."

"She's not my type." He stared into the flames.

"You sure? Because if you find a woman here you think you'd like to get to know better, just tell me and—"

"No." He looked at her. "You're the only woman I'm interested in. Here or anywhere else."

"Okay." She went back to the sheaf of paperwork, but her mind lingered on his words. Had he clarified that statement for her sake? Or for his? She wasn't sure, but there really wasn't time to dwell. She had pages of rules to read.

And a battle to prepare for.

CHAPTER SEVENTEEN

Charlie waved to Lazarus as they walked toward the food tent. He was a few yards away. He waved back. He and everyone else milling about had their lanyards on, entrant numbers visible.

Breakfast was being served under the tent and the smell of sizzling breakfast meat was strong. Charlie wasn't sure he could eat much, though.

He was nervous for Nasha. Himself, too. But what happened to her was now equally as important as what happened to him.

It was almost like the relationship they were playing at had started to become real. Almost. He wasn't really falling for her. He was just fulfilling his role. The fact that she was a tremendous kisser might be clouding his judgement, but that was it.

He knew she wasn't falling for him. And, he told himself a second time, he wasn't falling for her. They were just…friends.

"Ready to grab some grub?" Laz asked.

Nasha nodded. "Sure. How'd you sleep?"

"Like a baby. A cranky, colicky baby." Laz laughed. "Maybe it makes me less of a dragon, but I still prefer my memory foam mattress over the hard ground, although it wasn't that bad. And how did you sleep, Nasha?"

"Surprisingly well." She grinned at Charlie before looking at Laz again. "Did you know dragons snore?"

"I do not," Charlie said. Although he really wasn't sure. It had been a long time since he'd slept in his dragon form. He didn't even know if he snored in human form.

She gave him an innocent look. "Did I say you? I just said dragons."

He snorted. "Well, if I did, I'm sorry."

"Hey, at least the snoring isn't also accompanied by flames." Her brows lifted. "That would be trouble."

"Small victories." He hooked his thumb toward the tent. "Should we get some breakfast?"

"Might as well," Laz answered. "If I have to be up this early I should at least get a meal out of it."

He continued talking as they walked toward one of the lines that was forming up. "By the way, lunch is sausages and burgers on the grill and not until the first game is finished. Of course, we might not feel like eating after that."

Charlie hoped that wasn't the case.

"Have some faith," Nasha said. She lowered her voice as they got in line. "Any idea what the first game's going to be? From what I read, the women go first, then the men."

"That's right, but I have no idea what the game is." Laz frowned. "They've been pretty hush-hush about all of that. There has to be something to do with the games in those bundles over there. It can't just be supplies for the meals. There's too many of them."

Charlie looked in the same direction as Laz. Large pallets, stacked high and covered in camouflage netting and canvas tarps, sat in several long rows about twenty yards to the left of the tent. The camo hid them in plain sight remarkably well. From the sky, they were probably not visible at all. And they'd undoubtedly been brought in overnight, because they hadn't been there yesterday.

He turned his head slightly, trying to make out whatever was stenciled on the side, but the netting was in the way. "I could take a wander over there, see what I can see."

Nasha put her hand on his arm. "Don't. It could get you into trouble and knowing what's in there won't change anything. We can't stop what's coming."

"No, but we could prepare."

"Maybe. But the game will happen regardless of what we do."

"She's right," Laz said. "Better not to risk it. They could disqualify you. Well, maybe not over that small of an infraction, but with this council? Who knows."

Charlie and Nasha looked at him at the same time. Charlie had to know more. "Good point. Getting disqualified would be bad."

Nasha frowned. "You mean it seems like the penalty would be more than just not getting to play in the games?"

Charlie crossed his arms. "I don't know what this new council would do, but in the old days, you'd end up shunned for a year."

Nasha shook her head. "And that means what, exactly?"

Laz answered her. "You're considered dead, essentially. No other dragons are supposed to talk to you or have anything to do with you. Including your family."

"For a whole year? Harsh." She made a face. "Your society is pretty hardcore."

Laz looked past her at the table of councilmembers who were already eating. "We are dragons. We're supposed to be hardcore. It's not always the easiest of lives. This new council isn't helping, either."

Charlie spotted a dragon landing in the field behind them. The creature's coloring was a dead giveaway as to who it was. He nudged Nasha. "Look, your favorite person just arrived for breakfast."

She turned in time to see Verochka shift into human form. "Wow, that's some outfit."

Charlie had to agree. The Russian was in pearl-white leather from head to toe, including her boots, which had a tall, chunky heel. Not exactly the most practical outfit for a day of games in a field, but Verochka didn't seem to be concerned about practical.

Laz let out a low whistle. "Now that's a look."

"I feel underdressed," Nasha said.

Charlie looked at her and shook his head. "You look

perfect. She comes off like she's wearing a costume. Whereas you look like an actual badass."

Nasha did, too. She was dressed simply in a long-sleeve black T-shirt with a slim tactical-style vest over top, black leggings, and black combat boots. The little dagger earrings hadn't gone unnoticed, either.

She smiled at him. "Thanks. I hope I can live up to that assessment. But she looks pretty intimidating."

"You have nothing to worry about."

Laz leaned in. "Not to mention, if that outfit had ever seen any real trouble, it wouldn't be that pristine."

Nasha nodded. "Good point."

As the line moved and they got closer to breakfast, Verochka got closer to them. She smiled as she approached, and Charlie was pretty sure that smile was meant more for him than anyone else in his party.

"Good morning, comrade." Her accent was thicker than he'd expected. Her smile brightened as she passed. She shot one quick look at Nasha.

Charlie gave her a nod, nothing more.

Nasha snorted. "For someone who lives in L.A., she sure plays up that whole Russian angle."

"It's her schtick," Laz said. "I think her Instagram is literally @RussianBarbie."

Nasha narrowed her eyes. "You're teasing me."

"Nope. She totally owns it." He jerked his chin at her. "Look at her. She went straight to the front of the line and some shmuck she'll probably never speak to again just let her right in."

Nasha let out a soft, throaty growl that could have come straight out of a dragon, making Charlie smile, although he tried to hide it. "I can't stand her," Nasha said. "Or women like her. They use their looks to get ahead."

Charlie gave her a nudge. "Like you've never done that."

She cut her eyes at him. "You're being kind, but I don't have those kinds of looks."

He lifted his brows. "Those kinds of looks can be bought. You've got your own kind of beauty. Your own kind of dark charm. Plus, you've got something she doesn't."

One side of her mouth hitched up in an almost smile. "Yeah? What's that?"

"You look dangerous. Like a bad girl. Like the kind who might steal your car right after she breaks your heart and ruins you for other women." He glanced at Verochka. "That one? She mostly looks like she'll just empty your bank account."

Laz snorted. "You can say that again."

Nasha's half-grin went full blown. "You really know how to sweettalk a woman, you know that?"

Charlie laughed. "I just call 'em like I see 'em."

They'd reached the front of the line. Laz stepped out of the way so Nasha could go ahead of him. "After you."

Charlie appreciated the kindness and respect his old friend was showing toward her. He hoped that was the

Her First Taste Of Fire

same kind of treatment she'd get from the other dragons here.

Not Verochka, of course. But perhaps the men. The women...there was no telling. A lot would be determined by this first game and its outcome.

Something they were about to find out very soon.

They got their plates and found a table, which were big, six-seater picnics, meaning they only took up the end of it.

A few others joined them. Two women, sisters. And an older man on his own. They were cordial enough, but Charlie could sense they were taken aback by Nasha's presence.

It wasn't hard to tell Nasha wasn't dragon, he only wasn't sure how much they could sense about what she really was. She carried the subtle, sooty smell of dark magic, which he now understood why, since she'd revealed who her father was.

Did anyone else here understand it? He doubted it. His people were so insular that they rarely took the time to learn about other supernaturals. They generally only interacted with them as little as they had to.

Something he realized he'd been guilty of himself. Shadowvale had such a diverse population, and yet, other than the people who came into his shop, he hardly spoke to anyone else. He'd been keeping to himself because of his curse. That's what he'd told himself.

Now he wondered if that wasn't just an excuse. Everyone in Shadowvale was cursed, which was why no one cared what your problem was. The curses were a great leveler. Had he been avoiding others because it was something drilled into him all of his life?

He was really starting to question that.

He glanced at Nasha, who was listening to one of Laz's stories. He never would have imagined going out with her, let alone being involved with her the way he was now. This was her doing. She'd offered to help him.

Would he have done the same for her? Probably not.

He needed to work on that. If he ever got the chance to return to Shadowvale.

While they were finishing up their eggs, bacon, sausage, home fries, and toast, the councilmembers began directing the setup for what could only be the day's game.

Besides moving tables into several long lines, crates were being unpacked from the pallet bundles. Scales were being set up, along with stacks of small paper trays, the kind you might get a corn dog in at a state fair.

"This has to be for the game," Laz said. "But what on earth is it?"

Nasha shook her head. "Beats me."

The sisters at the table were watching the proceedings, too. One of them turned to the other and said, "Amarun berries."

Charlie nodded in understanding. "I know what this is. The first game is a contest to see who can stomach eating the most berries. That's why they're weighing them out. So everyone starts with the same amount."

"Amarun berries?" Nasha shook her head. "I've never heard of them and I bake with all kinds of fruit."

"You wouldn't have," Laz said. "That's their dragon name. Not sure if they have a different one, as no one really eats them. They're the sourest thing you can imagine putting in your mouth. They'll make you pucker so hard some people throw up after eating just one."

She made a face. "Then why are they using them for this contest?"

"Every traditional dragon holiday meal has a bowl of them on the table." Charlie remembered them well. He and his sisters always dared each other to eat one.

"But why?" Nasha persisted.

One of the sisters at the table looked at Nasha. "The legend of Mishka. She was a dragon taken captive by humans centuries ago, bound and held as a prize, shown off like some kind of trophy. The humans refused to feed her anything more than occasional scraps, fearing she'd grow too strong and escape."

The other sister nodded. "But Mishka found wild berries within reach of where she was chained, and despite their terrible bitterness, ate enough of them to get her strength back. She escaped her restraints and burned the village to the ground."

The sisters smiled.

Laz rolled his eyes. "Yeah, we eat them to celebrate how one of us overcame human persecution and triumphantly slaughtered those responsible *and* a bunch of innocents as a result. We're hardcore, remember?"

"Apparently." Nasha blinked a few times as she took all of that in.

Charlie put his hand on her leg under the table and lowered his voice. "You don't have to do this. You can just sit this one out."

She looked at him with amusement. "Please. Not only am I *not* going to sit this one out, I'm going to win it."

CHAPTER EIGHTEEN

Nasha found Charlie's skeptical look highly entertaining. She was looking forward to this game. Finally, an upside to her curse. And at the best possible moment. She did her best not to look too happy about the whole thing, because the dragon females around her all seemed pretty miserable.

One woman stood shaking her head, arms crossed, muttering to herself. "I'm not eating those things. You can't make me."

The sisters who'd been at Nasha's table stuck beside each other and seemed to be sizing up the competition, much like Nasha was.

Verochka stood off to one side, another fair blonde next to her. Verochka had an air of aloofness about her, like she couldn't be bothered to be bothered.

Nasha wondered just how well Russian Barbie would handle the sour fruit. Or maybe she was already so sour she wouldn't notice.

Didn't matter. Nasha was going to win. It wasn't a question. It was a statement of fact. Not only was this exactly the kind of contest she could win, a strong first-place finish would give her a nice lead and show the other women that she was a force to be reckoned with.

Granted, that might not be entirely a good thing, but better to intimidate some of them at the outset, even if it also made her a target.

She knew very well this contest was a gift to her. Whatever the other two games were, it would be highly unlikely that they'd be as tailor-made for her skills as this one. More reason for her to come out strong.

Thankfully, she'd read the rules very carefully last night, studying each one for any nuance or subtle wording that might help her. She had a plan in place, which she might not need, depending on what the other two games were. All the same, it helped boost her confidence to have a plan.

Had any of these women read the rules? Her gut said probably not.

A woman wearing a councilmember ribbon lifted a megaphone to her mouth.

"Women competitors numbers one through sixty should take their places at the tables."

Nasha was seventy-eight. She'd be in the next group to go. Good. This would give her a chance to observe and see how the first group did. It was always possible that someone here loved these berries and was going to eat them by the handful.

Doubtful, based on how everyone was reacting. But possible.

Verochka shifted, giving Nasha a chance to see her

Her First Taste Of Fire

lanyard. Russian Barbie was sixty-six. She and Nasha would be in the same group.

Interesting. But all that mattered was who ate the most berries by weight.

The first group was in their seats and the paper baskets of berries were being distributed. They looked like lemon-lime raspberries. Small, multi-sectioned fruits in pale green mottled with yellow. Not visually unappealing. Kinda cute. They'd make a great springtime dessert.

One woman was already gagging.

Could they really be that bad?

Charlie and Laz joined her as more men began to gather around to watch. This had to be interesting for them to see how the women would do and which of them were going to come out as front runners.

That gave Nasha a new thought. She looked at Charlie. "If I do well in this, does that mean the men will look at me differently? More like I'm mate material?"

"It could. A lot of them are still going to want a dragon first."

"Good." She nodded. "That's what I was hoping you'd say." She didn't want to attract the wrong kind of attention. Or any kind, really.

She just wanted her and Charlie to do well enough to go home together.

The woman with the megaphone was back. "This is a timed event. You have three minutes to eat as many amarun berries as you can. All the baskets weigh exactly the same. Raise your hand if you finish early. Any questions?"

No one responded.

"On your marks, then." The woman held a stopwatch up in her other hand. She pushed the button. "Go!"

There wasn't the enthusiastic start Nasha had expected. One by one, the women picked up a single berry, grimaced, and popped it into their mouths. Well, most of them did. A woman in the last seat at the farthest table just touched the berry to her tongue, then dropped it back into the basket.

As the women chewed, their faces contorted into masks of disgust and repulsion. They gagged and choked and coughed.

Nasha almost wished she could taste, just to see how bad the berries really were.

One woman appeared to be trying to swallow them whole, but she was struggling, and her eyes watered with the effort.

The seconds ticked by and, at last, the councilwoman lifted the megaphone to her mouth and announced, "Times up. The baskets will be weighed again, and the scores tallied. Remember, those scoring in the lowest percentages will be eliminated from the games."

Nasha looked at Charlie. "I don't remember that in the rules."

"It might not have been in there, but that's pretty standard." He glanced at Laz. "Isn't it?"

Laz nodded. "It's how they get to the cream of the crop in three games."

It took almost twenty minutes for the baskets to be weighed and the new baskets set out. It looked to Nasha like the new round of baskets had about half the berries in them that the first ones did. Probably because almost none of the first round had been eaten.

The woman who'd been swallowing them whole, number twenty-three, came out on top, with a grand total of three ounces eaten. Not a high bar.

"Women competitors numbers sixty-one through one hundred twenty-one, please take your seats."

Charlie gave her hand a squeeze. "You've got this."

She smiled back. "Thanks."

"What he said," Laz added. "Go show 'em how it's done."

She lifted her chin. "I plan to."

She walked over and took the first seat available. She had an instant of concern, wondering if there was a chance this berry might be the only other thing besides Charlie's chocolate that she was able to taste, and dismissed it. That was just silly.

She was old enough and had tried enough foods to know the odds of that were none.

She took a breath to calm her nerves and tried to see who else was seated around her. Because the tables had been lined up, no one could really see how anyone else was doing unless it was the person right beside them. Or unless you leaned forward to have a look down the row.

Verochka was at the opposite end. Nasha kind of wished she was closer, just so Nasha could see how she did.

It wasn't going to matter. Nasha was going to smoke all of them. Dragon pun intended. She was ready to do this.

Ready to win.

"All right, ladies. Just like before, this is a timed event. You'll have three minutes to eat as many amarun berries as you can. All the baskets weigh exactly the same, although we've gone with half the amount this time. Raise your hand if you finish early or you need more berries. Any questions?"

Again, there were none. Just cranky, scowling faces.

Nasha almost laughed.

"On your marks." The woman with the megaphone pushed the button on her stopwatch. "Go!"

Nasha took one berry, just to get a sense of the texture. It had some resistance as she chewed it, mostly a little pop as the sections burst under her teeth. Other than that, it was wet. Not much else. Thankfully.

She swallowed, then took a handful of the berries, tipped her head back, and dropped them into her mouth. She repeated that a second time, emptying her basket. The spectators closest to her, mostly men and some of the women from the first round, stared.

She raised her hand.

Megaphone woman came over. "Yes?"

Nasha held up her empty basket. "I need more,

please."

The woman's eyes rounded slightly.

The competitor next to Nasha pushed her basket over. "You can have mine. I haven't touched them, and after that, there's no point. I'm not going to eat more than you."

Nasha looked at megaphone woman. "Is that allowed?"

"Sure, go ahead. They all weigh the same."

"Great." Nasha downed the contents of that basket, then raised her hand again. She wasn't taking any chances that she might be beaten by a competitor yet to have their turn.

The crowd began to shift, moving closer to her end of the row. The whispers of amazement got louder.

Basket after basket, she devoured the berries, no real clue about how many she was eating, just determined to earn a score that couldn't be beaten.

Some of the other women in her round gave up and came over to watch.

Finally, the councilwoman raised the megaphone and announced, "Time's up. As before, the baskets will be reweighed, and the scores tallied. Lowest percentages will be eliminated."

Nasha leaned back and took a breath.

The crowd around her, some of them anyway, began to applaud. Charlie and Laz looked positively blown away. Proud, too, if she was reading them right. She smiled.

She didn't know what anyone else had done, but she felt pretty certain she'd accomplished what she'd set out to do. She got up and rejoined the guys.

Charlie hugged her. "That was amazing. *You* were amazing." Then, as if suddenly aware of all the eyes on them, he took her face in his hands and kissed her soundly.

She was fine with that. Maybe the other men would think twice about setting their sights on her if a legacy like Charlie was making it clear that he'd already claimed her.

When the kiss ended, she was still smiling. That had more to do with the kiss than the number of berries she'd just eaten.

"Outstanding work, woman." Laz nodded at her. "You definitely did what you set out to do."

"Thanks."

"Now we wait," Charlie said. He slipped his arm around her waist and kept her close. "How do you feel after all of that?"

She took a quick assessment. "Full, mostly. I probably could have eaten more if I'd skipped breakfast."

He laughed. "I love you. I mean, that attitude. I love that attitude."

"I know what you meant." She slanted her eyes at him. He looked ever so slightly pink. It could be that was just the way the sunlight hit him.

Officials got to work weighing the contestants' baskets and twenty minutes later, the results were announced.

Her First Taste Of Fire

Megaphone woman seemed to be having a good time. "We've got a new record, folks. Number seventy-eight with a total of three and three-quarter pounds of berries."

Verochka stepped out of the crowd. "How can this be? She is not dragon. Maybe the amarun taste differently to her. This is not fair."

Laz cupped his hands around his mouth. "No one likes a sore loser, sweetheart."

Charlie snorted in amusement as a buzz went up from the crowd. More people chimed in and things went from quiet to boisterous in a matter of seconds.

Megaphone woman raised her hand to calm everyone down. "We know for a fact that other species find the amarun just as sour and bitter as we do. If you have an issue with how things are being done, you're welcome to lodge an official complaint. No other discussions will be allowed. Those in violation of that rule will be subject to disqualification."

Verochka stared daggers at Nasha as she stepped back into the crowd.

"Oh, goody," Nasha said. "I've made a new friend."

Lazarus narrowed his eyes. "If she's your new friend, I'd hate to see your enemies."

"Two more days of games," Charlie said. "That's all we've got to get through."

"We can do that. Easy." But Nasha didn't think Verochka was the kind to let things go. Not after the woman had made a point of flying by the cave twice.

Nasha would be watching her. Closely.

CHAPTER NINETEEN

No one in the later rounds beat Nasha's score, but that didn't surprise Charlie. She'd set an impossible number to beat. He'd never been so proud of anyone in his life. What she'd accomplished was honestly unbelievable. She'd earned a lot of respect from others in the crowd, too.

Some enemies, as well. That much was plain. He brushed that thought off. Verochka seemed like a lot of talk, most of it designed to draw attention to herself. He doubted she'd risk disqualification by acting on any of that talk.

They helped themselves to lunch, going back to the table they'd sat at for breakfast. After this meal, it would be time for the men's portion of the games.

Nasha picked at her fries but hadn't put much else on her plate. She probably wasn't hungry after all the berries. "Are you guys going to have to eat that fruit, too?"

"Not sure," Charlie said.

"Probably not," Laz answered. "I overheard someone saying they like to switch things up. We'll have to eat something, but not berries. After all, that legend revolves around a female dragon, so that's probably why they chose it for the women."

She seemed to ponder that. "Any other legends involving a male dragon and a questionable food source?"

"Not that I can think of." Charlie looked at Laz.

He shook his head. "Me neither."

The sisters didn't join them at the table again, but the older man did.

Dressed in jeans, flannel shirt, and a worn-in leather vest, he sat at the far end. "Impressive showing today, ma'am."

"Thanks," Nasha said.

"If I were a little younger, and you weren't wearing that rock, you might be in trouble."

She laughed. "Good to know."

He raised his bottle of water. "Congratulations to the both of you."

"Thank you," Charlie said. "Where are you from?"

"Wyoming. Was hoping to find myself a missus here, but with this new system..." He rubbed at the gray stubble covering his jaw. "Not sure how that's going to work out. This council has some big ideas. Take my word for it, new blood isn't always a good thing. Not when they're trying to rewrite history and change traditions."

"Yeah," Laz said. "It's kind of messed up, right? But you might still find someone. There are a lot of women here."

"Maybe." He cut into the sausage on his plate. "Henry Grimstone, by the way."

"Nice to meet you, Henry. Lazarus Stratton. And these are my friends, Charlie Ashborne and his fiancée, Nasha Black, a.k.a. The Berry Killer."

Henry smiled. "Nice to meet you folks. You see any eligible older women who look like they could withstand a Wyoming winter, you send them my way."

Nasha laughed. "I'll keep my eyes open."

"Good," Henry said. "I ain't picky."

They talked about all sorts of things as lunch went on, and Charlie was surprised to find out that Henry had been on the council, nearly fifty years ago.

That explained a lot about why the man was so unhappy with the new council. Of course, Charlie hadn't heard anyone who seemed to be in full support of them, either.

As lunch wrapped up, an announcement was made on the megaphone calling for the first group of men to gather. He and Laz had numbers in the seventies, so they'd be in the second group, like Nasha was.

Henry had number eighteen, however. "Wish me luck," he said as he got up. "Not sure what fool thing we're going to have to eat."

"We'll be cheering you on," Nasha said.

They all got up and walked with him.

As they approached the tables, the food in question became clear.

Her First Taste Of Fire

Chili peppers. From the look of them, Carolina Reapers, the hottest pepper on record.

Henry shook his head. "I know we can handle hot foods better than almost any other creature, but do they not understand what spice like that does to an old man's system? Dragon or not, I'm going to suffer if I overdo it."

Laz put his hands on his hips. "I don't think it has anything to do with age. I'm not a fan of them myself."

Charlie shrugged. "I like spicy. To a degree. This won't be fun, but I should be able to finish with a decent score. I hope."

"Or..." Nasha began. "You could name me as your proxy and let me take your place."

All three men turned to look at her. Charlie blinked. "Pretty sure I can't do that."

Nasha looked confident. "Rule Five, section B. Proxies are allowed once per contestant per census without discrimination or prejudice based on age, gender, or species."

"She's right," Henry said. "Nothing like a woman who's done her homework."

"Okay, so they're allowed." Charlie still had his doubts. "You really think you can eat more hot peppers than I can? Those look like Carolina Reapers."

Laz groaned. "I hate Reapers."

Nasha was undeterred. "I don't care what kind they are. I can eat more of them than all three of you combined."

"This I gotta see," Henry said. "I wish we were in the same round so you could sit by me, ma'am."

"Hold up," Charlie said. "I don't know if this is such a good idea."

"Why not?" Laz looked at him. "Look what she did with the berries. I say if she wants to take on the peppers, let her. It's only going to strengthen her standing and make her more intimidating. Don't forget that head games are as much a part of this as anything else."

"I know but..." Charlie gave her a hard look. "You really want to do this?"

"Absolutely. My skill set is kind of limited compared to you guys. I can't fly, breathe fire, or shift into anything. But eating foods others find distasteful? I'm all over that."

He thought about it. "I suppose it would further cement our link as a couple if you proxied for me. And it might intimidate some of the other women."

Laz wiggled his brows. "Like a particular comrade?"

Charlie smirked. He was convinced. Still worried for Nasha, but he believed in her. "If you want to do it, then I'm in. Let's go tell them you're taking my place."

With Laz on the sidelines and Henry finding a seat for his round, Charlie and Nasha went in search of the councilmember in charge. They found a man holding the megaphone. His badge said Martin Harwell.

"Mr. Harwell?" Charlie asked. "Are you running this event?"

"I am. How can I help you? We're just about to get the first round underway."

Her First Taste Of Fire

"I wanted to let someone know I'm selecting a proxy to take my place. Are you the person I need to tell? Or is there some kind of form I have to fill out? Just want to make sure I do it right."

"A proxy?" Harwell seemed confused. "That's highly irregular, but I know the rules allow for it. Is there any particular reason for this substitution?"

"Do I need one?" Charlie asked.

"No. Just curious."

He glanced at Nasha and smiled. "My fiancée has a particular fondness for spicy things."

She grinned at him like that was an inside joke that everything to do with dragons and nothing to do with peppers. "I do."

"So," Charlie continued. "I'd like to let her take my spot."

"Fine with me. She'll need to wear your number as well as her own, but I'll see to it that the proxy is documented properly." He looked at Charlie's lanyard. "You're not up until the next round anyway."

"Right. Thank you, Mr. Harwell."

"You're welcome, Mr. Ashborne. I know you're a legacy, but I hope you know what you're doing."

"He does," Nasha said as she took Charlie's hand. "You'll see."

They went back to stand with Laz, who'd positioned himself as close to Henry as he could.

"Everything go all right?"

Charlie nodded. "She just has to wear my lanyard. I

can only imagine the ruckus it's going to cause when she takes a seat at the table."

Laz laughed. "I'm so here for it."

Baskets of the bumpy red peppers were being placed in front of each contestant.

"Come on, Henry," Laz shouted. "You've got this."

Henry smiled.

"Go, Henry!" Nasha gave him a thumb's up.

Charlie added a thumb's up himself for good measure. Then he leaned in toward Nasha. "This will give you an idea of how many you'll need to eat to win. But if you change your mind at any time, I'm okay with that, too."

"I won't. But thanks."

Harwell made the starting announcement, and the men were off. Some more reluctantly than others. Some with great enthusiasm.

"This is going to be a tough one," Charlie said.

Laz nodded. "Some of these guys look determined to place as high as possible. I think Nasha may have actually inspired some of them."

As the first round got under way, it became clear something had inspired at least a few of them. Three of the men in particular were eating with abandon. Nothing seemed to stop them, not their watering eyes, their red faces, not even the coughing and wheezing the peppers seemed to bring about. Nothing until Harwell called time.

After the weighing, the top three finishers had put

away almost two pounds apiece, or about four baskets worth. Henry had stopped at a basket and a half.

He joined them as the tables were being reset for the next round, hand on his stomach. "I might have to get some altitude after that so I can breathe some fire and get this heat out of my system." He smiled. "But I'm not going anywhere until after Nasha's had her chance. I'm not missing that."

"Thanks," Nasha said.

Charlie took off his lanyard and put it around her neck. "Remember, a basket is about half a pound."

She nodded as she made sure his badge and number were visible overtop of hers. "I plan to eat at least six baskets' worth, but I'm going to shoot for eight. I want a nice lead that will be hard to beat. Just like with the berries."

"Go get 'em," Laz said.

Charlie gave her a quick kiss before she headed off to find a seat at the tables. "You got this, babe."

Right on cue, there were complaints as soon as she sat down. Harwell shut them up with an announcement about the right of proxies and the importance of reading the rules. That quelled the loudest of them but did nothing to stop the dirty looks or mutterings.

Some of the men looked very much like they wished they'd figured that out for themselves.

Harwell lifted his megaphone and started the contest.

Again, there were those who ate with gusto and those who made the bare minimum effort. Nasha ate like a machine, raising her hand for a new basket before the one in front of her was completely empty.

Charlie couldn't believe what he was seeing. She seemed to amp up her pace as the clock ticked down, her movements almost a blur of supernatural speed.

When Harwell called time, she was halfway through her tenth basket.

CHAPTER TWENTY

Nasha slid off Charlie's back, landing between him and Laz on the ground in front of Henry's cave. He'd invited them over for dinner, an offer they'd immediately taken him up on. His cave was one of the very first ones at the beginning of the valley.

From the flickering light of the fire inside to the delicious aromas wafting out, it seemed like Henry had planned pretty well for company.

Maybe he'd been hoping that company would be female. Nasha felt for the guy. He was such a nice man. He deserved love.

She also wished she'd had something to bring. Maybe it was the baker in her, but on the rare occasions she got invited somewhere, she usually took one of her cakes or pies. "I don't like coming empty-handed."

Charlie, who'd shifted to human form, came up alongside her. "We didn't really have much to bring."

She frowned. That wasn't true. "Would it be a big deal if you took me back? I could get some of your chocolates. There's enough of those."

"That would put a big dent in your supply. You okay with that?"

She had pretty mixed feelings about it, actually, but not enough to stop her from sharing. "Absolutely. I want to do it."

"All right," he said with a smile. "Let's go. Laz, tell Henry we forgot something. We'll be right back."

"Will do."

Charlie returned to his dragon form and, in just a few minutes, she had the chocolates in hand and they were once again headed toward Henry's cave.

She felt much better. So what if she'd run out of chocolates sooner? Once she got back to Shadowvale, she'd never be without them again.

They walked in, and she instantly noticed the temperature change. It was practically balmy in Henry's abode. Not only was his fire twice the size of theirs, but his was built in the center of the space. A natural opening in the rock above it let out the smoke.

Around the fire were a single camp chair, another two-seater version, and a large trunk that looked like it might have been army issue. Laz was using that as a seat. A metal rack over the firepit held a big pot of stew, a pan of biscuits, and a pot of coffee.

A couple feet away was a cot that looked about as comfortable as any regular bed, with a thick foam mattress, a fluffy comforter, and a nice pillow. Next to it was a small folding table with a battery-operated lamp and two hardback books.

Henry clearly knew how to pack for a census. Or maybe he just camped a lot.

Her First Taste Of Fire

He greeted them with a big smile. "There you two are. Come on in. Lazarus said you'd forgotten something. Everything good now?"

She held out the chocolates. "Everything's great. It was so kind of you to invite us."

He took the box. "Candy?"

"Chocolates. Made by Charlie. He has a shop in our town."

"Outstanding. These will make the perfect dessert." He kissed her cheek. "I'm so glad you could all come."

"You seem pretty well prepared for company." Charlie looked around. "I like your setup, too. A lot better than what we started with."

"Thanks. The company I was prepared for was single and female, but you three will do. At least one of you's pretty."

They all laughed.

He continued. "As for my gear, well, I've been coming to these things enough years to know what I need. Although this isn't the cave I wanted. I'd heard there were a few here with natural pools in them. Couldn't find one, so I guess they got snapped up first."

Charlie laughed and raised his hand. "Guilty. We have one, but you're welcome to come over and have a bath anytime you like. Just give us a few minutes to vacate."

"Is that right?" Henry smiled. "A bath would be nice, but I don't want to put you out."

Nasha shook her head. "You wouldn't be putting us

out. Did you get to burn off all the hot peppers? You said you were going to fly."

"I did and I did." He patted his stomach. "Still brutal. And I might have burned off a few of my tastebuds, so if the stew is under-seasoned, you'll have to forgive me."

"I'm sure it'll be perfect." As if she'd know.

"Come on, have a seat." Henry gestured for them to move closer. "These biscuits'll burn if they stay over the fire any longer."

They joined Laz around the fire. Nasha took one side of the two-seat camp chair, patting the spot next to her for Charlie.

Henry went to work ladling up the stew. First, though, he handed Laz a spatula. "Give everyone a biscuit. There's butter and honey in the cooler over there. Bottles of water and beers, too. Hand it all out."

"I'd love a water." Nasha was amazed. "How did you get all of this here? It's a lot of stuff."

"Military grade cargo nets. I was an Army Ranger back in the day." He handed her a bowl of stew.

It smelled great. Bits of rosemary and black pepper flecked the rich brown sauce bathing big chunks of carrot, potato, onions, and beef. Nasha hated that she wouldn't be able to taste it.

"Smart," Laz said as he passed a bottle of water to Nasha, then a beer to Charlie. "Might have to look into one of those myself. Although I suppose it'll be another five years or so before there's another census."

Henry finished handing out stew, then sat down with

his own bowl. "Not from what I hear. This new council wants a census every year. It's their way of forcing marriages and trying to increase our population."

He shook his head. "I say let things take their natural course. Forcing people together is only going to end up poorly. But those idiots—"

"Well, there you are." Lakshmi Stoneheart strode into the cave.

Henry set his bowl down and stood up. "What do you want?"

"Not you, grandpa." She looked at Charlie. "Mr. Ashborne, the council has reconvened and in light of your fiancée's performance today, we feel the allowances made for her are unnecessary. The thirty percent increase in points will not be given."

Charlie got to his feet. "That's unfair."

Lakshmi pursed her lips. "She proved herself more than capable of competing. In fact, some might say her performances today were unfair."

Laz snorted. "You mean some like that plastic Russian?"

Lakshmi glared at him. "Complaints have been made." She shifted her attention back to Charlie. "It's the council's job to listen and respond."

Henry growled softly. "It's the council's job to do what's right and just, not give in to the whiniest of our lot. Being a councilmember isn't about being popular. It's about protecting our way of life and the things we hold dear."

She narrowed her eyes and focused on Henry. "Maybe if the council had done its job when you were on it, we wouldn't be in the situation we are today with falling numbers and a diminishing population."

Henry stepped forward, but the fire pit blocked him from going farther. As he moved, he began to look more menacing. His dragon was showing through, Nasha realized. He glared at Lakshmi. "If you paid any attention to our history, you'd get what those of us who are old enough to know better understand. Our numbers have *always* fluctuated. It's just the cycle of our kind. But you and your friends think it's the end of the world."

He shook his head. "You wouldn't know the end of the world if it showed up tomorrow."

Nasha twisted her father's ring around her finger, smiling at Henry's words and wondering how the dragons would react if her father came riding in.

Lakshmi snorted softly. "Don't worry about me, old man. Worry about yourself."

Laz jumped up. "Don't talk to him that way. He's an elder and he's served his people. He deserves your respect."

She frowned and walked out.

Nasha made hexy hands at Lakshmi, the way she'd seen Em do when someone got on her nerves. Of course, Nasha didn't actually have any magic to throw at the woman, but it made her feel better all the same. "Boy, is she a piece of work."

"Good job, Laz," Charlie said. "She needed to hear that."

Laz stared after her. "I doubt it'll sink into that thick head of hers."

Henry sat back down, shaking his head. "I appreciate it, but I'm afraid she'll make you pay for that, son."

"So what?" Laz took his seat on the trunk. "I'm not trying to win these games." He glanced at Charlie and Nasha. "It's you two I'm worried about. Especially now that Nasha's not getting any exemptions."

She shrugged. "I suppose I did that to myself with my performances. But what else could I do? That was my only chance to get out ahead. I wasn't going to let it pass me by."

"No," Charlie said. "But maybe you shouldn't have proxied for me."

Nasha was starting to think that, too.

"What's done is done," Henry said. "I'm not going to let that flying heifer ruin my evening. Neither should you. Whatever comes tomorrow, we'll deal with it."

Nasha leaned forward. "If what you said about the dragon population always fluctuating is true, why is the council so gung-ho on solving it now?"

Henry picked up his bowl. "Because they're young and they think they know everything."

He didn't seem like he wanted to talk about it anymore. Nasha respected that. "You're right about tomorrow. Whatever happens, we'll deal with it."

Charlie raised his beer. "Here's to our gracious host

for inviting us over and not throwing us out for causing trouble."

Henry laughed and raised his own beer. "Here's to making new friends with the best troublemakers in camp." He winked at Nasha. "The best-looking, too."

As they laughed and drank and enjoyed the rest of the evening, Nasha couldn't help but think about tomorrow.

What would it bring? What kind of game? Something told her it was going to be the kind of thing that would require real dragon skills. The very ones she didn't have.

Her gaze kept returning to her father's ring. Would she have to call upon the worst of her powers? The ones that marked her as her father's daughter? She'd vowed never to use those powers. Never to reveal that side of herself.

She looked at Charlie and knew two things. She cared about him an awful lot.

And saying "never" had been a dumb thing to do.

CHAPTER TWENTY-ONE

Charlie woke up as dawn was lightening the sky. Nasha was asleep, curled up on her cot with her back toward the fire. She'd be up soon. She'd been up before him yesterday. Bakers hours, she'd said.

Maybe yesterday's activity had worn her out. They'd had a late night at Henry's, and she'd mentioned she usually went to bed early because of having to be at the bakery before the sunrise.

He glanced at the pool of water. She'd probably love a hot bath. She'd asked him to heat the water yesterday but he'd brushed it off, telling her they should get down to the field early. He'd felt bad about that. He hated lying to her. But the truth was worse.

She'd think less of him. And he wouldn't blame her.

As quietly as he could in dragon form, he walked over to the water. Hard to say how much fire it would take to warm the pool up because the bottom wasn't visible. And it was clearly fed by a spring, so cold water would keep flowing in.

Better to overheat it, then let it cool to the right temp.

With that in mind, he charged up a good breath and let it rip, blowing fire across the surface.

Steam rose as the fire traveled, warming the cave with it.

A soft clink, barely noticeable over the sound of the fire rushing out of him, reminded him that his curse was very much active.

As the water began to bubble, he quickly shifted into human form and looked around for the scale he'd lost.

What he found was Nasha standing behind him, wearing pajama pants and a tank top, her hair rumpled from sleep. She held up a familiar blue-green object. "This fell off you. Is that normal?"

He stared at the scale in her hand as he tried to shove down his mortification. "I thought you'd like a hot bath."

She nodded. "I would. But seriously, I didn't know dragons lost scales when they used fire. Or is that like a natural shedding thing that just happens? Because if so, I'm going to keep my eyes open. I'd love to go home with a bag of these. Better than seashells. Or would that be weird?"

He sighed and looked away. She wasn't going to let this go. And if he didn't explain it, she'd be out in the field trying to find more of them. He could just imagine how that was going to go. "It's not natural. It's not a thing. It's..."

He couldn't finish. He just stared at the scale in her hand and frowned.

"Your curse?" Her quiet words seemed to reverberate through the cave like a church bell pealing.

He didn't want to answer. Didn't want to admit it. In

fact, all he wanted to do was walk outside, shift back to dragon, and fly as far away as he could. "Yes," he choked out.

When she moved toward him, he couldn't bring himself to look at her. She wrapped her arms around him. "It's okay."

"It's not okay. It makes me vulnerable."

"Not if no one knows. And I won't tell a soul. That's why we live in Shadowvale, right? We're all cursed. How long does it take for them to grow back?"

"About a day." He looked at her. "You're cursed?"

"Yep. I can't taste anything. I never have. All my life it's been that way. My father's the same way, but you have to promise not to say a word to him that I've told you."

Astonishment filled him. Everything became clear. Well, almost everything. "You can't taste? That's how you won the games yesterday."

She nodded. "Please don't say anything to anyone. A baker with no ability to taste..." She swallowed. "Not good."

He pulled her closer, holding her tight and completely understanding what she was feeling and how hard that confession had been. But there was one question he had to have answered. "Then why do you want my chocolate recipe?"

She suddenly burst into the biggest, brightest smile he'd ever seen. "Because I can taste it. I don't know why or how or what magic makes it possible, but I can taste your chocolate. I need your recipe because, frankly, I'm hoping to figure out what special ingredient you use that makes it possible. Then I want to use it to solve my problem."

He shook his head. "I hate to tell you this, but there's nothing special in it. It's a pretty standard chocolate mix. Raw cocoa, sugar, cocoa butter, a little vanilla, touch of salt, sometimes a few other spices depending on what kinds of chocolates I'm making. All organic. But no magic. No special ingredients. I'm sorry."

She deflated in his arms, putting her head against his chest.

"I'll still give you the recipe. You probably wouldn't be able to recreate it anyway. I use my dragon fire to heat and temper the chocolate."

She looked up at him. "That has to be it then. That has to be the secret ingredient. But why do you lose a scale when you use your fire?"

He took a breath and frowned. "I wish I knew. It's been that way since right after I got my fire. I wouldn't wish it on my worst enemy."

"Why? What's so awful about losing a scale?"

"Like I said, it makes me vulnerable. It gives me a weak spot. A dragon's hide can't be pierced. But if there's a scale missing? That hide become penetrable."

"Oh." She nodded. "I suppose it's not something you'd want anyone here to know, either."

"No."

She smiled up at him. "You know your secret is safe with me."

Her First Taste Of Fire

"Yours, too." He kissed her forehead. "I promise that I will never let you run out of chocolate."

Her grin widened. "Thank you."

"I heated that water up for you. You should probably get in it before it cools off any more."

Her arms tightened around him. "Are you joining me?"

"Are you telling me I need a bath?"

She bit her lower lip and looked up at him through her lashes. "Yeah. You need this bath. Trust me."

He didn't know what to say to that, but his internal temperature responded by shooting up several degrees.

She wiggled out of his embrace and walked over to the pool's edge, dipping her toes in. "Oh, that's perfect."

As he watched, she shed her pajama pants, revealing a pair of black string bikini underwear. She knotted the bottom of her tank top and gave him a long look. "Get the towels and the soap, will ya?"

Then she jumped in.

He stood there, mesmerized. Then he sprang into action, grabbing the towels, and the soap from his own toiletry kit. He dropped them both by the pool's edge.

Because he'd slept in his dragon form, he hadn't needed pajamas, but he was in jeans, a T-shirt, and a jacket, the same outfit he'd worn to Henry's.

And while he'd brought swim trunks, now did not seem like the time to go get them. He stripped off everything but his boxers and joined her, jumping in just as she was going under again.

The water was warm, but he could feel the cold current rising up around them. She surfaced next to him. He caught her eye. "You want it warmer? I can bring it up a few degrees if you like."

"Definitely." She nodded. "I like it hot enough to take off the top layer of skin. Figuratively."

"Got it." He charged his internal furnace and let the heat radiate through his body.

"Hey, I can feel that." She swam closer, her hand reaching out to touch his chest. "Wow, you're really hot."

He grinned. "You're pretty hot yourself."

She blushed as she laughed. "This isn't getting either of us any cleaner."

He found a ledge of rock and planted his feet on it. "Is that what we're supposed to be doing in here?"

She swam closer still, putting her hands on his shoulders. "Something like that."

He found her hips and held onto her. "Warm enough?"

She nodded. Her hair hung in damp waves around her face and tiny drops of water jeweled her lashes, making her look like a siren ready to sing him to his death.

He'd never been less afraid. Or more captivated. She knew his secret and she didn't care. She hadn't once looked at him like he was irreparably damaged. She made him want to be bold. "I don't feel like pretending anymore."

She tipped her head. "No?"

"No. I want this to be real." He could only hope she felt the same way.

Did she?

She held his gaze, her eyes big and liquid, her face unreadable. Then she grabbed him and kissed him with the kind of ferocity that was all the answer he needed.

CHAPTER TWENTY-TWO

Nasha floated through breakfast. She wasn't entirely sure if she was really in love or just in deep infatuation or under the spell of some kind of dragon magic, but she didn't care. She was happy. About as happy as she'd ever been in her life. Maybe happier. The happiest? Whatever, Charlie was simply amazing.

And now he was really hers.

Laz sat across from Nasha at the picnic table. Charlie was beside her, and Henry was in line getting coffee. Laz had enough food on his plate for several people. He looked at them like something was wrong.

"What's up?" Charlie asked. "You're staring."

Laz shook his head. "I can't help it. Why do you two look like that?"

"Like what?" Charlie forked up a piece of fried potato.

Nasha giggled, realizing too late the sound had actually come out of her and not just been in her head. Which only made her laugh again.

"Okay, something's going on." Laz glanced at Henry as he came to the table. "Do you know what's up?"

"With what?"

Laz tipped his head at Charlie and Nasha. "With these two. They look weird."

Henry peered at them. A big smile broke out on his face. "It's called being in love, son." He took a seat. "Nice to see, if you ask me."

Charlie nodded. "Thank you."

Unable to stop smiling, Nasha stared at her food. She wasn't all that hungry, but she needed to keep her strength up for whatever today's game was. All she really wanted to do was spend the day with Charlie.

She was completely ready to go back to Shadowvale and get on with their lives. She knew that wasn't possible. Not until the census was over and Charlie was truly hers. She changed the subject. "Any thoughts on what today's game will be?"

Henry looked up from his plate. "There are ring mounts set up at the far end of the valley. I flew over them on my way in this morning. Probably going to be a race to test speed and agility."

That took the smile off her face. "Speed and agility? I can't compete against dragons in those areas. And what are ring mounts?"

Laz answered. "Metal poles that hold a small ring off the ground. And I mean small. It's usually about the diameter of a silver dollar. The test will probably be to see who can fly down, get the ring, and come back in the fastest time."

Charlie groaned softly. "This is a game that favors smaller dragons. The bigger your talons are, the harder those rings are to pick up. Especially when you can't really see what you're doing."

Henry swallowed the bite he'd just taken. "It favors the fastest, too. But being fast won't help if you can't pick up the ring. I've seen lightning-quick dragons lose because they knocked the ring off and couldn't find it in the grass."

"Yeah, good point," Charlie said. "It's not like they ran a mower over this field."

Nasha turned to look in the direction of Henry's cave. At the very end of the valley, she could just make out a series of poles sticking up in the air. The rings were too small to see. "How am I going to do this?"

Henry was spreading strawberry jam on his wheat toast. "Two ways I can think of. You either send Charlie in as your proxy, or you run as fast as you can and hope a good bunch of them either drop the ring or miss it entirely." He glanced at her. "How fast can you run?"

"Not as fast as a dragon can fly." She looked at Charlie, her appetite now completely gone. "And if I send you as my proxy, I'm worried that the last game will be something so dragon specific I won't be able to do it at all, then I'll really need you and won't have the option. At least this one, I'm able to compete in. Maybe not well, but I'll still be able to finish."

The expression on his face said he didn't know what to do either. "I'm ready and willing to step in for you, but I see your point about the last game. If we knew what it was going to be…"

"This sucks," Laz said. "They really should make some kind of allowance for you."

"Lakshmi already chimed in on that," Nasha said.

Henry shook his head. "It's not right." He got up suddenly. "I'm going to talk to Reynaldo Rossi. He's an old-school guy like me. There might be something he can do."

Nasha didn't want Henry to get into any trouble on her behalf. "Henry, I appreciate that, but we talked to a guy earlier, Xavier Redwing. He sympathized, but couldn't do anything. Not to mention, you're only going to draw more attention to yourself. And it might not be good attention."

"Xavier's all right, but he's no Reynaldo. As far as drawing attention, at my age, I don't give a fig what happens." He winked at her. "Besides, it's for a good cause. If I'd stood up to some of this nonsense when it first started happening, we might not be dealing with the mess this new council is trying to ramrod down our throats. Be right back."

Charlie sighed as Henry left. "He's a good man."

"Yeah, he is," Laz said. "I wish we could find him a woman."

"I know a couple he might like," Nasha said. "One of whom is Cherry Webb. She comes into my bakery almost every day. Usually buys a loaf of pumpernickel, and something sweet for her dessert after dinner. She's a widow, about Henry's age, I think. She volunteers as a crossing guard and helps out one day a week at the library. Of course, he'd have to come to Shadowvale to meet her..."

Charlie smiled. "I think we could get him to visit. Would her curse be compatible with him being a dragon?"

"What curse?" Laz asked.

Nasha hesitated. They'd probably said too much. And not just because it wasn't generally accepted to talk about other people's curses. They'd talked about the town, too. The very place that was a safe haven because no one knew about it. "It's nothing."

"It's okay," Charlie said quietly. "Laz has his own curse to deal with. Or did." He looked at his friend. "I hope you don't mind me saying that. Nasha knows about mine."

Laz's brows bent. "You're still dealing with that?"

Charlie nodded. "Aren't you?"

Laz took a long, deep breath before answering. "Yes. I almost didn't come to this because of it, but I figured it was that or have the council banging at my door."

"Same," Charlie said. "Maybe you should come to Shadowvale, too. It's a safe place for people like us. People who have a burden to bear."

"Yeah?" Laz seemed interested. "Maybe I will. Tell me more about it."

Charlie started. "Everyone there has some kind of curse or trouble or jinx or whatever you want to call it, but it's pretty much an unwritten rule that you don't talk about it. People live their lives like nothing's wrong."

"Until something is," Nasha added. "And then you

just deal with it and get back to your life as best you can. Like Charlie said, no one talks about curses. The fact that we are right now is sort of overstepping."

"All right, then. Back to the lady you think might be right for Henry. What's her problem?"

Nasha shrugged. "I have no idea. I'd never think of asking her, either. Some people's troubles are obvious. There are folks who have storm clouds following them, some who spontaneously burst into flames. Dr. Jekyll even lives there and it's pretty obvious what his curse is. Some people, you'd never know they were cursed. Some never show signs of anything. The beauty of Shadowvale is it doesn't matter. You can live your life."

Charlie nodded. "You can be left alone if you want to. Or not. There's a great community there." He looked at Nasha. "One I need to get more involved in."

She smiled at him. "Me, too." Mercy, he was fun to look at. She made herself turn back to Lazarus. "What kind of work do you do?"

"I have a small construction company. Home repairs, some remodeling, simple additions, stuff like that."

"You could totally do that in Shadowvale. Plenty of houses there to take care of." Nasha realized the only setback might be if the town decided not to let Lazarus in. If he really had a curse of his own, she doubted that would be a problem.

"Yeah?" Laz seemed to be considering his options as Henry came back.

They all looked up at him. Nasha couldn't really read

his face, though. He looked about as cranky as he had when he'd left. Probably not a good sign. "You don't look like you got very far."

He sat down at his spot again, letting out a sigh as he did. "I didn't. I'm sorry, Nasha. Reynaldo agreed that you're being treated unfairly, but he's in the minority. He has very little ability to influence the others. And the older members that agree with him are in the same boat. They're outnumbered."

Fire flashed in Henry's eyes. "I am so sick of this. We never used to be like this. And maybe our numbers wouldn't be dropping if we had more new blood in the gene pool. So what if not all of it is dragon. Is that really the end of the world?"

A few people at other tables looked at Henry. He glared back at them.

Nasha reached over and put her hand on top of his. "Thank you for trying. Charlie and I were just saying that you should come visit us in Shadowvale. What do you think? We'd love to have you."

He smiled at her, his eyes returning to normal. "I think you're sweet for trying to distract me. If that's a real offer, I'd love to visit."

Charlie snorted. "You'd better believe it's a real offer. Nasha's already playing matchmaker and coming up with women to introduce you to."

Laz nudged Henry with his elbow. "I'm going to visit, too. Maybe we can coordinate and come at the same time."

"That would be great," Charlie said. "I have plenty of room."

Henry's brows lifted. "Plenty of room and a matchmaker, huh? Well, then, I might be there sooner than you think." He shifted his focus back to Nasha. "That doesn't answer the question about what you're going to do for this race. Have you decided? Will you have Charlie be your proxy?"

Nasha took a few breaths as she gave that question some serious thought. "No. I can run this race. I might not do that great, but I bet I won't come in last. Plus, I have a healthy lead from the first game, and I think I should save my proxy for the last round, in case it's really something I can't do." She took Charlie's hand and looked at him. "You okay with that?"

"Absolutely," Charlie said. "It's a smart decision. We'll be cheering for you the whole way."

She smiled. "Thanks." The support would be great, but what she really needed was wings. "Can you take me back up to the cave? I'd better get my sneakers on."

Chapter Twenty-Three

Charlie stood on the outcrop in front of their cave, staring down at the valley. He was in dragon form, which made it easy to see the poles and rings from here. Dragon eyesight was especially keen at long distances.

Being able to see the poles and rings didn't help him guess what Nasha's chances might be. He hoped she'd surprise them all. He didn't care if that was because other dragons screwed up or because she tapped into some speed she didn't know she had, he just wanted her to finish high enough that she could remain in the top ten.

Otherwise, everything would rest on the final game, and they had no idea what that might be. If he had to be her proxy, so be it. That could potentially make his own competition harder. Especially if it involved fire.

There was no way he'd be able to hide his curse. The judges watched things far too closely for him to lose a scale and hope it wouldn't be noticed. It would be. Then the real trouble would start. Thankfully, the scale he'd most recently lost was under one arm and impossible to see.

He tipped his head into the sun, letting the warmth wash over him.

Her First Taste Of Fire

"I'm ready."

He opened his eyes and turned his big head to see her. "You changed."

She nodded, looking down at her strappy black sports bra and skintight leggings. She'd braided her hair back, too. But her engagement ring sat proudly on her finger. In one hand, she carried a big gray sweatshirt. "I was trying to be more aerodynamic." She did a quick spin. "Too much?"

"Only if distracting the men and making the women jealous isn't a problem." He grinned. "You look *very* aerodynamic. Among other things."

Her mouth curved in a grin as she walked closer. "Thanks."

He lowered his head to see her better. "Ready to fly?"

She put her hand up, touching his face. "Almost. Your dragon form is so beautiful. I could look at you all day."

Thankfully, dragons weren't susceptible to blushing. "No one's ever said that to me before. Thank you."

"Good. I'm glad I was the first." She went up on her tiptoes and kissed his snout. Then she pulled her sweatshirt on. "Just need to climb up."

"Take all the time you need." She thought he was beautiful. Why that made him as warm and gooey as melted chocolate inside, he had no idea. Maybe because he cared what she thought?

Or because he was falling for her so hard he couldn't imagine his life without her.

She patted his side. "I'm up."

He answered with a nod and the spread of his wings. He launched off the shelf and caught the wind, sailing them higher.

There were other dragons circling the skies, no doubt checking out the course below where more of them were gathered. Already the first group of women milled around the starting point.

The course wasn't that long. About three-quarters of a mile down and the same back. It would be harder on Nasha since she had to run it, but some dragons would need a quarter of that length just to get airborne. A lot depended on the wind, which was decent when you were aloft or jumping off a mountain face, like he'd just done.

But on the ground? It had been fairly still this morning so far.

He wondered if the short distance would actually work in Nasha's favor. He hoped so. What could happen was that a lot of the contestants would struggle with having to judge the right height to grab the ring while trying to keep themselves in the air. If things went that way, Nasha's much more straightforward approach could really pay off.

He landed some yards behind the starting line, waited for Nasha to slide down, then turned human again. There was very little breeze.

She held her hand over her eyes to shield them from the sun. "Where are the guys?"

Charlie found Henry and Laz off to the right. He pointed them out to Nasha. "Over there."

Her First Taste Of Fire

"Great." She took his hand as they started watching the first round of competitors get ready to race. "I'd kind of like to watch from the end of the course. Where the rings are."

"You want to see who gets their ring and who doesn't."

"Yes. Not that watching that will give me any strategic advantage, but I think seeing a few of them miss might give me some confidence, you know?"

"Sure. Hearing their times should help, too."

"You think any of them will run it?"

"Not a chance. They're dragons, and dragons fly. But just because they're flying doesn't mean they're going to be as speedy as you think."

She glanced up at him, brows knitted in disbelief. "Come on now."

"No, really. Think about the turn at the end of the course alone. First of all, you've got to fly over at the right speed and altitude to snag that ring. If you get it on the first go, great. But now you've got to turn. Dragons don't turn on a dime. We're too big. Most of us turn in wide loops. That's going to add time, no matter how you look at it."

"Hmm. Good point."

"Then what if you miss the ring? Do you turn and come back around, hoping the second time's the charm? That is, if you haven't knocked it off the pole. If that's the case, you either shift into human form and start the scavenger hunt for it in the grass or that's the end of your round. Let's say you haven't knocked it off and you make a second pass. Now you'll have to turn even wider to give yourself enough time to get into position. And that's all split-second decision making. This is harder than it looks, trust me."

She was smiling now. "Okay, right. I see what you're saying. As long as I run at a good pace and don't screw up getting the ring myself, I might not do too bad."

"Not at all." That's what he was hoping. "So let's definitely go watch them at the end. In fact, we can fly down there so you stay fresh for the run."

"Okay."

They reached Henry and Laz, and Charlie filled them in. "We want to watch by the rings."

Henry nodded. "Good. I want to watch from down there, too."

"Flying?" Laz asked. "Otherwise, Nasha will have to walk that twice. Might waste energy."

Charlie agreed. "Yep. No point of that."

All three men shifted and Nasha got herself seated on Charlie's back again. They weren't alone. Others were shifting to head in that direction, too. Some were taking to the skies, though. They'd be watching from above.

Not a bad idea, Charlie thought. Great vantage point. It would also help keep the judges on their toes. He wanted to think the judges would be impartial and completely fair. Then again, with this new council, he was no longer sure of anything.

They landed by the rings, shifted, and joined the rest of the crowd who'd assembled there to watch.

Nasha leaned in to whisper at him. "The poles are higher up than I thought. Grass is really long out here, too."

He nodded. "Yes, to both of those things. You think either will be a problem?"

"The pole height won't matter too much. I can jump pretty well. But running through tall grass will definitely slow me down. Not much I can do about it, though."

She looked worried again, which only served to remind him that she was doing all of this for him. And sure, for his chocolate recipe, but this was still on him. "You're going to do great. I bet you surprise yourself."

"I hope so." She chewed at the inside of her cheek.

He took her hand again. "Hey, don't psych yourself out. Whatever happens, happens. Just do the best you can. No one expects more than that. Certainly not me."

She smiled, not quite convincingly. "Okay."

He put his arm around her and held her closer. Maybe he shouldn't have come to the census. Maybe he should have taken his chances with the council.

Maybe Shadowvale wouldn't have let them in.

Laz craned his neck like he was trying to see better. "They're all lined up."

Henry glanced skyward. "Traffic's gotten a lot thicker. They must be getting ready to start."

Charlie looked up. The sky was filled with dragons.

Just then, the pop of a starter pistol announced the race had begun.

Under his arm, Nasha tensed, her audible inhale filling his ears. "I wish I could see better."

An impulsive idea came to him. "You want to sit on my shoulders?"

She laughed. "Like it's a rock concert?"

"Hey, if it helps you see better, why not?"

She nodded. "Okay."

He bent down. "Climb on."

She practically vaulted into place.

He took hold of her feet. "That was impressive."

"Years of gymnastics."

"Then why did you need my help climbing up to ride the first time?"

"Um...partially because I had never ridden a dragon before. I wasn't sure how slippery you might be. Or where to grab. And not grab. And also because you were more than a little intimidating."

"Me?"

"In that form? Hello, yes."

He grinned. Beautiful, confident, wickedly witty, brilliant Nasha thought *he* was intimidating.

"Look," Henry said. "They're more than halfway and some of them are just getting air under their wings. There's no breeze and it shows."

Charlie tugged on Nasha's left foot. "Told you."

"Yep, you did. But they're coming in fast now."

They were, too. Standing at the end of the course made for an interesting viewpoint. Especially when that meant sixty dragons were headed straight for you.

Her First Taste Of Fire

Some of the crowd started to back up, but Charlie held his ground. "Tell me if you want me to move."

"Are they going to hit us?"

"They shouldn't."

Laz looked over at them, laughing. "I bet there'll be a serious amount of wash coming off them. We might get pushed back some."

"Maybe I should get down," Nasha said. "The last thing I need is to be knocked on my butt right before I have to run a mile and a half."

"Up to you," Charlie said.

She put her hands on his shoulders and dismounted with the same grace she'd showed getting on. "Thanks anyway." Her eyes were on the approaching dragons. "Definitely a better vantage point."

"Incoming," Henry yelled.

And just like that, a long, uneven string of beasts barreled toward them, dropping in altitude as they aimed themselves at the slim poles holding the objects of the game.

Nasha grabbed Charlie's hand and squeezed. Out of fear or excitement or both, he couldn't tell.

Wings tilted as the dragons grew closer, pushing against the air to slow themselves. Talons extended in a blind reach for the rings. Seeing beneath yourself in dragon form was nearly impossible. Picking something up was done on instinct and generally not that difficult. Except when that thing was only slightly larger than a standard coin.

Air rushed toward the crowd of onlookers, blowing their hair and clothes back. Charlie held his ground. Nasha did too, staying pinned to his side.

The turbulence made the poles sway slightly. The rings quivered, but none fell off their mounting. How much would those swaying poles throw off someone's aim?

They were about to find out as the dragons closed in. Here and there, people in the crowd ducked.

A few dragons managed to grab the rings. But just a few. As Charlie predicted, the rest either missed or knocked the rings off the poles to disappear into the grass.

Nasha looked up at him and smiled.

CHAPTER TWENTY-FOUR

Watching from the poles had been the right choice. Nasha felt more confident having seen so many rings fall into the grass. And then so many wide turns. And so many desperate faces as they searched.

The times had been less than impressive for all but a handful of contestants.

Charlie had flown her back to the starting area. She shucked her sweatshirt and claimed a lane.

As she positioned herself at the starting line, her badge tucked under the shoulder strap of her sports bra to keep the lanyard from flying up into her face, she was ready to do this. More than ready, she was eager. Even without the field being mowed.

Please don't let there be snakes in that grass. Bugs I can deal with, but please, no snakes. Or large spiders.

The dragon beside her, a dove gray creature with a slight blue iridescence, snorted. "You're running?"

Nasha shrugged, unbothered. Almost amused. "Yep. Poor old me. Not a dragon, and no wings, so no other choice."

The dragon's gaze went to the ring on Nasha's index finger. Her father's ring. "What are you then? *Human*?"

The word came out of the dragon's mouth as though it was poisonous.

Nasha was in a mood. Full of herself and without a fig to give about who knew what about her. And she certainly didn't care what this haughty creature beside her thought. "Not exactly. I'm the daughter of one of the Four Horsemen. You know, *of the Apocalypse*." With that last word, she let a little of her father's power into her eyes.

The ring vibrated with the use of that power. She could feel it flowing through her. Knew the whites of her eyes would have turned fully black by now, just like her father's did when he took on the role of Famine.

But that was enough. Just a hint for the sake of showing she wasn't someone to be messed with. Quickly, she released the power back into the ring.

No point in overdoing it.

The dragon had jerked back. To cover her reaction, she returned to flexing her wings.

"Good for you," the dragon on the other side of her whispered.

Nasha glanced at her. "Thanks."

The dragon nodded. "You're welcome. And ignore Katya, she's not nice to anyone. Except Verochka."

"Friends, huh?"

"Yeah. Birds of a feather and all that. I'm Marissa, by the way."

"Nasha. Nice to meet you."

"You, too. My dad's a dragon, but my mom's a basilisk.

She would have had to run this, too, if she was competing."

"A basilisk, huh?" Nasha took in the dragon's serpent-like hide. She had much smaller, finer scales than Charlie's, with a dark green background overlaid with a black diamond pattern. Nasha hadn't seen another dragon with skin like it and now she knew why. Marissa's tail was especially long and whiplike, too. "You get your coloring from her, then? The snake pattern? It's very pretty."

The dragon nodded. "Yep. And thank you. You have a good eye."

"Thanks. Good luck to you."

"You, too." Marissa smiled.

She seemed pretty cool. Maybe Laz ought to meet her.

"On your marks," the official called out. The megaphone made his voice slightly sharp.

Nasha crouched in a runner's position. Her heart pounded with the surge of adrenaline. On both sides of her, dragon wings went up, ready to move major amounts of air to get aloft.

"Get set."

Pop! The starter pistol went off and Nasha shot forward, pushing herself as hard as she could. The rush of air behind her sounded like a distant freight train. She couldn't help but glance back.

Not a single dragon was off the ground yet. All of them were running forward as well, pumping their wings and trying to get airborne, talons digging into the ground and throwing up clods of earth.

She had a chance to make some headway. To gain a small advantage. She called up every ounce of speed she had. Running through the tall grass was tedious. It whipped at her legs, wound around her feet, and did its best to trip her up.

She wasn't entirely sure the grass hadn't been bespelled on purpose to be difficult. The only upside to how much effort it required was that it was affecting the dragons the same way.

She pushed on, made herself forget about what was going on behind her, and concentrated on the poles up ahead.

Digging deeper, she raced forward, cutting through the grass as best she could. Behind the poles, she could see Charlie, Laz, and Henry rooting her on.

She made them her focus, keeping her eyes on them and nothing else. Driving harder and harder.

The sound behind her faded.

Then all around her, dragons sailed past. They seemed so high up, considering that the poles were only eight feet off the ground.

She ran harder. Her pole was getting closer. She could make out the ring sitting on top, cupped by a hollow, U-shaped bracket welded to the end of the pole. It wouldn't take much to knock it off, as she'd seen.

Her plan was to launch herself from a few feet away, grab the ring and the pole, then use the pole to swing herself around so that she'd land headed in the right direction.

If it worked, she'd cut seconds off her time.

If it didn't, she'd end up knocking the ring into the grass like the rest of them.

It was going to take a combination of gymnastics and supernatural power.

Charlie, Henry, and Laz were going to go hoarse shouting for her, but their encouragement made her faster, surer, stronger.

She was within twenty feet of the pole. The dragons were already there. And just like before, a few managed to snatch the ring, but far more knocked it into the grass.

Ten feet from the pole. Heart thumping. This was it. She gathered her energy, opened herself to the additional power of her father's ring, and leaped into the air, hands out.

It was as if time slowed. That was a gift of the ring, that ability to sharpen her actions as if each second had been stretched out. She grabbed hold of the pole just below the ring. The ring wobbled, tipping to one side.

She snatched it before it could fall, then kicked her legs out to use her momentum to swing wide.

The pole bent, but held fast, righting itself as her movements arced her around. The extra energy of the pole's flexion shot her forward. She landed on her feet about three yards from the pole.

Behind her, Charlie, Henry, and Laz erupted in cheers, yelling her name.

With a smile on her face and the ring clenched securely in her hand, she dug deep once again and started for the finish line. Three dragons crept into her peripheral vision, gaining slowly. The whoosh of their wings urged her forward. She called upon her father's ring for more speed.

Two of the dragons passed her, but she crossed the finish line at the same time as the third.

Energy spent, her knees began to buckle. Charlie was there to catch her as she fell.

She smiled up at him, shaking from her exertions. "How did you get here so fast?"

"I took flight as soon as you made that incredible turn." He helped her to her feet, keeping his arm around her waist. "Come on. You should probably walk a little so you don't cramp up."

"Yeah, okay." She glanced back. More dragons were sailing over the finish line now. "I think I did all right."

"You did phenomenally. You should be proud. I am. Now we just have to wait through the rest of the rounds so we can see where you'll finish."

That took a good while. She and Charlie returned to the pole end of the field to watch. That was where all the action was anyway. Especially in the fourth round, where two dragons collided during the turn, fell to the ground, shifted back into human form, and started slugging it out.

Both were disqualified, but it was very entertaining.

At the end of the last race, they all went back to the

starting line to await the announcement of the final placements.

Charlie held her hand.

Henry gave her a sweet smile. "You did great."

"Thank you," she said.

Laz nodded. "That turn was something to watch."

She laughed. "Good to know those years of gymnastics finally had a practical use."

But she was still nervous. There had been lots of good finishes. Some very smooth races. It was impossible to say where she'd ended up. She tugged at the hem of her sweatshirt. She hoped it was a decent finish.

While they waited for the judges to tally things up, she found something else to talk about. "Laz, do you know a dragon by the name of Marissa? She was next to me in the race. The green and black dragon, not the nasty gray one with the attitude."

He shook his head. "No, I don't."

Charlie frowned. "Was the gray one mean to you?"

"Just snooty, really. Marissa said her name was Katya and that she's a friend of Verochka's."

Henry huffed out a breath. "Sounds about right then."

"That's what I thought. Marissa was very nice, Laz. Maybe we should look for her. See if you two hit it off. Problem is, I don't know what she looks like in human form. She got in line beside me already shifted. She's very pretty in dragon form, though. Green with a black diamond pattern. Her mother is a basilisk."

He smiled. "I'll start watching nametags at lunch.

Although I'm not sure I want to date a woman who may or may not have the power to turn me to stone."

Nasha hadn't thought about that.

The official who'd run the game left the judges' table to address the crowd. "Ladies and gentlemen, the results are in."

She squeezed Charlie's hand as the official read off the top ten.

Nasha's nerves made it impossible to keep still. She alternated between holding her breath and trying not to pass out. The smells of lunch cooking in the distant tent almost turned her stomach, she was so on edge.

Then she heard the announcement she'd been waiting for.

She had come in eleventh.

Chapter Twenty-Five

Charlie let out a shout of excitement as he picked Nasha up and spun her around, barely able to contain his excitement. "You did it!"

"Did what?" She frowned at him. "I didn't make the top ten."

He set her down. "Sweetheart, it doesn't matter. You came in eleventh. With your finish in the first game, you're still very easily in the top ten."

"Oh." She gave that a moment of thought. "I guess I hadn't done the math."

A pretty redhead came over to speak to Nasha. "Sorry to interrupt. I just wanted to say congratulations."

Nasha stared blankly at the woman. Charlie didn't know her either.

The redhead laughed softly. "Sorry, I'm Marissa."

"Oh!" Nasha grinned. "Thank you so much. This is my fiancé, Charlie Ashborne."

He shook Marissa's hand. "Nice to meet you."

"You, too." She raised her brows slightly. "I've never met a legacy before."

Nasha grabbed Laz's arm and pulled him over. "And this is Charlie's best friend, Lazarus Stratton. Laz, this is my new friend, Marissa..." Nasha shook her head. "Sorry, I don't know your last name."

"Steelsong," Marissa filled in.

Laz shook Marissa's hand. Maybe a second longer than necessary, Charlie thought. He didn't blame Laz. Marissa was cute. And Laz had once had a thing for redheads. "It's a pleasure to meet you, Marissa."

Charlie clapped his hand on Henry's shoulder. "This is another friend of ours, Marissa. Henry Grimstone."

Marissa gave Henry an odd look, just for a second. "You served on the council, didn't you?"

Henry nodded. "You know your history, young lady. I did indeed."

She smiled. "I'm not that good at history, but my aunt, Martha Carrington, was on the council about the same time."

"I remember Martha. Our terms overlapped by a year. Lovely woman. How is she?"

"Retired and doing well. Currently sailing through the Caribbean."

Henry nodded. "That sounds like a nice retirement."

Impulse took hold of Charlie. "Why don't you join us for lunch, Marissa? If you don't have other plans."

"I don't, and I'd love to. Thanks."

They found a table and claimed it. Charlie shooed everyone off to get their food while he stayed to hold the seats. Fortunately, it wasn't as crowded as it had been for breakfast. Not everyone who'd showed up to participate in or watch the morning game had stayed for lunch.

Some had limped off to tend to their wounded egos.

But there was still a good crowd present, especially now that some of the men were trickling in, as they'd be up next.

Charlie stared into the crowd without seeing anyone. He was focused on his own upcoming turn. He was seriously thinking about a new strategy for getting the ring. Sort of half dragon, half-Nasha style.

What if he just—

Someone blocked out the sun. "Do you mind if we sit with you?"

He looked up to see Verochka and a friend, no doubt Katya, if her pale gray leathers were any indication, sitting down at his table. "Yes, actually. These seats are all reserved."

Verochka pouted. "Are you truly sending us away? Do you know who I am?"

"I know you're not my fiancée." If she thought that was going to work with him, she was laughably wrong.

She grunted in disgust. "Your fiancée is the little human one, no?"

"No. She's the little badass one."

Katya sniffed and leaned in toward her friend. "She was next to me in the race. She *ran*. No wings. So sad."

Charlie narrowed his eyes. "You both need to go. Now."

Verochka's lip curled. "You're making a dreadful mistake, legacy. You should be with a dragon. Especially another legacy."

He barked out a laugh. "You mean like you? Someone who's also shallow and self-absorbed? No thanks. I'd much rather spend my time with a real woman. One who's caring and kind and as beautiful inside as she is on the outside."

Verochka hissed at him, her eyes alight with dragon fire. "You won't get that choice when I win, legacy. I will choose you just to prove to you what you're missing." She smiled. "I look forward to making your life miserable."

"You're completely insane, you know that?"

She picked up her food tray. "But at least I am not tainted with the dark magic that possesses your girlfriend's soul. You know that about her, don't you? That she's the daughter of a man whose only purpose is to bring suffering to this earth. If that makes you proud, then perhaps you are not the man for me after all."

Charlie couldn't argue against that. Nasha's father was a Horseman.

"In fact," Verochka continued. "I am thinking I should mention this information to the council. Seems to me like something they may have interest in, don't you think?"

"Who I'm involved with is none of their business."

"It is very much their business. After all, it is their job to protect our race. And you are a legacy." She lifted her chin as though she'd won something. Then, with Katya at her heels, she strode away.

Blast it all. Verochka was only going to make more trouble for them. How had she found out about Nasha's father?

Her First Taste Of Fire

He had to talk to Nasha and let her know. He was about to stand up and go find her when she and Henry approached the table.

She gave him a curious look. "Everything okay?"

"I'm not sure. We need to talk."

"Go," Henry said. "I'll keep an eye on the table. Laz and Marissa will be here in a minute anyway."

"Thanks." He took Nasha's hand and led her away from the crowd.

"What's up?"

"While you guys were getting your food, Verochka and Katya tried to sit with me. I let them know I wasn't interested, and she got testy. To the point that she threatened to tell the council who your father is."

Nasha made a face. "How would she even know who my—oh."

"Oh, what?"

She took a breath. "I told Katya who my father was when we were waiting for the race to begin. She was so full of herself and putting me down and I just wanted to shut her up."

"I completely understand. I had the same feeling about Verochka. Especially when she said she was going to win and choose me to be her husband."

"Ew." Nasha screwed up her face in pure disgust. "Can you imagine? She'd probably expect you to hold her purse when she goes shopping. Or her little dog. She seems like the type who'd have a little dog strictly as an accessory. Maybe I should go have a talk with her."

"I don't think that would help. It would be fun to watch, though."

Nasha smirked. "Honestly, does any of her bluster mean anything unless she wins?"

"The part where she might tell the council about your father does. That could cause trouble."

Nasha crossed her arms. "Yeah, not if the council is smart. Which, granted, they don't really come off that way, but the only thing that information should do is make them treat me better. The Four Horsemen of the Apocalypse are no joke. My father and his three brethren could make life very difficult for those yahoos."

"Would they, though? Just on your behalf? That seems like it might be an abuse of power."

"They're the Four Horsemen. They're not the Mormon Tabernacle Choir. Abuse of power is probably in the job description." She sighed and looked away for a moment. "They wouldn't be happy about being involved in such petty stuff, though."

"Would there be repercussions? If your father became aware of all of this, I mean?"

She shrugged. "Hard to say. But then again, depends on his mood. He is very protective of me. I'm his only child, you know. I'm the heir to his position. He's not about to let me get hurt."

Charlie wasn't so sure after all that he wanted to meet the man when they got back. "But that's just standard father behavior, right?"

"I don't know. He's the only dad I've had. I have

nothing to compare him to. My gut says it's a little more than standard. Putting all of that aside, what could the council do to you? Anything? Could they affect your status as a legacy?"

"I don't think so." He shook his head. "That stupid inheritance is more trouble than it's worth."

"What is it worth, if you don't mind me asking."

He genuinely wasn't sure. "I don't have any idea. The last time it was inventoried, which was in the '90s, it was approaching a billion dollars."

Her mouth fell open. "That's a lot of money."

"It is, but it's not really spendable. Some of it is, but the Crimson Treaty Hoard is such a big deal because it represents the price paid to secure the peace between two warring dragon clans. The Ashbornes and the Bloodwings. It goes back centuries."

"And your family holds the hoard because?"

"Because we won the war, essentially. We were more powerful. Despite that, the Bloodwings killed more of our clan. Therefore they owed us a great debt to keep us from wiping them out. Pretty barbaric stuff, but that's how it was with my people back then."

"I see. It all makes sense now. Why you're treated the way you are, I mean. Not only are you worth a freaking fortune, but you've got all this history behind you. I take it your dad deals with all of it right now, though?"

"He does." Charlie exhaled, wondering what his father would think about all of this. Actually, Charlie knew. "He'd be livid if he knew what was going on."

She seemed concerned suddenly. "Would he take your inheritance away from you?"

Charlie shook his head. "He can't. I'm his eldest child." Not that it made a difference in their relationship. "Besides that, it's called a legacy for a reason. He has no control over it passing to me. That was written into the treaty documents long before either of us existed."

She nodded like that answer satisfied her. "Good. Then if anything happens and word spreads about your...*you know*...he won't freak out over that, either."

Charlie's mouth firmed into a hard, terse line before he responded. "Oh, he's already freaked out over that. And trust me, if he could take the hoard away from me, he would."

CHAPTER TWENTY-SIX

Nasha stood quietly with Henry as they waited for Laz and Charlie's race to begin. Marissa was at the starting line, wishing Laz good luck. Those two had certainly hit it off.

Meanwhile, Nasha was still trying to process the information Charlie had given her. How could a father want to punish his son for something that wasn't his fault?

It seemed like the opposite of what parenting was supposed to be. Where was the unconditional love? The support?

If she'd been born completely human, without any of her father's abilities, she couldn't imagine her father loving her any less. In fact, he might have been pleased about it. Her being completely human might have spared her the need to take over from him.

Then again, maybe not. There had been human Horsemen.

She couldn't stop thinking about Charlie. About the look in his eyes when he'd spoken about his father. His eyes had held pure pain. Hurt, too. Mixed with sadness, shame, and regret.

She could only imagine the true nature of their relationship and how deeply scarred it was for him to look like that. Just thinking about it made her ache for him. It also made her love him that much more. She wanted to take care of him and make it all go away, but she didn't have a clue how to fix his curse.

Or if it was even possible. That kind of magic wasn't something she knew anything about.

"You okay?" Henry asked. "You look like someone just ate your dessert."

She smiled half-heartedly. "Just thinking about Verochka and her nonsense." Charlie had explained most of what had happened to the whole gang over lunch. Thankfully, he'd left out the part about Verochka threatening to tell the council who Nasha's father was.

For now, they were trying to keep that under wraps. If Verochka made good on her threat, it wouldn't matter.

"Don't worry about her," Henry said. "You and Charlie are doing fine. One of you will end up in the top ten and you'll be able to pick the other as your mate. And as long as no one else picks them, too, you'll be fine. Seriously, you'll probably both be top ten and your worries will be over."

"I hope so." But she couldn't shake the unsettled feeling in her gut. It was like waiting for the other shoe to drop. Except that shoe could very well blow up and bring about the end of the world.

She lifted her head, determined to ignore that unsettled feeling long enough to cheer Charlie and Laz on. "You're sure we're in the right spot?"

Henry nodded. "Yep. Charlie's in the lane directly in front of us and Laz is one over. If you want, I'd be happy to take you up to watch from the sky."

"Thanks, but this is fine. I'm afraid I'd lose my grip in all the excitement."

Henry smiled. "Can't have that, now."

In the distance, they could hear the official telling the contestants to get lined up.

New nerves zipped through her. She hooked her arm through Henry's. "This makes me so nervous."

He patted her hand. "I know. Me, too. But Charlie's whip fast and I think he's got some kind of strategy figured out. He was cagey about it at lunch, and I don't blame him. Too many people around to talk about something like that without being overheard."

"I hope whatever it is works."

"Me, too. I'm pretty sure he filled Lazarus in on his plan."

The starter pistol went off, making Nasha jump slightly. She stared down the lane.

Sixty dragons headed toward them, all lumbering forward, wings pumping for all they were worth. Charlie and Laz both got up in the air quickly, but so did a few others.

Nasha let go of Henry to cup her hands around her mouth and yell, "Come on, Charlie! Come on, Laz! You've got this!"

To the far left, one of the dragons veered into the path of another, sending him off course. It looked deliberate. The second dragon responded with a tremendous burst of fire, causing two more dragons to go sideways. The whole left side of the course was a tangle of wings and fire and screeching beasts.

Charlie flew steady on, about halfway now. Laz trailed slightly behind, but not by much. Beside her, Henry yelled encouragement to both of them.

She held her fists to her mouth, almost wishing she could close her eyes until it was over but there was no way she wasn't going to watch. She was riveted. "Come on, Charlie," she whispered. "You can do this. You have to do this."

Suddenly, he shifted course downward, almost touching the ground. Then she saw Laz was doing the same thing.

"What in the devil are they doing?" Henry said. "It's too soon to—"

Charlie shifted into his human form and hit the ground running. Two lanes down, Laz did the same thing.

She kept her gaze on Charlie. As he approached the pole, he jumped up, snagged the ring, then used the pole to pull himself around toward the finish line. He kept running as he shifted back to his dragon form. He was aloft in seconds, using the momentum to push himself skyward.

She checked on Laz. He was lifting off, too, having done the same thing.

"Genius," Henry breathed out. "They copied you."

Nasha couldn't stop staring, open-mouthed. She was stunned by what they'd done, as were a lot of the people in the crowd around them, who just seemed to be staring in amazement.

"Those two are going to cross the finish before some of the others have even turned." She grabbed Henry's arm. "Get me down there."

With a nod, he was in dragon form.

She didn't wait for an invitation, just climbed on. Henry got out of the crowd and onto the sidelines, where he took flight. Less than a minute later, they were landing again.

Nasha slid off. "Thanks, Henry."

"No problem."

She scanned the finish line for Charlie. He was walking toward them, hands on his hips, taking big gulps of air. She raced toward him. "Charlie!"

Behind him, Laz was crossing the finish toward Marissa.

Charlie grinned. "How'd you like that?"

She ran into his arms. "That was amazing."

He kissed her cheek as he took hold of her. "It worked out better than expected. Took a ton of energy. I feel like I could lay down and sleep for about three days, but it worked. Did Laz make it?"

"Yes. It worked like a charm." She kissed him back,

full on the mouth. "You know the next round is going to be full of dragons doing that now."

He nodded. "Let them. We did the best we could."

"You sure did. They'll all just be copycats, anyway. And I bet you got a fantastic time."

He took a deep breath. "That was the plan. And you were my inspiration."

"Babe, you were the first one across the line."

He glanced back toward the finish. "I was?"

"And it looked like Laz was second."

Dragons were clearing the line now, one after the other, some neck and neck.

Charlie ran a hand through his sweat-damp hair. "Then it worked better than I thought it would."

Henry came up to them. "Outstanding job, son."

"Thanks."

Laz and Marissa joined them. Laz had his arm around her shoulders. "I don't know about you, Charlie, but I feel like I just ran a marathon. That much shifting in that short amount of time, plus the takeoffs..." He shook his head.

"Yeah," Charlie said. "I feel it, too. Completely wrung out."

Nasha smiled, thrilled they'd both done so well. "You know what we should do tonight? Skip the communal dinner in favor of figuring out food on our own and a soak in the pool at our cave. After it's been sufficiently heated up, of course."

"That does sound good," Charlie said. He looked at

the group. "What do you guys think? Pool party at our place, say around seven? That will give us a little time to chill on our own. I'm just not sure what we can rustle up for dinner."

"If you don't mind steaks and baked potatoes, I think I can help in the dinner department," Henry said.

"Mind?" Charlie laughed. "I feel like we should pay you for that."

"Nonsense," Henry said. "I wouldn't dream of it."

Marissa grinned. "As it happens, my mother packed me a whole cooler full of desserts." She rolled her eyes. "I love sweets, but there's only so much cheesecake a girl can eat. I'd be happy to bring it."

Laz made a show of patting his stomach. Despite how much he ate, it was remarkably flat. Dragon metabolism at work, apparently. "And I will be happy to bring my appetite."

Nasha clapped her hands. "Then it's a plan. Bring a suit, a towel, and an appetite." The idea of them all being together made her very happy. Almost as much as not having to risk the possibility of running into Verochka.

"That will be a nice evening," Charlie said. "Now all we have to do is wait for the final results and we can get out of here."

Wait they did. It took another hour and a half for the races to be over and the scores to be compared.

The group ended up sitting at the picnic tables by the main tent. It was still near enough to hear the announcement when the official made it. When he started to speak, they got up and moved closer.

Nasha was more nervous than she'd been waiting for her own results. She couldn't keep still, clenching her hands and fiddling with the tail of her braid.

Charlie held out his hand. She took it and tried to breathe.

"Whatever happens," he said. "You and I are leaving here together. You can count on that."

She nodded, wanting to believe him with everything in her.

The official read off the top ten.

Laz was tied for second with another dragon.

Charlie had come in first.

Chapter Twenty-Seven

After about half an hour of doing nothing but relaxing by the fire, which felt amazing, Charlie finally got up and stretched. "We should change into our suits. The gang will be here shortly."

She nodded. "You want to go first?"

"No, I need to get more firewood and build this fire up. How about I go do that and you can have the cave to yourself for a bit?"

"Okay." She got up and went to her duffel, presumably to find her swimsuit.

He went outside to get more wood, taking the small ax he'd brought. He chopped some extra to give her more time, and when he got back, she was changed. She'd put her clothes back on over the suit, but the ties of her bikini top hung out through the neck of her sweatshirt.

He stoked up the fire, adding on a few more pieces of wood. The rest he stacked nearby. Then he changed while she stood at the entrance, her back to him.

"Done," he called out as he pulled on a T-shirt. Between the crackling fire and the candles, the cave was warming up nicely. Her mylar wall had been genius.

She came back in and got to work right away on

getting things ready for their guests, arranging seats around the fire for all of them. "Are you going to heat the pool now?"

He nodded. "I figure I'll get it good and boiling, then by the time they get here it should still be plenty warm."

"And if it needs heating up after that?"

He could tell she was concerned about his curse being revealed. It was incredibly sweet. "There will be three other dragons here. Two who have no problems making fire. We'll figure it out."

"Okay."

Charlie walked over to the pool. He breathed fire across the surface until the water bubbled and steam wafted up. He made sure to gather the scales he lost in the process. Three in total, one for each time he'd created fire. He looked himself over. None had come from super obvious spots, which was good.

On the other side of the cave, Nasha set up more candles and lanterns. She was spacing them out to spread the light.

He watched her for a moment. Losing the scales bothered him, but not nearly as much as it used to. Hard to get too worked up over a thing like that when he'd finished first in today's game. Even harder to be upset about it when the woman he was falling for wasn't bothered by it, either.

That helped a lot. Just being around her made him feel better in all kinds of ways. He couldn't remember when he'd been this happy. And that was in the midst of this stupid census. He could only imagine what things would be like when they got home.

Assuming she was still interested in him when they returned to Shadowvale. Did she understand that when he'd said he wanted this to be real, he'd meant for longer than while they were here?

She was up on her tiptoes arranging three candles on an outcropping of rock.

He cleared his throat. He needed to know. "Nasha?"

She looked at him and smiled. "What? Need me to do something?"

"Just one thing."

She went flatfooted again. "What's that?"

"Tell me that this isn't going to change when we get home."

"You mean us?" Her smile didn't waver.

He nodded. "When I said I wanted it to be real, I meant that. I really like you. And I would very much like to keep seeing you."

She walked over to him, took hold of the drawstrings on his swim trunks and tugged him closer. "I'd keep seeing you even if you stopped making chocolate."

He laughed. "Well, I already promised to keep you in the stuff, so I can't go back on my word now, can I?"

"Nope."

He bent to kiss her, but the kiss was interrupted by the sound of a dragon landing outside. He kept his forehead pressed to hers, not entirely ready to give up the contact. "Someone's here."

"Henry," she said. "He's the most likely to arrive early."

"Agreed."

And it was. Henry arrived at seven on the dot, carrying a cooler packed with the steaks and baking potatoes he'd promised. He'd also brought a smaller, second bag and a grill specifically made to go over an open fire. "I hope you don't mind me bringing my own equipment, but I wasn't sure if you had a grill screen to go over the fire pit."

Charlie looked around and shook his head. "That might be the one thing I didn't buy. Good thinking."

Nasha joined them as Henry dug potatoes out of the cooler. They were already wrapped in aluminum foil. "Catch." He tossed them to Charlie, one by one. "Those need to get buried in the coals. They'll take about an hour if we don't help things along. Which we can do."

"No problem." Charlie pushed the potatoes into the glowing embers, making a ring of them along the stone wall of the pit. "Did you bring your suit?"

"Yep. Got a towel in the other bag, too."

Nasha touched Henry's arm. "I'm so glad we're doing this instead of joining the crowd, aren't you?"

"You betcha," he said.

Laz arrived next. He was in sweatpants and a sweatshirt, but Charlie could see the drawstring of swim trunks sticking out of the waistband of his pants. He had a towel over one shoulder. "I'm sorry I didn't have anything to bring."

Her First Taste Of Fire

"You're here," Nasha said. "That's all that matters. Where's Marissa? I thought you two would be coming together."

"She had to get her desserts." Laz was smiling. "She's something, isn't she?"

Charlie laughed. "Lovestruck already?"

Laz shrugged. "What can I say? I'm a sucker for a pretty redhead."

The whoosh of wings announced Marissa's arrival a few moments later. Like Henry, she'd come with a cooler and another small tote bag. "Hi, all! I brought the cheesecake and the strawberry sauce my mom packed. No whipped cream, though."

Laz gazed at her with moonbeam eyes. "You're sweet enough already."

Charlie almost rolled his. He shook his head. "Did you wear your suit, or do you need to change?"

"I wore it," Marissa answered. She took a look around. "Wow, this is a nice cave. One of the nicest, I'd say. And that pool is amazing. How on earth did you score this place?"

Charlie shrugged. "We just got here early. I actually picked it because it has a path that leads down to the valley. I figured that would be easier on Nasha."

"Good thinking," Marissa said. "Otherwise she'd be stuck up here." She looked at Nasha. "Assuming you can't teleport or something cool like that."

Nasha laughed. "Safe assumption. Come on, let's test the water and see if it needs to be warmed up again."

Marissa went back to the pool with Nasha.

While the women did that, Henry approached Charlie and Laz by the fire. He kept his words quiet. "Reynaldo came to see me right before I left. He says Verochka has approached the council about disqualifying Nasha."

Charlie straightened. "I've about had enough of this."

Laz nodded. "I agree. But do you really care if Nasha gets disqualified? She's not a dragon. What can the council really do to her?"

"Nothing," Charlie admitted. "But they could use her as a way of punishing me."

Henry frowned. "That they could. Reynaldo says nothing's set in stone yet. The council realizes that your position as a legacy has to mean something, or they set a dangerous precedent."

"Except Verochka's a legacy, too."

"True," Henry said. "But her hoard isn't worth half of what yours is. The council wants to upset you less than they want to upset her."

"Well, tomorrow is the last day of games." Charlie tossed one final chunk of wood onto the fire, sending up a shower of sparks. "Then we have to wait for the final placements. The good news is, this will all be over soon."

"Yeah," Laz said. "But don't forget, we also have to wait to see how the council's going to pair up anyone who didn't make top ten or get picked by one of the top ten."

Laz stared toward the pool, where Marissa and Nasha were now sitting on the edge, dangling their feet in. "I want Marissa. I mean, I want the chance to at least get to know her. When I first got here, I was kind of okay with the council matching me with a mate. Now? I'm not. It's my life. I should be able to decide who I spend it with."

Henry nodded. "You should. There has to be more of us who feel this way, don't you think?"

"Sure," Charlie said. "But are they brave enough to do something about it? To stand up and voice their disagreement? That's the real issue. The council has a stranglehold on us."

Laz was still looking at Marissa. "So what are we going to do?"

The three men were quiet until Charlie said the only thing he could think of. "We wait and see how tomorrow goes. Maybe we even wait to see how everything finishes. Where we place, how the matches are made, and if the council truly decides to flex its muscle, we flex back. Even if we have to do it alone."

Henry looked concerned. "I don't care what happens to me, but you two are young. You have a lot more years ahead of you. The last thing you need is the council breathing down your necks the rest of your lives, making things hard on you. Or worse, deciding to disqualify you."

Charlie shrugged. "I can handle it. I've been living like I was already disqualified for about five years now. Laz?"

He was quiet, like he was thinking. "Is Shadowvale really a safe haven?"

"It is," Charlie answered.

"Then if I get disqualified, I'll move there and start over. Maybe I can talk Marissa into coming with me."

"Speaking of the women," Charlie said. "We'd better join them or they're going to think we've forgotten about them."

"I'm ready," Henry said. "These old bones have been looking forward to a hot soak."

Laz headed straight for the pool. "How's the water, ladies?"

Charlie and Henry followed him.

"Getting cool," Nasha said. She glanced at Henry. "Would you do the honors and heat it up again?"

"Happy to. You'd better get back."

She and Marissa got up and moved to stand with Charlie and Laz.

Henry let loose, breathing fire across the surface until the steam began to rise again. "What do you think? Good enough?"

Nasha went over and stuck her toes in. "Deliciously hot. Thank you."

"You're welcome." He pulled off his long-sleeve shirt.

Everyone else stripped down to their suits as well and slipped into the water. Marissa and Nasha clipped their hair up to keep it from getting wet.

Laz went straight to Marissa, diving under and bobbing to the surface next to her.

Henry hung by the side, arms outstretched on the rocks, head back, eyes closed. "This is nice."

"Agreed," Nasha said. After a few minutes of just floating and enjoying the water, she swam closer to Charlie, smiling at him. "You boys seemed to be having a big conversation by the fire. Something going on?"

He didn't really want to spoil the evening with more talk about the council and Verochka, but Nasha had a right to know. "Verochka is trying to get the council to disqualify you. It's not something that's going to happen anytime soon. My legacy status means they have a lot to think about."

Treading water to hold her position, she shook her head as she looked at him. "Aren't you tired of caring what they think?"

"I am. Really tired." Boy, was that an understatement. "But it's not just about me. Anything that happens to me will reflect poorly on my family. I'm most worried about my sisters."

Nasha's gaze seemed to hold some questions. "Do you think they're most worried about you? How often do you talk to them? How often do they reach out to you to see how you're doing?"

He let out a sigh. "I get your point. The truth is, I haven't talked to anyone in my family in a long time. And they haven't made any effort to talk to me. It doesn't matter. I can't help my concern for them."

"That's because you're a decent person. I wouldn't want anything bad to happen to your sisters or your parents, but they're all adults, right?"

"Right."

"So at some point, maybe you need to put yourself first."

"Maybe." He knew she was right. But it was a hard thing to do. Depending on how this census went, the decision might be taken out of his hands.

She came closer. "Do you think Verochka's going to tell the council about my father?"

"I think it's a very real possibility. Especially if you continue to do well in tomorrow's games."

"I hate that," Nasha said. "She shouldn't be in charge of who knows what about me. That's my information to share when and if I decide to share it."

"I agree. She gets her power from crap like that."

"Then I guess I need to take that power away from her. At least in some small way." Nasha twisted to face Laz, Marissa, and Henry. "You guys? I need to tell you something. Something that Verochka is probably going to hold over me, so better you hear it from me than her warped version."

Henry opened his eyes, instantly concerned. Laz and Marissa swam over, so Henry joined them.

"What has that heifer done now?" Marissa asked.

Nasha took a breath. "It's my fault. I made the mistake of letting her friend, Katya, know who my father was. She was making me mad at the starting line and I decided to explain how not human I was. Now Verochka is very likely going to use that information to have the council disqualify me."

Marissa raised her hand out of the water. "To be honest, I overheard you. Not much, but enough that I think I know who you said he was."

Charlie snorted. "Unlike Verochka, you aren't using that information to hurt Nasha."

"Never," Marissa said.

Charlie went on. "Well, Verochka actually threatened as much at lunch, right before you guys came back from getting your food. I didn't think it was my place to share all of what she'd said."

Laz's gaze held intense curiosity. "That was solid of you."

"It was," Nasha said. "But I've had enough. I don't care who knows about my father. I'm certainly not ashamed of him or who I am or the kind of magic that runs through my blood. I also know that not everyone feels the same way, so if what I'm about to tell you changes your mind about me and you want to leave or to stop being friends with me, I understand. It wouldn't be the first time. I'll have no hard feelings about it, either. I'm past all that."

Henry frowned. "That's not going to happen."

"I hope not," Nasha said.

Charlie hoped not, too. Laz had enough of his own troubles to judge someone else, but Henry was old school. At least Marissa didn't seem to care. If she'd actually overheard Nasha correctly. If not...

Nasha paused, like she was steeling herself for their reaction. "My father is one of the Four Horsemen of the Apocalypse. And I'm next in line to take over as Famine."

CHAPTER TWENTY-EIGHT

Nasha braced herself as the silence became deafening. They were all looking at her with unreadable expressions. Maybe telling them wasn't a good idea. Maybe Marissa hadn't really overhead Nasha's boast to Katya.

Marissa was the first to speak. "It didn't bother me when I heard it the first time, and it doesn't bother me now. I mean, as far as we know, Verochka's father might be the devil, so..." She shrugged.

Everyone laughed. Nasha was instantly relieved. "Thank you."

Then Laz spoke. "That's pretty heavy. I can't imagine growing up with all of that on your shoulders."

"It was, at times," Nasha admitted.

She looked at Henry. "You haven't said anything. You have any thoughts about who my dad is?"

He shook his head. "Not much to say. Except that it hasn't changed the way I feel about you. I think you're one of the nicest people I've met in a long time. Who am I to judge your father? If he had anything to do with raising you, he can't be that bad. Look how you turned out."

"He had everything to do with raising me." She

almost teared up. "And he's not bad at all. He does a very hard job. All of the Horsemen do. And they're all good men at heart. If they didn't do their jobs, someone else would. Someone who might not care as much or be as judicial."

Henry nodded, the wisdom of his years shining in his eyes. "I can understand that entirely. Sometimes good men have to do hard jobs. He did a fantastic job with you."

She swallowed the emotion thickening her throat and smiled. "Thank you all for being so understanding. Not everyone is."

Marissa shrugged like it was no big deal, sending ripples through the water. "We're dragons. You think everyone likes us right away? Most people are scared of us. The fact that you came here to support your fiancé and immediately jumped into the games despite not having the same skill set as the rest of us says a lot about who you are."

"She's right," Charlie said. "You've done an amazing job here."

"Watch," Laz said. "You'll be top ten after tomorrow's games for sure."

"Maybe," Nasha said. "So long as it's something a non-dragon can do."

He nodded. "True. Anyone have any idea about the game tomorrow?"

"Nothing," Marissa said.

Henry folded his arms on top of the rock edge, letting

the rest of himself hang in the water. "There's a good chance it will be very dragon-specific. That would be an easy way for the council to deal with Nasha on the sly. Trust me. We were not above doing the same thing back in my day. Tweaking the games, that is."

Nasha sighed. "Good thing I have my proxy left."

"Whatever you need, babe, I'm there." Then Charlie held up his hand. "Although I might be done in here. My fingers are all pruned up. Not to mention, my stomach is rumbling."

Laz shot him a look. "Is that what that noise was? I thought we were having an earthquake."

Charlie pushed a wave of water at him, making Marissa shriek with laughter as she tried to swim out of the way.

Henry chuckled as he climbed out of the pool. "I'll get those steaks working while you kids play. Baked potatoes should be close to ready soon anyway."

Amused by the horseplay, Nasha just shook her head. It was good to have friends. Of any age. She was glad she'd told them about her dad. It felt like a weight had been lifted off of her. Now, if Verochka tried to use her father against her, at least it wouldn't be a surprise to everyone.

Nasha got out of the water, wrapped herself in a towel, and headed toward the fire pit to help Henry. "What can I do?"

He was situating the grill rack over the fire pit. "This is a little embarrassing for me, since I like to think of

Her First Taste Of Fire

myself as a pretty decent cook, but I have a feeling I left the salt and pepper back at my place. Any chance you have some?"

"We do. Charlie bought out the local camping goods store when he realized I couldn't exactly curl up and sleep dragon-style like him. One of the things he got was a seasonings kit. Salt, pepper, sugar, ketchup, mustard, and hot sauce."

None of which had been opened. Seasonings made no difference to her, and they'd been eating most of their meals down in the field with everyone else.

"Way to go, Charlie," Henry said. "I will definitely take that salt and pepper. We'll need it for the baked potatoes, too. Maybe even that hot sauce. It's not bad on a potato. Not as good as butter and sour cream, but I don't have either of those, so we'll have to make do."

She opened up the package and handed the salt and pepper to him. "Here you go. Can I ask you something?"

"Anything."

"You have a nicer bed setup than I do. How come you don't sleep on the ground like the rest of the dragons?"

He laughed. "Because I have old bones that prefer some comfort. I'm not the only one, either. You'd find cots in a good number of these caves."

"Oh." She hadn't thought about that.

He started liberally seasoning the steaks on both sides. "How do you like your steak cooked?"

She really didn't know. "Whatever you think is good."

He made a funny face. "I'm dragon. I think rare is

good. You sure that's what you want? Wait. You're not a veggie person, are you?"

"No, I'll eat just about anything."

He laughed. "I suppose you proved that in the first game, didn't you? So how'd you like that steak? Rare? Medium rare? Please don't say well done."

She wasn't sure what to say but at least he'd helped her eliminate one possibility. "How about a little more done than rare? Medium, like you said."

"You got it. Want to check with the others and see what doneness they'd like?"

"Sure." She went back to the pool. Charlie was out and drying off. Laz was giving Marissa a hand to help her out. "How do you guys want your steaks? Henry wants to know."

"Rare," Charlie said.

Laz nodded. "Same."

"Yep," Marissa agreed. "For me, too."

"All right, I'll tell him." She went back to Henry. He had the steaks on the grill rack, and they were sizzling up a storm, smelling delicious. If only they tasted like that to her. "Everyone said rare."

"As I thought." He had a long barbeque fork out. He set it on the side of the fire pit. "Don't worry about the game tomorrow. Charlie will handle it if you can't. And if Verochka does say something to the council about your father, I'm going to file a formal complaint against her."

"Henry, you're going to get yourself in trouble." She

Her First Taste Of Fire

liked him too much to see him suffer at the hands of the council.

"I don't care. If they decide to make me a target, I'll move to Shadowvale, too. You and Charlie like it well enough there. And it sounds like there's a couple eligible women I ought to meet, so why not?"

She smiled. "There are at least two I can think of. Probably more if I asked around. But what if you don't like Shadowvale?"

"What do you think I wouldn't like about it?" He sat in the nearest camp chair.

"Well, there's no sun. It's permanently overcast. The witch who created the town did that to protect her vampire lover."

His eyes widened slightly. "Talk about a gift of love. That's something. So it's gloomy all the time, huh?"

"Not gloomy, exactly. There are some pretty bright days. To be honest, I thought I'd hate it, but I don't. In fact, I hardly even notice it anymore. Maybe it wouldn't matter as much to you anyway, seeing as how you can just go for a spin above the clouds whenever you want."

"True. Tell me more about the cursed part."

She hesitated, hoping he wasn't going to ask about hers or Charlie's. "Most everyone has one, but I don't think it would be a big deal for you to live there without one. Maybe having the council after you could even be considered a kind of curse."

"With this council? I'd say that definitely qualifies.

Why do so many cursed people end up there? Just to get away from everything?"

"That's a reason, but also because somewhere in the depths of the Enchanted Forest exists a magical book. If you can find that book and write your name in it, your curse will be gone forever."

His lips parted in amazement. "How about that? Is it just a legend? Or is it true?"

"Oh, it's true."

"Have you ever looked for it?"

She smiled and stared into the fire. "When we first moved there, I used to look all the time. I haven't in a few years now. I guess I just stopped caring if my curse ever got lifted." That wasn't really true. She'd just stopped believing it was possible.

Charlie joined them. He had his T-shirt back on and Nasha's sweatshirt in his hand. He held it out to her. "You warm enough, sweetheart? I brought you your sweatshirt."

"Thanks." She took it and pulled it over her head. "I'm pretty dry now. I should get my leggings on, too. I definitely feel the cold more than the rest of you."

"Or the four of us could just radiate a little heat and warm the place up." Charlie nodded at Henry.

"We can absolutely do that for the lady of the house. Er, cave," Henry said.

"Do what?" Laz asked as he and Marissa joined them.

"Radiate a little heat to keep Nasha more comfortable," Charlie answered.

Her First Taste Of Fire

Marissa sat on the stump Charlie had brought in earlier for just that purpose. "It does get chilly here at night, doesn't it?"

"Chilly?" Nasha laughed. "There was frost on everything this morning. Fortunately, it warms up pretty well once the sun's been up a few hours."

"How's that work in your town?" Henry asked. He picked up the long fork and started flipping the steaks. "Without the sun, is it chilly? Not that it matters so much to me, being thick skinned and all. Which is probably why I don't mind living up in the mountains of Wyoming like I do."

"Our seasons are about what you'd expect for the Carolinas." She looked at Charlie. "Wouldn't you say?"

He nodded. "You'll see for yourself when you come visit, Henry. Same with you, Laz. And Marissa, you're invited, too."

She leaned in. "What's this now? Where are we going?"

While Charlie filled them in, Nasha drifted. Her mind was on tomorrow's game and Verochka and her father. She couldn't help but think that something was going to happen. Something that might change everything.

She had no idea what, of course, but she hadn't come this far to give up. She twisted her father's ring around on her finger. If that meant digging into her darker powers, then maybe that was what she'd do.

She knew she was kidding herself.

There was no maybe.

Chapter Twenty-Nine

By the time Henry, Laz, and Marissa left, Charlie was stuffed with food and questioning the amount of cheesecake he'd eaten. He was utterly content, however, despite having overindulged.

Nasha looked pretty much the same as she lazed by the fire in one of the camp chairs. She glanced up at him with heavy lidded eyes as he came back in from seeing everyone off. "I feel like I could sleep for two days."

He nodded and sat beside her. "Me, too. That was a good night."

"It was," she agreed. "I haven't laughed that much since we ate at Henry's. They're all such fun company. Was the cheesecake as good as everyone said it was?"

He let out a long, satisfied sigh. "Probably better. Did you see how much of it I ate? It was fantastic. You should get her mom's recipe. Or do you already make cheesecake in your shop?"

"Not as a rule, no. If I had that recipe, I'd definitely add it to the menu." Her eyes held a mischievous glint. "Of course you'd know I don't offer cheesecake if you ever came into my bakery."

"Didn't you just come into my shop for the first time a few days ago?"

She laughed. "True."

He winked at her. "I promise, your bakery will be my first stop when we get back."

"No," she said. "Your first stop will be to your store to make me more chocolate."

He held up his hands in surrender. "Yes, ma'am."

Smiling, she slipped down in the camp chair so she could rest her feet on the edge of the fire pit. "What a nice group of people they are. I'm so glad I've gotten to know them all. I really do hope they come visit us in Shadowvale."

"Us." Charlie smiled. "I like when you say that."

She reached out and interlaced her fingers with his. "I like saying it."

"I like hearing it." He kissed her fingertips and stared into the flames. "We should probably turn in. I'll add a few more logs to the fire so that you're nice and warm."

She yawned. "Thanks. I need to change and get out of my bikini."

"No comment other than you look pretty good in that thing."

"I already like you, you know." But she was grinning. She tipped her head slightly. "Are you really comfortable sleeping on the ground? I know you're in your dragon shape and all that, but it's basically stretching out on hard dirt and rock. Henry says it's hard on his bones."

He glanced toward the side of the cave where he slept.

"It's very comfortable for me, but you're right that it probably shouldn't be. I guess it's a dragon thing. Which will apparently change as I get older."

"Hey, as long as you're happy." She stood up and moved in front of his chair, bent down, cupped his face in her hands, and kissed him. "I'm going to change, blow out the candles, and turn off the lanterns. Sleep well."

"You, too." As she left, he got up, added some logs to the fire, then walked over to his spot, where he shifted into dragon form. He settled his big body down, curling his tail around him. He focused on how he felt. Very comfortable. Odd how dirt and rock really made for a pleasant sleeping place when you weren't human.

He could hear her somewhere behind him. When she came into view again, she was in an oversized T-shirt that hung to the tops of her thighs. It had a slightly menacing horse head on the front with the words Black Horse Bakery wrapped around it.

She wandered over to him and stretched her hand up to touch his face. "Good night, Charlie."

"Night, Nasha."

She stayed there, staring up at him. Then she climbed up and nestled herself into the valley between his curled tail and his chest, settling into the dip there as if it had been made for her. "I'm not as sleepy as I thought I was and you're warm and I'm chilly. I tried sleeping in leggings but they're too restricting."

He smiled as best he could in his current form. "That's all right."

Her First Taste Of Fire

As she lay there, she hummed something, not a tune he recognized, but it was soft and soothing and it began to lull him to sleep.

He woke sometime later. The cave was dark as the fire had died down. A few flames flickered, though not nearly at the strength they'd been earlier. It was mostly coals. Nasha was in her cot, her sleeping bag pulled tight around her.

Charlie hadn't felt her leave, but obviously she had. He raised his head. Had it gotten cold in the cave with the fire dwindling? As tired as he was, he shifted into human form and went to add logs to it. Nasha mattered more than sleep. She mattered more than a lot of things, he realized as he carefully placed new logs on the glowing embers.

Like this stupid census.

He wasn't sure what they'd face tomorrow, but they'd come through it. No matter what happened, they were leaving together. The council could go hang. And his family would just have to get over any repercussions as best they could.

So what if he'd fallen for a woman who wasn't his own kind? Was that so terrible? And was it really so terrible that he lost a scale every time he breathed fire? He couldn't help it.

While the thought of that secret coming to light struck fear in his heart, he knew he'd survive it.

So long as this woman was by his side.

He kissed her on the cheek and went back to sleep.

Morning came bright and early and *cold*.

He found that out because Nasha was snuggled against him again, this time in her sleeping bag. There was no way to move or shift without waking her. The fire was down to embers. Not nearly enough to battle the drop in temperature.

Beyond the cave's entrance, frost covered the ground.

"Hey," he said softly. His breath puffed out in wisps of icy vapor. "I'll get the fire going again. And start some coffee." Maybe for her sake, he'd put a little chocolate in it. If there was any left.

She nodded and mumbled something that sounded like, "Okay." Hard to make out the word through her chattering teeth.

As carefully as he could but with real urgency, he moved her to the ground, then shifted to human. Instantly, he felt how truly cold it was. Besides being able to see his breath, the pool had a thin layer of ice on it.

No wonder she'd come back to make use of his heat. And now, with him no longer in dragon form, she'd be even colder. She shouldn't have to wait until the fire was roaring. That would take too long.

He faced the back of the cave and breathed fire until a cloud of flames filled the air. He lifted the stream toward the ceiling, heating the rocks so they'd diffuse warmth. Next, he brought the pool to a boil. The temperature within the cave rose instantly.

With every blazing breath, a scale fell. He was probably leaving a trail of them, but he didn't care. Nasha needed to warm up.

He stacked logs high in the fire pit, then blasted them with a breath to get them going. He filled the coffee pot and set it on the rocks nearby to heat.

With that done, he shifted back to dragon and wound himself around Nasha. "Better?"

She nodded, snuggling closer.

"Sorry."

From the depths of her sleeping bag, she shook her head. "You don't control the weather. It's not your fault. I should have worn the leggings to sleep in anyway."

He blew more fire toward the stone ceiling. It was a pretty efficient way to heat the cave. But maybe he could do better. He breathed fire onto the floor wherever there was no danger of melting anything.

Two more scales slipped off his hide. He let them lay where they fell. The frost near the entrance was starting to melt, and to him, the cave felt pretty comfortable. He wasn't sure that was sufficient for Nasha. "How's that? Want more?"

She pushed the sleeping bag down. "Actually, that's pretty good. Once I get the feeling back in my toes and fingers, I'll be golden." She glanced toward the fire. "I can smell the coffee. That'll help, too."

"That might need a few more minutes."

She sat up, her gaze on the fire. Or so he thought. "Wow. You sure went through some scales. They're all over the ground."

"I'll get them in a minute."

"They're so pretty. What do you do with all of them?"

"Nothing. I have a drawer full of them at my shop."

As they were looking, a shadow blocked the light coming in through the entrance. A dragon approaching.

Charlie tried to see who it was but the view from his position didn't give him much. "Someone's coming."

"I'll get dressed." Nasha wriggled out of the sleeping bag and started picking up the scales.

A pearl-white dragon landed in front of their cave.

Verochka.

He glanced down at himself. None of the missing scales seemed to be in obvious places. At least that he could see. Not much he could do about it now. He needed to keep the Russian from seeing inside. He didn't want her entering their cave. He positioned himself partially in the cave's mouth, using his size as a screen. "What do you want?"

She turned human before answering him. She was in her pearl leather outfit again, hair in braids. "Such a friendly greeting from my future husband."

"That's never going to happen."

"Oh, I think it will. Verochka gets what Verochka wants."

He shifted to his human form, trusting that had been enough time for Nasha to gather the scales. "Have you ever been tested for psychological problems? I'm pretty sure talking about yourself in the third person is a sign of that."

She laughed like he'd made a joke, moving closer to run her finger down his chest.

He shoved her hand off before she got halfway. "The privilege of touching me belongs to my fiancée. Why did you come here?"

She made a strange face, which he suddenly realized was her attempt at looking coy. "To make a truce with you."

He doubted that. "What kind of truce?"

"You become my mate and I won't say anything about the little human's father." She shook her head with mock concern. "I don't think the council would take it lightly that you've brought such treacherous magic into our gathering. This is meant to be a place of safety. Her very presence endangers us all."

"You've lost your mind, you know that? You think you can blackmail either one of us?" Then he felt something behind him. The unmistakable prickle of magic.

Verochka paled.

He turned to look. Nasha was walking out of the cave. She looked very different than he'd seen her before. Power radiated off her.

She'd shifted into a much darker version of herself. Still wearing black head to toe, but the bones of her face were more pronounced, the hollows under her eyes and cheekbones deeper, giving her a gaunt, haunted appearance. Her eyes were completely black, and darkness swirled around her like an ethereal cloak of smoke and soot.

She no longer looked human. In fact, she seemed like a nightmare come to life, but he had no fear of her. Nothing but undying respect and a surprising sense of pride. She was ridiculously scary. And yet, also crazy hot. He smiled. "There's my beloved now. I think she's got something to say to you."

As Nasha reached them, she tipped her head slightly, narrowing her eyes. "You shouldn't have come here, Verochka."

Verochka swallowed.

Nasha lifted her hand to tuck a loose strand of hair away, causing the heavy silver ring on her finger to glint in the morning sun. Even without the ring, there was no question whose daughter she was or what kind of magic infused her blood.

She raised her brows, her black gaze pinning Verochka. "Nothing to say to me?"

"Don't you threaten me—"

"If you confuse good advice with a threat, you need to be a better listener." Nasha took a step forward. Verochka took one back. Nasha never dropped eye contact. "Talk to my fiancé again and I'll consider *that* a threat, understand? Now fly away home. Before you make me mad."

A vein protruded from Verochka's forehead. "I will win today. Then I'll take him from you."

Nasha laughed, but it sounded like there were other voices laughing with her. Eerie was the only word he could think of to describe it. "Oh, Verochka. You silly twit. You're not going to win today."

Verochka retreated another half-step. "You don't know that."

Nasha's smile disappeared in a hot second and her face turned even darker and more skeletal than it had been before. "Not only do I know it. I'm going to make sure of it."

Chapter Thirty

Charlie stared in amazement as Verochka shifted into dragon form and took flight, clumsily getting airborne with as much speed as she seemed capable of.

As she sailed toward her side of the valley, he shook his head. "That was impressive."

Nasha rolled her head around and as she did, her appearance returned to normal. She rubbed the back of her neck while staring at Verochka's vanishing form. "Thanks. I've never actually shown that side of my magic to anyone before."

"Really? I'd never have guessed that was your first time. You really owned whatever that was."

She didn't seem as pleased by his compliments as he'd expected. "That was me as Famine. I suppose I'll look like that all the time when the day comes that I take over for my father in that role." She finally made eye contact him with. "Not very pretty, I know."

"Pretty? Who needs pretty when you can look like that? To be honest…"

She grimaced.

"I thought you looked remarkably hot. Is that weird? I guess I just have a thing for powerful women."

Her First Taste Of Fire

She blinked a few times. "You might actually be the perfect man for me."

He laughed, long and hard. "We do seem well-suited, don't we?"

She nodded as she slipped her arm around him. "Thanks for not being scared of me. I was so afraid you'd freak out if you saw me like that but I thought it was time Verochka got put in her place."

"Hey, I'm a dragon, remember? I'm usually the one that freaks people out. Now, we should get you back inside before you freeze to death."

She leaned into him and looked up as she patted his chest. "You might do all right meeting my dad after all."

He scooped her into his arms and carried her into the cave. "Looking forward to it."

He was happy to feel that the temperature inside the cave hadn't dropped that much. He set Nasha on her feet. "Still warm enough in here for you?"

"Yep. I suppose we should get ready and go down soon, huh?"

"Probably. I think we have time for at least one cup of coffee first."

"Good. Because I could really use a cup." She went to the fire and poured two mugs full.

He joined her, sitting beside her in the camp chair. "I can't get over how impressive that was."

"Yeah, well, I may have screwed myself over with that show. She might really have a bug up her butt to tell the council about me now."

"Maybe." He sipped the scalding hot brew without burning himself, one of the many dragon benefits. "But do you care?"

She looked sideways at him, a smile finally breaking out on her face. "Not really."

"That's a good feeling, isn't it? Not caring?" He nodded, his next words as much for himself as for her. "I need to get there, too."

"You mean about your curse?"

"Yes."

She set her cup down to take his hand. "Would it help if you talked to your dad? Or maybe your sisters? Someone in your family?"

He stared at the fire. "They'd have to be willing to talk to me, too. And that hasn't been the case in many years."

"When's the last time you tried?"

"Long time." He thought about that. "Since before I moved to Shadowvale."

"Then maybe it's time to try again. What have you got to lose?"

He let a few breaths pass before answering. "Nothing. I'll call them tonight. I promise."

She squeezed his hand. "You don't have to promise me anything. I just want you to be happy."

"Thanks. I'm not sure anyone's cared about my happiness in a long time. It's nice."

"Well, you are my ticket to a lifetime supply of delicious chocolate, so..."

Her First Taste Of Fire

He laughed. "I don't remember saying anything about a lifetime supply."

She sat up straighter. "You know what? We should totally do a collaboration."

"What do you mean?"

"Like I could make chocolate chip cookies using your chocolate for the chips. We could sell them in both shops." Her eyes were wide with interest. "A Black Horse Bakery-Chocolate Dragon mash up. What do you think?"

"I've never made chocolate chips, but it can't be that hard. You don't actually sell anything, though, right?"

"Right, but I charge for the coffee. It's only fair, since Deja Brew is right down the street from me. Giving away coffee would hurt their business and I'm not trying to do that. We could sell our cookies and donate the profits to a worthy charity."

"Such as?"

She sat back and sipped her coffee. "There aren't too many desperate causes in Shadowvale, thanks to the gem mines that help pay for everything."

"True. But I like the idea. There has to be something we can think of."

She shrugged. "Doesn't have to be cookies. Could be pain au chocolate. Or cupcakes. Or some kind of chocolate tart. Or—"

"Okay, now I'm hungry." He grinned. "And I don't even eat sweets in the morning as a rule, but if there are danishes down there, I may have to grab a few."

"I can be ready to go in five minutes."

He looked at his watch. "Good, because I'm pretty sure that will still make us five minutes late to meet the gang."

She hopped up. "Two minutes, then."

It took them four to get out of the cave and another minute to fly down, but no one seemed upset when they found Henry, Laz, and Marissa holding a table. Kindly, they'd gotten coffee for everyone.

"Sorry we're late," Nasha said. "Nice of you guys to get us coffee." Then she clarified, "We had a visitor this morning."

"Yeah," Charlie said. "An uninvited one." He checked the crowd for Verochka. Thankfully, it appeared she hadn't arrived yet.

"Oh?" Marissa said. "Who was that?"

"Let me guess," Henry said. "Tall, blonde, and full of herself?"

Nasha touched the tip of her nose. "We have a winner."

Laz rolled his eyes. "What was that all about?"

"Oh, the usual," Nasha said. "Threats, intimidation, promises she won't be able to keep."

Charlie wrapped his arm around Nasha's shoulders. "Verochka pretty much shut up when Nasha let her black light shine."

Nasha snorted and gave him a look. "You have such a way with words."

"Black light?" Marissa asked.

Nasha nodded. "I just let Verochka see what I was

capable of. After all, she showed up in dragon form. I gave her a glimpse of what I inherited from my father."

"Dang," Henry said. "Sorry I missed that."

"Stick around," Nasha said. "You may get to see it later today if Verochka doesn't behave herself. Now why don't you boys go get your plates. Marissa and I can hold the table."

"No way," Laz said. "Ladies first."

"But Charlie's hungry." Nasha looked at him. "I can wait."

Charlie shook his head. "Laz is right. You two go. We'll stay here until you get back." He leaned in. "But if you see a good-looking pastry, feel free to grab me one."

She smiled. "Will do. Come on, Marissa."

Marissa got up and the two women went off to get into line. Charlie sat with the men. "You really did miss it, Henry."

"Tell us," Henry said.

Charlie flattened his hands on the table. "I've never seen anything like it in my life. She looked like a nightmare. I don't mean that in a bad way, but I don't know how else to describe it. She was all dark and menacing. It was terrifying and impressive, and I've never wanted a woman more in my life. The way she stood up to Verochka was just extraordinary."

Laz leaned in. "You really think we'll get to see it again?"

"Maybe. If Verochka pushes Nasha, it might not take much."

"What did she come see you about this morning?"

Charlie frowned. "That fool woman told me that if I agreed to be her mate, she'd leave Nasha alone. It's that stupid hoard. I'm surprised I don't have more of them after me."

Henry snorted. "You know why that is, don't you?"

Charlie glanced at him. "No. Why?"

"Because Verochka's made it clear that you are hers. They're not going to cross her."

Charlie looked away to find Nasha in line. "Nasha isn't going to bow down to her. Not even a little bit."

Henry sighed. "Good for her. But I fear that's not going to end well. For either of them."

CHAPTER THIRTY-ONE

"You have to show me later," Marissa said. "I am dying to see what you did."

Nasha smiled. "I will, promise. But consider yourself warned. It's a little freaky. Maybe more than a little." She hadn't lied to Charlie when she said she'd never shown that part of her magic to anyone before. She hadn't.

She'd only manifested it twice before. Both times in front of a mirror in her own home.

Never where anyone else could see. In fact, she'd promised herself she'd never let anyone see her like that.

Now she was thinking about doing exactly that twice in one day. How things changed.

Marissa shrugged. "You've seen me in all my snakeskin glory and you handled that just fine. I'm sure I can deal with whatever you've got."

Nasha almost laughed. "Does your snakeskin bother people?"

Marissa made a face. "In this crowd? Did you just get here? Some of these people are pretty hardline about anything that's not pure dragon."

"Yeah, I did pick up on that." Nasha grabbed a plate as

they moved forward, then scooted up so Marissa could get one, too. Everything smelled really good.

Marissa seemed more amused than bothered. "I'm beyond caring. I'm perfectly happy with who I am, my family loves me, I have friends, a cat named Lexi who thinks I'm her mom, a good job. What more could I want?" She grinned and looked back at their table. "Except maybe Lazarus."

Nasha snickered as she put a couple of pancakes on her plate, then moved on to the fried potatoes. "You guys are getting along pretty well, I take it?"

"We are." Marissa grabbed some pancakes, too. "Between us, I'm kinda crazy about him, but I don't want to go overboard with how much I like him and scare him off."

"He doesn't mind your snakeskin, does he?"

Marissa blushed. "Nope."

Nasha gave her a closer look. "Um, why did that make you go all pink and girly?"

Marissa's grin went supernova. "He thinks it's sexy. Said it makes me look a little dangerous."

"Men really like that, don't they? At least the ones in this crowd." Nasha snorted as she added a ladle of blueberries in syrup to her pancakes. "I guess he's gotten over his fear of you turning him to stone. Is that really a thing, by the way?"

"Oh, sure," Marissa said. "But it's totally controllable. It's not like I'm about to do it accidentally or anything."

Her First Taste Of Fire

"Really?" Nasha's brows lifted. "That's such a cool talent to have."

"It is, but I haven't used it since I was a kid, and my mother had a stern talk with me about responsibility and abuse of power."

"Why? What happened? If you don't mind me asking." Nasha used the tongs to get several slices of bacon. She spotted the pastries up ahead.

"Let's just say there are a lot of stone ants and frogs around our old house. And that I learned my lesson."

"Oh. Well, that's what kids do, right? Test the limits of things?" Nasha took a smaller second plate and selected two of the pastries that looked the best. Some kind of apple fritter and a blueberry turnover, both glazed. She figured whichever one Charlie didn't want, she'd eat.

Using all that magic had given her an appetite. No ability to taste anything, of course, but it wasn't that often she really felt hungry. Might as well give in to it.

"Yep," Marissa said. She took what looked like a spice muffin. "You want anything else? My plate is full. We can always come back for seconds, I guess."

"I'm already carrying two plates, so yeah, I'm done."

They headed back to the table. Nasha put the pastries in front of Charlie. "Take your pick."

"They both look good." He grabbed the turnover as he got up from the table. "Thanks. You guys eat, don't wait for us to get back. Your food will get cold."

Nasha took her seat in the middle of the bench. "You're sure?"

"Of course." He took a bite of the turnover. "Okay, I'm getting another one of these."

Laz touched Marissa's shoulder and nodded. "He's right, don't wait."

"Okay," she said.

As the men left, Nasha cut into her pancakes. "You think your parents would like Laz?"

Marissa looked at him and nodded, smiling. "They won't care who I end up with so long as I'm happy and they know the guy's going to treat me right. What did your parents think about Charlie?"

Nasha swallowed the bite she'd just taken. This was tricky territory. "My mom died when I was a baby. And my dad hasn't met Charlie yet. That's going to happen as soon as we get back."

Marissa stopped eating, fork in midair. "I'm sorry about your mom, but how on earth has he not met your dad yet? Does he not live nearby? Your dad, I mean."

"No, we live on the same piece of land, actually." Nasha shrugged. "It just hasn't happened. My dad's a pretty busy guy." Not a lie. Also not the reason he and Charlie hadn't met.

"I can understand that. I just think my father would have had a small coronary if I'd gotten engaged to a guy he didn't know. Not judging. Just saying."

"My dad knows about Charlie. It's just been a logistics thing."

Marissa nodded and was about to say something else when they were interrupted.

Verochka *and* Katya.

Verochka sneered at Nasha. "You have a lot of nerve showing your face here."

Katya sniffed. "Yeah."

Nasha scrunched up her face like she didn't understand. "At breakfast?"

"You know what I mean," Verochka huffed.

Nasha didn't, but she was over all of this woman's nonsense. She rolled her eyes. "Just go away, will you? Both of you. Just leave. The whole intimidation thing might work on other people, but not me. You scare me about as much as a blow-up doll."

Marissa snorted, then quickly stopped like she hadn't meant for the sound to come out.

Verochka turned to look at her. "And you. A dragon, keeping company with this...abomination. How could you? But then, you're not pure-blooded, so I don't know why I expected differently."

"Wow," Nasha said loudly. "You really want to antagonize a woman who can turn you to stone? I guess I was wrong to think you were smarter than that."

Verochka whipped around, snarling. "You are the one who's not smart. Flouting our ways and carrying on like—"

Nasha called up enough magic to change her eyes to pure black while she stared at Verochka. "Shut your mouth and go sit down. No one wants to hear you anymore. Understand?"

Verochka seethed quietly for a couple of seconds. Her eyes narrowed. "I am going to crush you today."

Nasha forked up another mouthful of pancakes. "Doubtful, *comrade*."

Verochka glared for a second longer, then stalked away, Katya in tow. Nasha let go of the magic and ate her pancakes.

Marissa's eyes went wide. "What a freaking piece of work she is."

"I know. They should both be disqualified for being giant, dragon-shaped idiots."

Marissa laughed as she leaned in. "And your eyes! That was amazing."

Nasha smiled a little. "Thanks. That's just the tip of the iceberg, really."

Charlie, Henry, and Laz walked up to the table.

"Okay," Laz said. "Clearly we just missed something."

Marissa nodded enthusiastically. "You missed Nasha making Verochka look like a fool."

"Again?" Charlie took a seat beside Nasha. "You'd think she'd have learned her lesson."

Nasha shrugged. "Maybe she thought she'd do better in a crowd. Or without you here. Who knows? She's not a quitter, I'll give her that much."

Henry laughed as he settled in on the other side of Nasha. "The games are going to be interesting today."

"I'll say," Laz said. "Any clue what they are yet?"

"Nope." Henry cut into his stack of pancakes dripping with butter and maple syrup. "But the lanes they used for the races yesterday have been divided into a lot of larger squares."

Charlie turned to look in that direction. "The poles are down, though."

Nasha was curious. "What could it be?"

Henry shook his head. "I don't know. I guess we'll find out soon enough."

Nasha couldn't let it go. Her mind was spinning in too many different directions, none of them good. "You don't think it's some kind of battle royale, do you? Like the last dragon left in their square wins?"

Marissa's brow furrowed. "I hope not. I mean, they do know I can turn people into statues, right?"

Laz snorted. "That's going to make for a short contest."

She swatted him, clearly in good fun. "I wouldn't actually do that! Being turned into stone is permanent, you know. There's no magic look that brings you back."

He shrugged, clearly amused. "I know. I just hope they put you next to Verochka. That's all I'm saying."

Nasha laughed, Henry chuckled, and the subject soon changed to how good the pancakes were.

Nasha was fine with that. Dwelling on what-ifs wasn't going to help. And as much as she wanted to know what the game was going to be, they were very close to finding out.

Didn't mean her brain wasn't trying to figure it out. Unfortunately, all she could think of was that it was some kind of contest that involved flying over and dropping something into a specific square. Like an accuracy kind of thing.

Why she was stuck on that, she wasn't sure. If that's really what it was, she'd have no choice but to make Charlie her proxy.

He was willing, she knew that. She also really wanted to finish these games out having done every one herself. Not just to prove to the council that she was capable, but also to shut Verochka up once and for all.

Wouldn't that be something?

CHAPTER THIRTY-TWO

Charlie was fully prepared to step in for Nasha in whatever capacity was necessary. He stood beside her as they waited to hear what the game was.

Marissa stood on the other side of her, then Laz next to Marissa, and Henry beside Laz. Charlie was glad they were all together. He was even happier that Marissa and Nasha had become friends so quickly. He liked that. At first, he wasn't exactly sure why, but then he realized that Marissa's approval of Nasha made him feel like his own affection for Nasha was validated.

As if Nasha being liked by another dragon meant she was a good choice. Silly, but he couldn't help what he felt.

Maybe that would help him talk to his father, even if he already knew what his father's reaction would be. His mother, Charlie wasn't so sure about. She probably wouldn't say much. She rarely did, letting his father make most of the big decisions.

Maybe she didn't like fighting with him. Charlie sighed. He needed to call his father. He'd meant to do it already, but the morning had gone differently than planned, what with needing to warm the cave and then Verochka showing up.

But he would. Tonight. Because it was high time this friction between them was resolved. And if not resolved, at least brought to some kind of conclusion. He was no longer willing to spend the rest of his life in this dreaded limbo. He either had a family and was part of their lives or he wasn't, and he'd move on.

He smiled at Nasha. If that was the case, he could make his own family. She'd agreed to keep seeing him when they got back to Shadowvale. He wondered how soon she'd be ready for more than that.

He felt ready for more.

Of course, he'd need to meet her father. Charlie wanted to do things right. He wanted to make it plain that Nasha would be his first concern. That he would provide for her in whatever way she needed. Chocolate, mostly, he assumed.

That thought made him laugh out loud.

Nasha looked up at him. "What are you laughing about?"

He shook his head. "Just thinking about you and your chocolate addiction."

"Any chance you brought a secret stash I don't know about? Because I ate the last piece before we left for breakfast this morning and to be honest, knowing I'm out is making me a little cranky."

"No, sorry. But don't let that crankiness go to waste. If the opportunity presents itself, use it."

She seemed amused by that response. "You have no idea what you're telling me to unleash."

He stuck his hands in his pockets and rocked back on his heels. "Oh, I think I do."

She laughed and leaned in closer. He put his arm around her. She'd bundled up this morning. Beanie hat, gloves, and a scarf. She looked cute. But then he'd reached the stage of infatuation where she was permanently beautiful.

Even seeing her in Famine mode had done nothing to change that, except maybe intensified his feelings.

"Warm enough?" he asked.

She nodded. "Better now that the sun has had a chance to work its magic."

"Good." The sun had definitely warmed things up. The frost was gone, leaving the tall grass to sway in the slight breeze. Very cool, but a lot more bearable than it had been first thing this morning.

He stared at the field, watching the grass.

It wasn't easy to see the lines that had been made to mark off the squares unless you were right on top of them. Yesterday's lanes were more visible because they'd been trampled some from the previous game's activity.

He supposed the lack of demarcation wouldn't matter too much. The council had to have allowed for that. He imagined so, anyway. Hopefully, whatever game the council was planning today would make sense once they found out what it was.

Henry nodded at something. "The official's coming out. Game's about to get underway, I suppose."

Nasha went up on her tiptoes, Charlie imagined there

were too many people in front of them for her to really see the woman with the megaphone. Putting her on his shoulders didn't seem like something she'd go for right now. At least she'd be able to hear.

The official lifted the megaphone to her mouth. "Ladies and gentlemen, welcome to the last day of games here at the census. We hope you've been enjoying the competition as much as we have."

A couple of cheers and a smattering of applause went up. Charlie heard a few boos, too. Dissent for the new council and their nonsense was starting to show and he was glad about that. It was good to know he and his friends weren't alone.

"Our game today focuses on a skill that we excel at as a race."

He felt Nasha stiffen.

"As you can see, we have divided yesterday's lanes into a field of squares. We've done the same at the far end of the field as well, where we'll be holding the men's competition. Because of how today's game will work and only having so much space, we are limiting the number of contestants to the top one hundred."

That got the crowd to make some more noise. One woman immediately shouted out, "That's not how this is supposed to work."

A man shouted, "Stop making stuff up as you go along."

That seemed to encourage more people. The jabs kept coming. "What's wrong with the old ways?"

Her First Taste Of Fire

"The new council sucks."

"We all play or it's not fair."

The official tried to regain control, but got shouted down.

Laz glanced at Charlie. "Looks like some chickens are coming home to roost."

He nodded. "About time, too."

A burst of flame filled the air, and the crowd went silent. Lakshmi stepped forward. "That's enough. Today's game is settled. It will only be played by the top one hundred men and women. If you don't like that, you're welcome to make your complaints to the council after the games are over. If you're one of the contestants who won't get to play because you aren't ranked high enough, then I suggest you take a look at your own failings and try harder next year."

Low snarls answered her. Charlie took a look around. There were a lot of angry faces in the crowd.

He leaned toward Nasha. "We don't have to do this. There are enough upset people that if we left now, we probably wouldn't be alone."

She shook her head. "It's not my call to make. These are your people, not mine. I'll go along with whatever you decide, obviously, but we don't even know what the game is yet."

"True." He wondered what Laz and Marissa thought. Henry looked pretty riled up. Before Charlie could ask them, the official started speaking again.

"As soon as I explain the rules of today's game, I'll call

out the numbers of those who made the cut." More groaning and a few snarky comments filtered through from the crowd, but she didn't let that stop her. "Each participant will be assigned a square. The first participant to *decimate* that square through whatever means they see fit will win. Time and thoroughness are everything in this game."

Nasha crossed her arms. "Nice use of the word decimate. They probably figured if they said burn I'd argue about it being unfair, but this way they've included me. Although clearly the game was designed to favor those with built-in blowtorches. You know, a skill your race excels at."

Charlie scowled. He didn't like this at all.

The official went on. "Judges will be monitoring from the field as well as from the sky. As soon as you believe your square to be cleared, raise your hand and it will be checked."

"Put me in as your proxy," Charlie said. "I can do this."

Nasha frowned at him. "I know you can, but at what cost?"

It would be much harder to hide the loss of a scale on a square of burned earth. Especially with all of those judges watching. He shook his head. "I don't care about the cost."

She continued to frown. "I do. And while I appreciate your offer to proxy, I can handle this."

Her First Taste Of Fire

"But how? You don't have fire."

She stared out at the field with a calculating gleam in her eyes. "I don't need fire. They said decimate, remember? Well, I can do that. In fact, I can do it in such a way that they'll be sorry they set this game up."

CHAPTER THIRTY-THREE

Nasha knew Charlie might not understand that, but she didn't want to explain. Mostly because she wasn't entirely sure how well her plan was going to work. Using magic she was unfamiliar with was risky. If there was ever a time to do so, this was it.

If things went the way she thought they would, she'd not only win, she'd make a pretty bold statement.

More importantly, she'd protect Charlie and Laz from having to use their fire. Two birds, one stone.

If things didn't go the way she hoped, she'd lose. Big time. And she and Charlie would be in a lot of trouble.

She glanced down at the ring on her hand. She knew what her father was capable of. What power flowed through her veins.

On her eighteenth birthday, he'd promised her anything she wanted.

She'd used that promise to ask for something she knew he'd never anticipated. To accompany him on one of his jobs.

He'd balked. Tried to refuse. But a promise was a promise. She'd argued that if she was supposed to take over for him one day, she deserved to know exactly what she was getting into.

He hadn't been able to disagree with that. And so, reluctantly, he'd agreed.

She'd joined him, the two of them on Domino, riding into a strange country ruled by a tyrant. Then she'd watched as her father had become Famine and unleashed his power upon the land.

She imagined that what she'd seen that day might have scarred a lot of people. She wasn't a lot of people, though. She was Famine's daughter. And she'd already had a pretty good idea of what to expect.

Even so, the scenes that played out before her had imprinted themselves on her memory like clips of a movie. They were horrifyingly crystal clear. And not just when they showed up in her dreams.

That day had cemented within her two things. First, the understanding of just how hard her father's job was and how seriously he took it. Secondly, that day had laid upon her the full realization that someday his great and terrible power was going to be hers.

She hadn't imagined she'd be using it this soon—she looked at Charlie—or to protect the man she loved. But those were her circumstances.

She hoped her father would understand. And that he wouldn't be angry with her for using those powers. He'd never said she couldn't. Never even implied they were forbidden in any way. He'd only cautioned her that with such power came great responsibility.

Much like she imagined Marissa's mom had done with her.

Unlike Marissa, Nasha had never practiced the gifts she'd been given. Calling her powers gifts seemed like a generous use of the word.

"Contestants, please choose a square," the official announced.

Before Marissa and Nasha could head to the field, Charlie grabbed Nasha's hand. "You sure you want to do this?"

"Yes."

He nodded. "Then go for it. Give it everything you've got. I believe in you."

She smiled and squeezed his hand before letting go of it. "Thanks." She glanced at Laz and Henry. "Brace yourselves."

She and Marissa started for the field. Marissa looked worried. "We should take squares next to each other. That way, if you need help, I'll be right there."

"I appreciate that, but I'm pretty sure they'd consider that cheating."

Marissa glared at the first judge they passed. "I'm not sure I care."

Nasha laughed softly. The support from Charlie and her new friends was amazing. "It's okay, I've got this."

Marissa looked at her. "You're positive?"

"No. But I'm still confident. I've never used this magic in this way before, but I've seen it done. I am my father's daughter, so fingers crossed."

Her First Taste Of Fire

Marissa gave her a small smile. "I hope it works even better than you think it will."

"Thanks. Me, too."

"Can I give you some advice? I know you didn't ask and we're different kinds of creatures, but—"

"Absolutely you can. What is it?"

"Start sooner than you think you need to. When I was learning to use my stone gaze, I learned pretty fast it took a second or two to warm up, so to speak. Not now. Now I can do it instantly. Since you said you were new to this..."

Nasha grinned. "You're very smart, you know that? Thank you."

"You're welcome." Marissa was all smiles.

They reached two open squares, so Nasha stopped. "These okay?"

"Sure."

Nasha touched her arm. "Don't get freaked out by what I do. You won't get hurt. I promise."

Marissa nodded, then crossed the first two fingers of her right hand over the first two fingers of her left hand, like a hashtag. "Team Nasha. One hundred percent."

With Nasha laughing, Marissa went to stand in the middle of one of the squares. The grass came to just below her knees.

Nasha took the other. The grass was slightly higher on her legs.

They'd chosen a spot near the center of the designated area, slightly to the right-hand side. The original lanes had been pretty wide to accommodate the size of the dragons. Now divided, each square was about twenty feet by twenty feet.

And all of them were quickly getting filled in.

Marissa's advice about not waiting was incredibly smart. Nasha had seen her father use his power and it had been instantaneous, but he'd been using it for years. She'd never attempted anything like this before.

Timing and thoroughness mattered, the official had said. Nasha had to be on her game, or it wouldn't matter what she did.

With that in mind, she closed her eyes and allowed a partial measure of the power seated deep within her to rise up and show itself. She used the ring to get focus and control just like she had this morning, so the power didn't take over completely. Not yet. Not until it was time.

Across from her, she heard Marissa gasp.

Nasha opened her eyes.

Marissa's mouth was open in amazement. She quickly gave Nasha a thumb's up and a nod of approval, then mouthed the words, "So cool."

A couple of seconds later, Marissa shifted into her dragon form. She lifted her head and blew a big plume of flames into the sky, as if to announce she was here to win.

Nasha grinned. This was going to be interesting.

All around her, the women took on their dragon forms. Perhaps following Marissa's lead, many of them breathed fire toward the sky. A show of their power, Nasha imagined.

Her First Taste Of Fire

And why not? It was kind of the dragon equivalent of trash talk.

The best Nasha could do was make eye contact and let the other women see her new look. A lot of them were staring, so obviously it was having some effect. The expressions on the ones in human form were easy enough to read. They were either repulsed or afraid.

Dragon faces didn't express as much emotion. Not to Nasha anyway. Probably different if you were a dragon yourself.

"If you're not in a square when the starter pistol fires, you will be disqualified," the official said over the megaphone.

A few more women raced by, fighting the tall grass the way Nasha had the day before.

"Get ready," the official said.

Nasha closed her eyes and sank into the magic that had come alive inside her. She let it swallow her completely, until she and the magic were one. There was no beginning or end in either of them, just a loop of power that pulsed through her as automatically as breathing. She was the magic. She was Famine.

She opened her eyes, taking in the surroundings with her new vision. The grass moved to a rhythm now. The earth beneath her feet vibrated. Even the air had become visible, like the currents of water.

The dragons around her had diminished, going gray and blurry, as if seen through a clouded lens.

They were not her concern.

She leaned forward and brushed her hands over the swaying grass. The tips danced against her palms with a frantic, pleading movement. Begging her to let it live.

She sucked in a breath at that realization. All around her, nature knew what she was about to do.

Did her father face this every time he used his power?

She swallowed and shook her head. She couldn't let herself be persuaded to change her mind. She clenched her fists at her sides.

The blast of the starter pistol cracked through the stillness.

Nasha crouched and planted her hands flat on the ground. "Sorry," she whispered. Then she poured her deadly power into the earth.

CHAPTER THIRTY-FOUR

Nasha had been there one moment, gone the next. Charlie strained to see her. Where was she? It was like the grass had swallowed her. Nothing else had changed. The grass was still waving in the breeze, the dragons around her had begun breathing fire into their squares, the ones overhead staying close to monitor the action.

What on earth had happened to—then he realized the patch of grass she'd been standing in was going oddly dark. No, not just dark. It was withering and dying.

As the grass fell away, it revealed Nasha, crouched in the midst of it, head down, hands pressed into the earth, surrounded by a whirling darkness as menacing as anything he'd seen.

In the time it took for him to exhale, the destruction spread out from her like a black wave, destroying every blade of grass and weed it touched.

The speed of the destruction was incredible. In seconds, the entire area of lush, green squares turned into nothing but dried, shriveled scrub already crumbling to dust.

The devastation kept going. It ripped past the spectators, leaving dead vegetation and cracked earth under their feet. Dust whirled in tiny funnels where the wind picked it up.

The crowd turned as a whole, watching as the tsunami of ruin continued past them. In a few more seconds, it destroyed the entire valley, finally stopped at the river. Only the forest beyond was spared.

The shocked silence was deafening. The landscape had become a battlefield. The forest that survived looked like an oasis now.

No one seemed capable of words. Charlie certainly wasn't. What could he say? He'd never seen destruction like it in his life. Not even wildfires worked so completely or so quickly. All around him, stunned faces seemed to echo that feeling.

He turned around to find Nasha again.

She was standing, hands loose at her sides, eyes as black as a starless night. The wisps of sooty blackness spinning around her were fading into the air. Despite the determined set of her jaw, she looked spent. While he watched, she lifted one arm high into the air.

A soft curse of understanding slipped from his lips. She was signaling for a judge.

The dragons around her seemed to grasp that, too. They began to shift into human forms. As he continued to watch, the shroud of Famine left her altogether, turning her back into the woman who'd walked out onto that field.

Pride and admiration filled him.

Nasha had done what she'd said she was going to do.

Her First Taste Of Fire

He had no idea what it had cost her, but she'd made her statement. The council would have to come up with a new game now, if they intended to finish what they'd started. There was no grass left for the men to burn down.

In a matter of seconds, the Valley of Fire had become the Valley of Death. He smiled. She'd really done it. Dragon magic was apparently no match for Apocalypse magic.

"I can't believe it," Henry breathed out.

Charlie looked at his friends. Laz was just staring and shaking his head.

Henry made eye contact with Charlie. "You ever seen anything like this before?"

"No. You?"

He shook his head. "I've seen land that looked like this. Never seen magic that turned it into this." His brows went up. "That woman of yours has a serious amount of power. More than I realized."

"Me neither." He wasn't sure he was a worthy mate for a woman like Nasha. Being a dragon and breathing fire was one thing, but she was at a whole different level. She might actually qualify for superhero status.

It was easy to see why her power was considered dark magic. It was clearly destructive. But was it any worse than dragon fire? Power was only bad when wielded with evil intent.

Nasha had done this to protect him. The weight of that was staggering.

People all around them were finding their voices. Talking in hushed whispers, but the words still traveled over the now barren ground. Words that expressed their astonishment, fear, respect, and, in some cases, anger.

A few more interpreted what Nasha had meant to do in a way that wasn't entirely wrong. They got that she'd made a point. To them, that point had been that only allowing the top one hundred to play hadn't been fair. The way they saw it, Nasha had put an end to all of that.

A new word reached his ears. *Hero*.

The council was not going to be happy. That alone kept the smile on his face. "I think she did great," he said to Henry.

Henry nodded. "I'd follow that woman into battle."

"I don't think that fight would last very long." Laz glanced over at Charlie. "Did you know she could do that?"

Charlie shook his head. "No idea."

Laz whistled, long and low. "I'm man enough to admit I'm a little afraid of her."

Charlie chuckled. "I think that's probably healthy."

Nasha's hand was still up. The judges were either ignoring her or too afraid to approach. Charlie wasn't having that.

"Hey," he shouted. "The woman's waiting for a judge. Send her one already."

"Yeah," someone else shouted.

Henry added his two cents. "Your game. Your rules. Better play by them."

Her First Taste Of Fire

People continued to chime in until Lakshmi herself picked her way across the dead ground. She stopped a few squares in. Not even close to Nasha. "It's become very obvious that one of our contestants has made a mockery of these games—"

"No, she hasn't," Charlie shouted as he took a few steps forward. Anger curled hot around his spine. "She did exactly what the council asked the participants to do. She decimated her square."

"Yeah," Laz added. "Decimated it good."

Lakshmi glared at Charlie. "She destroyed the entire valley."

"Was there any instruction not to?" He glared right back.

"Nope," Laz said.

Charlie continued. "At the beginning of the game the official said, and I quote, the first participant to *decimate* that square through whatever means they see fit will win. Time and thoroughness are everything in this game."

Henry grinned and planted his hands on his hips. "Looks like thorough decimation by fit means to me."

Heads nodded all around them.

Laz smirked. "There was no mention of staying inside the lines either. None. Zip. Zero."

In the middle of the field, Marissa, now human again, left her square to stand next to Nasha, shoulder to shoulder. "We need a judge out here right now. If one doesn't show up soon, these games will no longer mean anything."

Another woman came to stand with them. Then another. And another. The crowd around Nasha grew to at least twenty-five.

Lakshmi frowned, and Charlie figured she knew she was beat. After a few more long, tense seconds, she sighed. "Can a judge please make a ruling?"

The judges who were out in the field all looked at each other. Obviously none of them wanted to be that person. There was no right decision for them. If they said Nasha had won, they'd invoke the wrath of Lakshmi. If they said Nasha was disqualified, they'd invoke the wrath of a large percentage of the watching crowd.

"Come on," Charlie said softly. "There has to be one willing to stand up to her."

Henry nudged him and pointed skyward. "There is."

A large, gray-green dragon was flying down toward the field. One of the judges who'd been assigned to watch from above. As the dragon landed and took a few steps, it took human form.

Henry's friend Reynaldo.

He walked straight toward Nasha. "Clear the square, please. Except the contestant."

The women gathered there got out of his way, leaving Nasha to stand alone. He introduced himself to her, then went to the perimeter of her section. He walked the border, then moved slightly inward, covering each inch of the square.

Charlie supposed Reynaldo was doing his due diligence so that no one could say he'd skipped a step or shown any favoritism. He had to know every eye was upon him. Both good and bad.

Finally, Reynaldo reached Nasha. He said something to her that was too quiet to overhear. She nodded.

Then he turned to face the crowd, Lakshmi included, took hold of Nasha's hand, and raised it high in the air. "We have a winner."

The crowd erupted in cheers, surprising Charlie. He hadn't thought there was that much support, but the council hadn't made themselves easy to like, either.

Lakshmi's face looked like a storm cloud. There was fire in her eyes. Angry fire. "*No*. That cannot be."

Reynaldo frowned as he let Nasha put her hand down. "Are you saying I'm wrong?"

Lakshmi shook her head as she sputtered and tried to find her words. "She's...not..."

"Dragon?" Marissa said. "So what? I'm only half dragon. I'm sure I'm not the only one, either. You have a problem with that, too?"

Lakshmi pursed her lips, clearly stymied by the resistance she was facing.

A man stepped forward from the crowd. "I'm only a quarter dragon. You want to discuss that with me?"

A pair of people came out of the crowd a few feet away. The older woman spoke first. "I'm not dragon at all. My husband is. We're here because our eldest son was required to register and join the games this year. He's only nineteen and if you think we're happy about any of this, you're completely wrong."

The man beside her, no doubt her husband, nodded. "You can assign him a mate all you want, but we won't enforce it. He deserves to make that choice himself. *After* he's done with college."

The fire in Lakshmi's eyes died, replaced by panic. "We are dying out as a race. Don't you see how important it is that we find mates for the most eligible among us?"

Henry shook his head. "There's no happiness in that. Let people find love where and when they want to. If they need the council's help getting a mate, then they can ask. As for our numbers, if you paid attention to our history, you'd know our numbers ebb and flow like the tides. It's just the way of things."

Lakshmi looked downright perplexed, although still a little angry. "Fine. So the human, or whatever she is, wins. But she's destroyed the entire valley. How are we supposed to finish our games?"

Marissa rolled her eyes. "Are you even listening? No one wants to finish the games."

"Wrong." Verochka walked out of the crowd of contestants. "Some of us do. Those of us who understand the need for the right kind of mate and the importance of keeping the bloodlines strong."

Nasha shook her head and finally broke her silence. "You just want my fiancé because he's worth a lot of money. Let's be honest about that much, okay?"

Verochka spun around. "Don't talk to me, you black magic devil. You shouldn't even be here."

Charlie took a few more steps toward the field.

"Maybe none of us should be. Maybe those of us who want to leave should just go."

"Why?" Verochka shot back. "Because you know you won't end up with her? Because you know you'll end up with a real woman? That scares you, doesn't it?"

Charlie couldn't help but roll his eyes. "I have a feeling that if the results were tallied right now, the real woman I'd end up with is the one I arrived with."

"Fine." Verochka lifted her chin and snorted out a laugh as if Charlie had just made a joke, but her condescension was plain. "If you think that's the case, let's tally the results. And then we can see just how mistaken you are."

CHAPTER THIRTY-FIVE

Nasha didn't think Verochka was the tiniest bit amusing. In fact, Nasha was completely done with the Russian and her insane nonsense, but Nasha was also exhausted from the magic she'd just used.

The way she felt right now explained so much about why her father shut himself off in his house for several days after working as a Horseman.

All she wanted to do was lie down and sleep. Right there in the field. She didn't care what the council did, she just wanted to get back to the cave. She decided to tell Charlie as much. She called his name to get his attention. "Charlie?"

He strode across the field to stand at her side. "I'm here."

She looked up at him, at the concern for her in his eyes. At the indignation there over what was going on. He was such a good man. "Let them tally the results."

"You really think that's the right move?"

"It's got to happen sooner or later. Might as well be now. Does it really matter what the results are?"

"No. We're leaving together no matter what happens."

She smiled at him. "Good. Now I could really use a rest."

His eyes narrowed and he put his hand on her arm. "Are you okay? You do seem pale."

"I'm always pale. But I am very worn out. That took a lot out of me."

"I've got you." He moved his hand, sliding his arm around her for support. He looked at Marissa. "Thank you for standing by her."

Marissa nodded. "Absolutely. And I agree with her on the results. Let's get this thing over with."

Nasha leaned into him, happy not to support her own weight. She would have shut her eyes, except she didn't want to miss anything.

Charlie nodded. "Agreed. Enough is enough." He looked around at the crowd. "My name is Charles Ashborne, Jr., legacy of the Crimson Treaty Hoard, and I demand the council end these games now. With or without results. Who's with me?"

All around them, hands went up.

But a good number didn't.

Nasha wasn't sure what that was going to mean in the long run, but the new council wouldn't have gotten elected if they didn't have supporters. No surprise that Verochka's hand wasn't up. Katya's neither.

Then Lakshmi made her voice heard again. "If you want things brought to an end, then fine, that's what we'll do. The council will convene a special meeting and give you the results in the morning." Her lip curled in a sneer, the gleam in her eyes downright nasty. "This evening's dinner is cancelled. Fend for yourselves. It seems to be what you want."

With that, she turned and marched back toward the group of judges and councilmembers who'd gathered behind her.

Nasha sighed. "I don't think this is going to go well."

Charlie shook his head. "Probably not, but I'm done caring. I just can't do it anymore. Whatever the consequences are, I'll deal with them."

"Same here," Marissa said. She smiled at them. "You think Shadowvale could use a third-grade teacher? That's what I do back in Indiana."

Nasha smiled. "I have no idea, but I promise to do everything I can to help you find a job."

"Thanks." Marissa bit her lip. "It's scary to think about moving and starting brand new somewhere else, but it's kind of awesome, too."

"What's kind of awesome?" Laz asked as he and Henry joined them.

Marissa took his hand. "Nasha's going to help me find a job in Shadowvale. I think it's time for a change."

Laz looked like he'd just won the lottery. And maybe he had – the girlfriend lottery, anyway. "Feels that way, doesn't it?"

She nodded. "I'm ready for this new chapter."

"Me, too," he said. He looked at the rest of them. "Whatever the council announces tomorrow morning, there are going to be a lot of unhappy dragons. I'm sure you guys feel the same way, but I'm not about to let them dictate my life." He gazed adoringly at Marissa. "Not now that it's finally going in a good direction."

Henry put his hands in his pockets. "Well, I'm not passing up the chance to meet all those eligible women Nasha told me about. I'm in for Shadowvale. Provided the cost of living is reasonable enough and I can find a decent place to live."

"Hey," Laz said. "I can do any remodeling you need."

Charlie's arm around her tightened. "The cost of living there is very reasonable. You'll see."

Sleep wasn't just calling Nasha, it was screaming in her ears, but she was reluctant to interrupt her new friends' enthusiasm for moving to her town. "Just follow us home tomorrow and we'll give you the tour. Right now, I really need to lie down."

"Go," Henry said. "You've earned it."

"We're out of here." Charlie looked at Nasha. "Will you be able to hang on until I get you back to the cave?"

She glanced toward their spot in the mountainside. "Um..."

"Okay, that settles that. Marissa, can you ride behind her and make sure she doesn't fall?"

"Absolutely."

"Thanks." Charlie gestured to Henry. "I want to get some distance from this crowd. Come hang on to her while I shift, then you guys can give her a hand up if she needs it."

"Lean on me, Nasha." Henry took her arm, his grip surprisingly strong.

In a matter of minutes, Nasha was up on Charlie's back with Marissa seated behind her and making sure she didn't fall asleep – and fall off – before they made it back to land. She knew why he'd wanted distance from the crowd. He was missing scales. The only real noticeable spots were near one of the spiney plates going down his back and another on his front foot.

The flight up to the cave was short. Marissa helped Nasha down, then gave her a hug, said goodbye, and took off to fly to her own place.

Nasha shed her coat, hat, and scarf as she walked inside. The day had definitely warmed to a mostly bearable chilliness. "Did anyone say anything about your missing scales?"

He was back in human form. He frowned. "No. Didn't mean they didn't notice. I figured if anyone said anything, I'd say I scraped myself against the rocks and hope they bought that excuse."

She nodded. "Good thinking." She glanced toward the cave entrance. "You think they'll all really come to Shadowvale? That would be so great."

"Laz is. He told me as much. You know, what you did to the field down there saved him a lot of embarrassment, too. He feels indebted to you."

She sat on her cot by the fire, which had mostly gone out but was putting off a bit of warmth. She yawned before answering. "I'm glad it helped him, but he

Her First Taste Of Fire

shouldn't feel indebted. I didn't do it so anyone would owe me. I did it because it seemed like the best possible solution to several different problems."

"It was." He stacked a few logs on the coals that remained in the fire pit. "It was also the most amazing display of power I've ever seen. I take it that was Horseman power?"

She nodded, feeling her lids droop as exhaustion got the better of her. She fought it, forcing her eyes open with a couple of good blinks, but knew it wouldn't be long before the sleepiness won. "Yep."

"You need to sleep. You're practically asleep now. Come on, let's get you settled, then I'll make sure the fire's going good."

She yawned again. "What are you going to do for the rest of the night?"

He laughed and kissed the top of her head. "I brought a book. I might read. Whatever I do, I'm not going to leave you alone. Promise."

"Okay." She lay down. She really needed to take her shoes off. She'd do that in a minute. Or maybe Charlie could help her. She wanted to talk to him about what he'd seen her do. And how that had made him feel.

She yawned. Did he still like her? Or was he afraid of her now? Didn't seem like it, but then again...Wait, she still had her shoes on. "I need...to take...my shoes..."

Sleep won.

Chapter Thirty-Six

"Off?" Charlie finished. Nasha was already out.

Smiling, he got her boots off, shaking his head at the pink socks patterned with purple cupcakes that were under them. He got her feet onto the cot, unzipped her sleeping bag, and used it to cover her like a blanket. He tucked the pillow under her head, too.

He hoped she was comfortable, but as quickly as she'd passed out, he supposed it was kind of a moot point.

The logs he'd put on the fire hadn't done much, so he added a few smaller pieces, then blew a few soft streams of fire over them to help them catch. He gathered up the scales that cost him, tucking them into the side pocket of one of the duffels.

He sat in a camp chair, watching her sleep and making sure the fire was burning nice and steady.

No one had ever done anything for him like what Nasha had done down in that field today. It was humbling to think she cared so much about him that she'd expend that kind of energy. Not only that, but she'd made it very clear in a very public way what kind of power she had at her disposal.

Her First Taste Of Fire

A lot of supernaturals he knew were reluctant to do that kind of thing for fear of making themselves a target.

And here she'd done it for him, despite never having done it before.

What on earth had he done to deserve that level of compassion and concern and care, he didn't know. It wasn't just because of the chocolate he made. There was no way. That wasn't enough.

Was it possible that she felt the same way about him that he felt about her? Did she love him?

He studied her face, marveling at how beautiful she was. How everything about her was just so perfect.

She shifted in her sleep, turning onto her side, and putting her hand near her face. The engagement ring he'd given her twinkled in the firelight. Would she want to keep it? Maybe it wasn't her style. He had no idea. She could pick out anything from his hoard that she wanted. Anything. And if there was nothing there to her liking, he'd sell some of it off to buy her a ring that suited her better.

If she wanted to keep wearing a ring from him.

He sighed. Maybe he was getting ahead of himself. After all, he'd yet to meet her father. What if he didn't want Nasha to marry a dragon? What if he had a specific idea about who his daughter should be with?

It was very possible. He knew that firsthand.

Which reminded him that he had yet to call his own father. He really didn't want to. He could predict how that call was going to go. If his father even answered.

But it needed to be done. Charlie was tired of the tension.

If he and Nasha were going to move forward together, he needed to eliminate some of the baggage from his life. And the biggest piece of that was his family.

As much as he wanted a relationship with them again, his sisters especially, he'd given up on that a long time ago.

Maybe if he and Nasha eventually got married, his sisters might show up. They'd love Nasha if they gave her a chance. Made him wonder if Nasha could be the person who brought them back together again.

He was getting ahead of himself, assuming he'd even be able to have a conversation with them.

Reluctantly, he got up and walked to the front of the cave to try to get a signal. He took his phone out of his pocket and dialed his father's number. Dread built in his chest like a bad case of heartburn.

Four rings. Charlie was about to hang up when the line was answered.

"Charles Ashborne speaking."

Did his father really not know his son's number? Or had it been so long that he didn't recognize it? "Dad? It's me. Charlie."

Silence stretched out between them, making Charlie wonder if the line had gone dead. "Dad? You still there?"

The gruff response came quickly. "If you're calling about money—"

"I've never called you about money. I do just fine on

my own." Charlie shook his head and stared at the sky. Why did things have to be this way?

"Then what is it? Has your curse been cured?"

"Nope, not that either."

"I see. What then?"

"I'm at the census. Here in the States."

"I'm aware that you moved."

That was news. Did that mean his father was keeping tabs on him, despite not wanting to talk? Charlie wasn't sure if that was a good thing or a bad thing. "Yes, I live in Shadowvale now."

No response, so Charlie kept talking. "Anyway, the reason I'm calling is that the census isn't going well. There's a new council with some very specific ideas about how we should be living our lives—"

"And naturally, you're against it."

Charlie took a breath, reminding himself that he shouldn't be frustrated. He'd anticipated having this conversation. Nothing about it was surprising. "I am against certain aspects of it. That's not the point. The point is so far I've been able to keep my curse a secret, but things may come to a head tomorrow. I don't know how everything's going to play out, but I wanted to give you fair warning that there may be trouble."

"Which you'll be in the midst of, no doubt."

Charlie's exasperation grew. "If you have a problem with me standing up for what's right, then I can't help you with that. But I have to take care of myself." He hesitated. "And the woman I love."

A few moments ticked by. "She loves you back?"

His father sounded so surprised. "I believe she does, yes. I know she cares for me."

"You found another dragon who doesn't care about your curse? Or doesn't she know?"

"She knows." Charlie braced himself. "But she's not a dragon."

His father snorted. "Well, that explains it."

"Why does it matter? You haven't cared about me in years."

"Because the hoard passes on to you, you know that. And someday to your eldest. That child should be a hundred percent dragon."

Charlie was starting to regret the call. "I can't guarantee that. I don't even know if I'll have kids. Who can predict their life? But you'd love this new council, I can tell you that much."

"I see nothing's changed. You're the same stubborn—"

"No, a lot has changed. For one thing, I don't care if none of you want to talk to me anymore. I've carried that hurt around for long enough. That's really why I'm calling. To warn you that things are probably going to get ugly tomorrow. And to let you know that I'm moving on with my life. I'm not happy about what you've done to me, but I have accepted that you don't want me in the family."

"What I've done to you?" His father was getting angry now. Charlie knew the dark edge to the man's voice all too well. "How dare you. You did this to *us*."

Her First Taste Of Fire

"You believe whatever you need to. You're wrong, of course, but hey, whatever gets you through. Anyway, you have my number if you ever want to talk. Tell Mom, Mia, and Suzanna that I said hello and that I miss them." He hung up.

His pulse was racing and his heart aching. The call had gone about as badly as he'd expected it to. He put his phone in his jacket pocket.

He sat on a rock near the cave's entrance and leaned his head into his hands. There were too many emotions coursing through him to name one.

Had he meant the words he'd said? Was he really over what his father had done to him? Was he ready to move on?

He nodded, answering himself. He was. Didn't mean he was okay with how his father had treated him. He simply couldn't live with that much weight on his soul anymore. The curse was *not* his fault.

And he was absolutely ready to move on. Especially with Nasha. Would they marry? Have kids? He had no idea. He was happy to let things take their natural course. If time brought him more, then he'd be even happier about that.

He had enough to worry about right now.

He glanced back into the cave. Nasha was fast asleep. He would have loved to have taken to the sky and flown fast and hard to get all the built-up energy out of his system, but he wasn't going to risk leaving her alone.

There were too many people on the side of the

council who might want to do something about the woman who'd upset their big plans for this census. He wasn't about to give them the chance.

Maybe Laz or Henry would come by later. Charlie got up and stretched. For now, he'd content himself with that book he'd brought.

Or maybe he'd get out his notebook and work on a few new chocolate ideas. He smiled. Even better, he would dedicate his new egg to her. That would be a fun thing to surprise Nasha with when they got back. An egg of her very own. Instead of the white chocolate egg he'd planned, he would make it a dark chocolate egg dusted with iridescent black luster dust. Then he'd wrap it with a black ribbon. The chocolates inside would all have complex, interesting flavors to represent how complex and interesting she was. Espresso bean, red wine, smokey bourbon, spicy orange, salted burnt caramel, black cardamon—things like that.

That got his brain fired up. Made him long for home, too, but that would happen soon enough.

He went back in, dug out his notebook, and sat by the fire scrawling down his ideas as fast as they were coming to him.

A name for the new egg came to him. He shook his head at the idea. It was all wrong for his shop.

And yet, it was perfect for an egg meant as a tribute to Nasha, the woman who'd stood up to all those who'd wished her ill at this census. Who'd remained strong and courageous in the face of difficulty. Who'd torn down the walls he'd been using to protect himself.

The woman who'd shown him there was more to life than his curse. The woman who'd shown him love didn't have conditions.

His pen remained poised above his notebook. Then he touched the tip to paper's surface and wrote.

Dragonslayer.

CHAPTER THIRTY-SEVEN

Nasha woke from a dream where the ground beneath her feet had been screaming. There had been more to it, but thankfully she couldn't remember the details. As she shook off the dream, she lay on the cot, staring up at the shadows that danced on the craggy rock ceiling. The flickering fire caused the shadows to move like they had a life of their own.

They were mesmerizing. She hoped if she watched them long enough, they'd help her fall back to sleep. She only seemed to grow more awake.

The play of dark and light above reminded her of something her father had once told her. "Horsemen tend to only see shadows. We have to remind ourselves to look for the light."

Remembering his words, she made herself watch the light instead. It wasn't easy. Her eyes were drawn to the darkness.

That made sense, didn't it? She was darkness after all. She'd proven that to herself and everyone else yesterday.

She turned her head just enough to look at Charlie. She'd hoped to find him awake, so they could talk, but he was definitely sleeping. She squinted in thought. Had he always taken up that much of the cave? She turned her head more and realized he'd positioned himself differently this time.

He'd been sleeping perpendicular to her, against the far wall. Tonight, he was parallel. Blocking the cave's entrance.

She pushed up onto her elbows. Had he just shifted during his sleep? That would be a pretty big move. It would also be the first time he'd done such a thing. It seemed more likely that he'd taken that spot deliberately.

If that was so, there were only two reasons for his new position that she could think of. To keep her in. Or to keep others out.

She continued to stare at him, but she was seeing the crowd from yesterday. Was she in danger because of what she'd done? There had definitely been a small, angry group that had sided with the council down there in that field.

Were they angry enough to do something against her?

The idea made her sit up. She'd never been one to back down from a fight if there were no other options, but she didn't love confrontation, either. Not the physical kind, anyway. Words were a far better way to resolve things.

She slid her legs out from under the sleeping bag and put her feet on the floor to sit at the cot's edge. One good thing about Charlie blocking the entrance was that he'd kept out a lot of the cold air. The cave had never been warmer.

Even so, she got up and quietly added two small chunks of wood to the fire, placing them carefully to avoid sending sparks into the air.

She checked her phone to make sure there were no new texts from Clara or Brighton, then she padded across the ground in her socks to where Charlie slept. She wanted to touch him, but she didn't want to wake him up. She placated herself with just looking at him and admiring how utterly beautiful he was.

Was he really protecting her? She wanted to think so. They hadn't had a chance to talk about what she'd done. Not much anyway.

Before she'd fallen asleep, she'd wanted to ask if what he'd seen her do had changed his opinion about her. Or his feelings.

She'd understand if it had. And while he hadn't acted like he felt any differently, she also knew that might have just been a show for the crowd.

She knew what her father looked like doing his job. Like a terror come to life. She imagined she looked very similar. If Charlie couldn't deal with that part of her, or didn't want to, he was allowed.

Her heart might break if he removed himself from her life, but she'd gotten through a lot of hard things.

Losing him would be no different.

"Liar," she whispered. Losing the man she'd fallen in love with would be *very* different. She might never recover.

That singular thought already caused pain to shoot

through her. She put a hand to her chest, her eyes hot with the beginnings of tears. The reaction surprised her. No one had ever caused her to feel like this before.

That's because this was love she was feeling. There was no other explanation. She wanted to have this talk with him right now, but she didn't want to wake him up. He had to fly them home tomorrow. He needed his rest.

If only they knew what the council's decision would bring them. A good result? Or more trouble?

She thought she knew the answer to that one. She stared up at him, her beautiful dragon. He was so peaceful in sleep. Also a little terrifying, but she kind of enjoyed that.

There was something very satisfying in knowing the big bad monster loved you best. Not that Charlie was a monster in his dragon form, but he was intimidating. She smiled. Was there really a chance he loved her? Or had he seen too much of her darkness to want her to be part of his future?

Her smile disappeared, replaced by a desperate longing that had no name. It filled her entire being.

"I love you, Charlie," she whispered. "I just hope you love me, too."

She supposed she'd find out soon enough. She turned and headed back to her cot.

"I do." The words reverberated through the cavern like a distant motor starting up.

She stopped and looked over her shoulder. "You heard me?"

He lifted his big head to nod. "I did."

She wasn't sure she believed him. She faced him. "You're not put off by what you saw me do yesterday? How I went all dark and creepy?"

He laughed, a low, rumbly sound that made the cave shake. "Apparently, I like dark and creepy. A lot."

"That works out for you, because that's all I've got." He wasn't afraid of her. Not only wasn't he afraid, he loved her.

"It does, doesn't it? I'm a lucky guy." He shifted, curling his tail around his body more tightly. "Are you going back to sleep?"

"I think I should. Big day tomorrow. Well, in a few hours now."

"Yes, it will be." Then his expression darkened. "I called my father."

She took a few steps toward him. "You did? How did it go?"

"As I expected. No change from him. I am on my own."

"Does that mean he'll take your inheritance away from you? Will you lose the hoard? Because if you're worried about money, don't be. I'm pretty well off." She had no problem taking care of him in whatever way that meant.

He grinned, showing off teeth that would send most people running. "Thank you, but no, he can't do that. It just means that I have no family. I no longer exist to them."

Her First Taste Of Fire

She went to him and reached up put her hand on his jaw. "You have me."

He closed his eyes and pressed his big head against her torso. She wrapped her arms around him, loving the feel of his smooth scales under her hands.

"And I'm so glad about that," he purred. "We should sleep."

She kissed his face and, without waiting for an invitation, curled up in the divot between his chest and his tail like she'd done before. The heat coming off him was glorious. "Don't let me sleep past breakfast."

He didn't. He nudged her awake some hours later with his snout. "Wake up, sleepy head. Time to get ready."

She yawned and stretched and wished a Keurig would magically appear in the cave. "Okay."

She climbed off him to stand on the ground and stretch again. While she was doing that with her back to him, he nudged her again and let out the same low rumbling laugh that he had last night.

"Hey." She turned around, but Charlie the man was standing there. "You sure are feisty in the morning."

He grabbed hold of her and pulled her in. "You have that effect on me." He kissed her, short and sweet. "How did you sleep?"

"Hard. All that magic exhausted me. I feel pretty good now." She smiled up at him. "You are so toasty to sleep on, you know that?"

"I'm glad I could be of service."

"Does that service extend to coffee making?"

He grinned. "I'm on it."

"Thanks, babe. I'll get ready while you do that. Could you heat up the pool?"

"Sure." He sent a long, hot blast over the water until steam rose off it. He picked up the scale he lost in the process. "We need to pack up, too, and make sure we get all this gear into that big duffel the outdoor store assured me it would fit into."

"Let's hope so. I might actually want to go camping again. This wasn't so bad." She dug through her bag for an outfit for the day. Something comfy. Leggings and a sweater. After her bath, she'd pair that with her short boots. She headed for the water with her toiletries and a towel.

His back was to her, and she knew he'd stay that way until she was done. "Really? More camping?"

The disbelief in his voice made her smile as she stripped down. "Sure, why not? Or are you not a camping guy?" Of course he wasn't. Otherwise, he'd have brought some of this stuff instead of needing to go buy it. "You're not, are you?"

"I could be persuaded."

She took a quick bath, got dressed and returned to the fire where he'd been working on the coffee, his back to her. "You know, we could just stay home for a while, too."

"Even better." He looked up and winked at her. "You think your dad will like me?"

"No." She laughed, hoping he knew she was teasing him. "Probably. Once he sees how happy I am."

Charlie smiled. "I'm glad you're happy."

"I am. Very."

"How about that diamond ring? Does that make you happy? Or would you like something different?"

She looked down at it, hand out, fingers splayed. "I think it's incredible." Then she frowned and stared at him. "Are you asking me if I want to keep this ring?"

"I am. Along with everything that comes with it." He looked unsure suddenly. "I mean me, you know. I'm asking you to stay engaged to me. If you want to."

She laughed. "I knew what you meant." The air seemed to leave her lungs with that admission. "Wow. Engaged for real."

"Too soon?"

She took one more look at the ring, then back at him. She was trembling with the emotion of this becoming permanent, of how good it all was. Of how right it felt. "No. It's not too soon at all."

Chapter Thirty-Eight

Despite the seriousness of what was about to occur, Charlie stood on the field smiling like a lovesick fool. Which, he supposed, he was. Well, if he looked like an idiot because he couldn't stop smiling, who cared?

Very shortly, he'd never see any of these people again. Except for Laz, Henry, and Marissa, who were the only ones who mattered.

He glanced at Nasha. Besides his fiancée, of course. His real-life fiancée. He almost laughed at how good that sounded.

Yep. He was losing it. And it was all Nasha's fault. His wife-to-be was turning him into a mental case.

He grinned at her. He couldn't wait to get home and build her the Dragonslayer egg filled with the most amazing chocolates he'd ever made. He was going to spoil her silly. And not just with chocolates.

"Ladies and gentlemen," Lakshmi's voice carried through the megaphone. "We are gathered this final morning to announce the results of our games. Regardless of those who wanted to complete our challenges, the council listened to the majority and tallied the results as

Her First Taste Of Fire

they stood. Because of these special circumstances, there will be no appeals to the outcomes. The results are final and permanent as read."

That got the smile off Charlie's face. Brows raised, he glanced at Laz, who was next to him.

Laz shrugged. "What did you expect?"

"Right." Charlie took a deep breath. Whatever. It was about to be over.

The councilmembers were lined up in a row behind Lakshmi. Some looked like they were gloating. Some looked completely frustrated. Others looked like they wanted to be anywhere but here.

She glanced at the paper in her hand, then raised the megaphone to her mouth again. "Our top ten women are as follows." She read off the names.

Neither Nasha nor Marissa were on the list. But Verochka was. Katya too.

Rage boiled up in Charlie. He stepped forward. "How is Nasha Black not on that list? Everyone saw the performances she turned in. No one else came close."

Lakshmi looked at him, her gaze cool and calculating. "As stated earlier, the results are final, and no appeals will be heard."

"I'm not making an appeal. I'm calling you a liar." A couple of gasps left the crowd behind him, but he wasn't backing down.

"The council deliberated long and hard, Mr. Ashborne, and due to the games being cut short, we felt it was in the best interests of everyone involved if only dragons were included in the results. Ms. Black has been disqualified."

Red edged his field of vision, his anger so thick he almost couldn't see. "You cannot make up rules as you go along."

"Mr. Ashborne, we are the duly elected council. Making rules is exactly what we do." She looked at her paper again, ignoring him. "Now for the men."

His first instinct was to blast her with fire and turn her into ash. Not the most legal or appropriate response, he knew that, but the fantasy gave him great satisfaction.

Nasha took his arm. "It's fine," she whispered. "None of this matters, remember?"

He nodded. But it did matter. She'd worked hard and put in the effort. Disqualifying her was the council's way of saying all of that was worthless. That she was beneath their notice. It was their way of slapping them both down. And it was unacceptable to him.

Lakshmi read off the top ten men's names. No surprise that he, Henry, and Laz didn't make that list either.

Henry looked about as cranky as Charlie had seen him. "Didn't expect to place myself, but you boys should have been there."

Laz nodded. "Except the council is just doing whatever they want now. There was no math involved in these results. Just favoritism."

Her First Taste Of Fire

Lakshmi raised the megaphone. "The top ten women will now come forward and make their choice for mates, then the top ten men, then the council will reconvene and assign mates to those who remain."

As the women gathered near the council members, Charlie took Nasha's hand. "We don't need to stay for this. Might as well go get packed and get out of here."

"Okay." She glanced at Marissa, Laz, and Henry. "You guys going to follow us home?"

Marissa nodded as she looked at Laz and Henry. "We are, right?"

"Right," Laz said.

"You bet," Henry answered.

"Then let's go." Charlie was done. This whole thing had become a mockery. A way for the council to get their agenda accomplished. He wasn't sticking around for anymore. He and Nasha started walking.

Lakshmi was on them instantly. "Please stay where you are until the selections have been made."

"Why?" Charlie barked back. "What's the point? You really think I'm going to break off my engagement to the woman I love because someone *you* picked decides I'm husband material?"

Lakshmi's eyes narrowed. "You actually believe one of these women would choose you then?"

"I *am* a legacy." Then he looked directly at Verochka as he kept speaking to Lakshmi. "But why don't you ask Ms. Lukin?"

"Fine." Lakshmi pursed her lips. "Verochka Lukin, who is your choice for mate?"

Verochka's smile was very cat-that-ate-the-canary. She stared at Charlie, drawing out the silence for effect, he guessed. "I will take the legacy. Ashborne."

Lakshmi frowned. "Very well."

"Not very well," Charlie said. "I refuse."

"By the laws that govern us, you cannot do that," Verochka pouted. "I have chosen you and now you are mine."

"The laws that govern us? You mean the ones the council just ramrodded into place? Those mean nothing to me. The only person who decides how I spend my life is me. Now, let me repeat myself. I refuse. I realize that decision comes with consequences." He glanced at Lakshmi. "So what are they?"

"This is unacceptable," she sputtered. "There will absolutely be consequences."

He was getting bored, but Nasha had a curious little smirk on her face that made it seem like she was enjoying this. "Right, all good with that. Just tell me what they are."

Lakshami was positively fuming. "Complete censure. If you refuse to obey the laws set down by this council, your name will be written on a piece of paper and burned, then the ashes scattered to the winds. You will be considered *drakona ostraka*."

The collective gasp that went up from the crowd spoke volumes.

He hadn't expected that strong of a response. To be

made *drakona ostraka* was to be considered dead. Not just for a year, either. Permanently. No other dragons would be allowed to speak to him or even acknowledge his presence for fear of reprisals themselves.

It was the strongest punishment his people had. He'd never known anyone who'd been the subject of it.

His father would never forgive him. Of course, his father hadn't forgiven him anything else, either.

Despite his convictions, there was sadness in Charlie's heart that things had come to this. He kept that from his face as he looked at Nasha and smiled.

"What's it mean?" she asked.

"It means I would be dead to them. No other dragons would be allowed to acknowledge my existence."

Her face fell. "What? All because you wouldn't marry that twit?"

"You love me, right?"

She nodded as she swallowed and seemed to be struggling with her emotions. "More than anything."

He winked at her. "Then we're good."

He gave her hand a quick squeeze and stepped forward, hoping he wasn't making the biggest mistake of his life. "I accept the censure."

"Idiot," Verochka shouted over the rumblings of the crowd. If her clenched hands weren't telling enough, the fire in her eyes was a clear sign of how angry she was at being so publicly rejected. "I would have given you everything."

Charlie looked at Nasha. "I have all I need."

Lakshmi looked positively dumbfounded.

Henry came to stand beside Charlie. He waved at Lakshmi. "You can write my name on that censure paper, too."

Charlie frowned at him. "You don't have to do this."

Henry laughed. "I want to. Besides, what better way to start fresh than by burning bridges?"

Hand in hand, Marissa and Laz joined them next. Laz stared Lakshmi down. "You can add our names as well."

A moment of silence followed as Lakshmi seemed to be attempting to process what was happening. That moment didn't last.

"Add ours, too." The couple who'd complained about their son being forced to participate in the games left the crowd behind as they came forward, defiance on their faces.

More people followed. Men, women, and other engaged couples. In a matter of minutes, more than half the crowd had joined Charlie.

Lakshmi stared at the scene before her, eyes round, mouth open. She had to know that actually censuring this many people would get her into serious trouble. "I, that is, we will convene a special session to decide how best to handle this...new development."

"Do whatever you want," Charlie said. "My fiancée and I, along with our friends, are going home."

"You can't leave until we declare the census over," Lakshmi said.

"Or what?" Charlie asked.

"Or...you will be censured as I stated."

"You've already threatened that. Just do it then. You can't censure all of us."

"Try me," she spat back.

He just shook his head at her arrogance. He looked at Henry, Laz, and Marissa. "Can we be airborne in forty-five minutes?"

They all nodded.

"We'll leave from our place." He looked back at Nasha. "Time to get packing, sweetheart."

"It's practically done," she replied.

He took a few steps away from his friends to make room, then shifted. Nasha got seated, and he took off. Below him, Laz, Marissa, and Henry were taking off as well. They weren't the only ones. Hundreds of dragons were doing the same thing.

Lakshmi was yelling for people to stay where they were. Very few seemed to be paying attention to her or any of the new council members.

He hadn't expected that to happen, but wow, what an outcome.

Nasha leaned forward, her arms around his neck. "That was the craziest thing ever. I'm so proud of you for standing up to her. To that whole nutso council."

"It was crazy." He smiled as he landed, thankful the flight to the cave was so short. He shifted as soon as she slid off. "Thanks. That was both scary and exhilarating. I'm probably still going to be censured."

"Better than being married to Verochka."

He grimaced. "That's for sure."

She laughed as she rubbed her hands together. "All right, let's break this place down and get our bags packed. Actually, I'm going to send a text to my employees first and let them know I'll be back soon. I am so ready to go home."

"Me, too."

They worked hard, but it didn't take that much effort to get things together. About half an hour later, as they were finishing up, Henry landed outside.

He shifted back to human and left his bags by the entrance. "You kids need any help?"

Charlie shook his head. "We're almost done. You ready to go?"

"I am. Laz is helping Marissa with a few things, but they should be here soon, too." Henry approached him. "You ever think about running for council, son?"

Charlie knew he'd heard the man right, but the question threw him. "You were down there just now. You saw what happened. I'm about to be censured."

"That might be true, but if they censure everyone who left, there's going to be a whole bunch of us who need to reorganize. We'll need a new council. One that understands what's really important to our kind. That could be you."

He hadn't thought about that, but he supposed Henry was right. While Charlie had never considered running for council, he knew it was often expected of legacies. Except those legacies weren't cursed.

Her First Taste Of Fire

He ran his hand through his hair and exhaled. "There's another reason I might not be council material. Something I haven't really talked about."

Henry tipped his head. "Have anything to do with your missing scales?"

Charlie swallowed. "You noticed those?"

"Mm-hmm. Didn't think it was any of my business, though."

"Do you think anyone else noticed?"

"Not that I was aware of. Probably too focused on the ruckus you all made down there."

Charlie sighed. He'd already been about to tell Henry, so carried on. "I lose one every time I use my fire. Have since I was a kid."

Henry shrugged. "I get up twice a night to pee. We all have our issues."

Charlie starred at him for a minute, then started to laugh. "You're all right, Henry."

"So are you."

Charlie continued to smile. "You really think I'm council material? Even with the scales thing?"

"I do, and I'd bet my hoard there's a whole bunch of other folks who feel the same way." He hitched up his jeans. "I'll tell you something else. My years of experience say this council isn't going to be around much longer."

"That would be the best possible outcome."

Henry's brows went up and he smiled. "Mark my words. When news of this census gets around, things will change one way or the other. What do you say? Would you run?"

"Do it," Nasha said. "Think of how much you could accomplish with some actual power."

"I don't know. It would mean a lot of time." Time away from her. He wasn't sure he wanted to do that right now. Actually, what he was sure of was that he *didn't* want to be away from her. He took a breath and looked at Henry. "I'll think about it. That's all I can say."

"Fair enough. I suppose you two have a lot on your plates, what with the impending wedding and honeymoon and all that. But I think the three of you should run."

Charlie's brows lifted. "The three of us? Me, Laz, and Marissa?"

Henry shrugged. "Why not? If you want things to change, the best way is to do it yourself. You kids are young and smart and forward thinking."

Charlie thought about that. Henry wasn't wrong. "It's not a bad idea. Ambitious, but not bad. I think it's a conversation we need to have as a group. Maybe at dinner some night after we get back?"

Henry smiled. "Sounds good. By the way, you sure you have room for all of us?"

Nasha zipped up her duffel. "Marissa can stay with me. I have plenty of space."

Charlie took her bag to add to their pile of stuff. "And you and Laz will bunk with me. I have a guest room and a pull-out couch in the den. It's all good."

Her First Taste Of Fire

Outside, Laz and Marissa set down.

Henry clapped his hands together. "Shadowvale, here we come."

CHAPTER THIRTY-NINE

Flying to the census had been a very cool experience but flying home with three other dragons in formation was something that made Nasha feel like she was living a dream. It was beyond cool. It was epic. She and Charlie led, with Laz and Marissa flanking him one length behind, then Henry at the back so they formed a diamond pattern.

This was probably how princesses traveled. The whole princess thing wasn't something she'd ever identified with when she'd been growing up. Having Famine for a father had a way of dampening that sort of fantasy life. As an adult, she figured princesses could be dark and creepy, too. Why not? There was no rulebook that said otherwise.

The only thing that kept poking at her happiness was the thought that Shadowvale might not allow Henry, Laz, and Marissa to enter. If that was the case, she wasn't sure what she and Charlie would do.

But Shadowvale would let them in, wouldn't it? They were just visiting this time. Sure, the town could be fussy sometimes and they weren't exactly entering in the most traditional fashion through the gates. Laz had his own troubles, so he should be all right.

It was Henry and Marissa that worried her the most. They weren't troubled in any way that Nasha knew about. She crossed her fingers and hoped for the best. Maybe they each had some secret problem that would grant them access.

Funny to wish for someone to be cursed. That had to be a first.

They rose above the clouds just like they had on the trip out. She closed her eyes and let the sun wash over her. Once they were back home, that would no longer be possible. She looked at the ring on her finger and smiled.

She didn't need the sun with a sparkler like that – and the man who'd given it to her – around. How crazy was it that she'd left Shadowvale pretending to be his fiancée and now she was returning with that charade as the truth?

Life was funny sometimes.

She settled in for the ride, growing drowsy as the sun and the rush of wind lulled her. She leaned forward and wrapped her arms around Charlie. "I might take a little nap. I'm pretty well seated, though, so I don't think you'll have to worry about me falling off."

"Okay," he said. "Even if you did fall, I'd catch you."

She smiled. She'd known that. "Thanks. Wake me up before we descend. I want to see the town from up here." That was a view she did not want to miss. In fact, if she remembered, she was going to take a few pictures, although she imagined Charlie would take her up any time she wanted.

"Will do."

She drifted off, content in the knowledge that she was well protected. And always would be.

Her dreams weren't all that pleasant. She woke a few hours later at Charlie's gentle insistence, plagued by the idea that her father was unhappy with her. With her use of power, or her choice of men. She couldn't quite be sure, but her dreams had been rife with her dad being unhappy about something she'd done.

He'd kept saying over and over that she knew what it was.

Was it just her subconscious giving in to a few minor doubts or was there any truth to it? She'd always felt her father would be fine with whomever she ended up with, so long as they were a good, decent person who made her happy.

Now she wasn't so sure. Stupid dream. But she couldn't shake the feeling she'd woken up with.

Her gaze went to the ring on her index finger. His ring. Would he think that what she'd done in that field was an abuse of her power?

Maybe it had been. There was nothing she could do about it now. If he was mad, she'd just have to listen and accept whatever yelling he needed to do.

Her father had never been the type to yell. He'd never needed to. His quiet voice, the voice she'd come to associate with his disappointment in something she'd done, was devastating enough.

"Descending," Charlie called out.

That was more for Laz, Marissa, and Henry than for her, Nasha realized. She got her phone out and brought up the camera, but even the magnificent views of Shadowvale below her couldn't displace the lingering feeling of dread.

She took a few photos, then switched to video mode and recorded their landing in Charlie's backyard.

Apparently, her fears about the town not letting their friends enter had been for nothing. They sailed straight in. She hoped her concerns about her dad went away just as easily.

She shut the camera off and slid down. Charlie quickly shifted into human form to make room for Laz, Marissa, and Henry to land.

He gave her an odd look. "You okay? You don't look happy."

She sighed and tried to smile. "I had a bad dream about my dad. I know it was just a dream, but I can't shake the feeling that he's upset with me."

"Why don't you go see him?"

"Right now?" Nasha asked. "I should get Marissa settled in at my house first, don't you think?"

"I'll make some lunch for everyone. It's about that time anyway. They can all hang out here while you do what you need to do."

Laz, Marissa, and Henry, who'd all landed and become human again, walked over.

Marissa nodded. "What he said. If you need to do something, don't let us get in the way of that."

"Okay," Nasha said. "I won't be too long." She smiled. "Then we can show you guys around and all of that."

"We have time," Laz said. "No need to rush."

Henry tipped his head, his eyes filled with concern. "They're right. You do whatever you need to and don't worry about us."

"Thanks." She gave them a wave, kissed Charlie on the cheek, and started off.

Charlie came after her. "Hey."

She stopped. "What?"

He glanced at her hand. "You might want to take that ring off before you go see him. As a matter of fact, maybe don't mention that we're engaged. I'd really like to talk to him about that first. That probably makes me old fashioned, but that's just how I feel about it."

She felt the smile on her face this time. She wiggled the ring off and handed it to him. "I love that idea. Why don't you hang onto this until that talk takes place then?"

"Okay." He took the ring and slipped it into his pocket, then he kissed her. "I love you, Nasha. Whatever happens, just know that."

She touched his cheek, so filled with love for him that she was surprised she had room for worry. "I love you, too. I'll be back as soon as I can. Text me if you go anywhere, all right?"

Her First Taste Of Fire

He nodded. "Will do."

She went straight to her father's house. The Enchanted Forest seemed darker and eerier after her time in the bright, sunny, very green Valley of Fire. Well, most of it was brown now, thanks to her, but that would change over time.

She parked and went up to his door, steeling herself for whatever awaited her.

He opened the door before she could ring the bell.

"Dad. Did you, like, sense the ring returning to you or something?"

He laughed. "Nothing that magical. I heard your car in the driveway. How was your trip? You're home early."

"It was good. And wild. And very interesting. I know more about dragons and dragon politics than I ever thought possible." He didn't seem mad. "It's good to be back. Did you miss me?"

His smile widened. "I always miss you when we're separated." A new light filled his gaze and he stepped out of the way. "Come in and tell me all about it. A dragon census has to be a pretty amazing thing to see."

"You have no idea." She entered the house. "But it's a long story," she warned him.

"That's all right," he said as he closed the door. "Start with that big surge of power I felt yesterday."

She sucked in a breath. "You felt that?"

"You had my ring on. Hard not to."

"Oh. Right." She twisted it off her finger and handed it to him. "Thanks for that. About the power...I really should start at the beginning. But first, are you mad I used my power?"

"Mad?" He squinted at her. "Why would I be mad? You're an adult capable of making your own decisions. If you felt it was warranted, then it must have been."

She exhaled, then hugged him. "Thanks, Dad. I've had the worst feeling of dread like I did something to upset you." She shook her head. "It all came from a dream, which I know is dumb, but I couldn't get rid of the feeling."

He put his hands on his shoulders. "Using a power like ours has side-effects. It will not only drain you physically, but mentally and emotionally as well. It takes time to recover, and if you don't, that exhaustion can seep into your life in ways you least expect it to. Bad dreams are just one of those ways."

"Really? So my dream was just a symptom of not enough recovery time?"

He nodded. "Most likely, yes. It's my fault for not explaining that more. You've just never seemed that interested in using your abilities, so I guess I thought I had time."

"I'm so relieved. In fact, just hearing that explanation has made me feel better."

"You probably need some good sleep and a day or two of doing nothing. As hard as that might be for a busy woman like yourself."

She shrugged, giving him a smile. "The crew at Black

Horse has handled things just fine while I was gone. I'm sure they can manage one more day without me."

"Good." He put his arm around her and together they started to walk toward the living room. "Now, once again, tell me all about your trip."

Chapter Forty

"I feel like I'm going to throw up." Charlie swallowed as he straightened his tie in Nasha's living room mirror. "I'm not, don't worry, but my stomach is in knots. Going up against the council didn't make me this nervous."

Nasha smiled indulgently. "Honey, I told you, my dad is looking forward to meeting you very much."

"That's what's got me worried." Charlie blew out a breath. Having the dinner party at Nasha's was helpful. At least her father wouldn't be judging Charlie *and* his home. "What if I don't live up to the hype?"

She snorted. "Okay, get a grip. He already likes you. I swear. I told him all about you."

"Did you tell him I like to do this to you?" Charlie grabbed her and nuzzled the side of her neck, planting a kiss right below her ear.

That made her squeal, which in turn, made him laugh and instantly feel better. At least for a few moments.

She swatted his arm. "No, I did not. Now behave yourself or I will."

He laughed and kissed her again, just because he felt like it.

Her First Taste Of Fire

Laz came out of the kitchen. "You two better cool it or we're not going to make it through dinner. You're not the only one nervous about meeting Nasha's dad, Charlie. He's one of the Four Horsemen. How could we not be nervous?"

"I'm not nervous," Marissa called from deeper in the kitchen. "But I'm not trying to marry his daughter, either."

Laz rolled his eyes. "Women."

"I heard that," Marissa said.

Laz grinned. "I'd better go see if Henry needs any help grilling those steaks. I already know Marissa doesn't need help."

As he disappeared, Nasha smiled at Charlie. "It was really nice of them to make dinner. Seeing as how I can't taste anything, it was probably the smart thing to do."

"It was nice, wasn't it? I'm glad they came back with us." Charlie also figured Nasha's dad might be less inclined to turn down Charlie's request to marry his daughter in the presence of other people. Maybe. At the very least, it was comforting to have friends around him.

"Me, too. They seem to like the town pretty well, don't you think? I know they've only been here two days, but still."

"No, they do. Laz and Henry are already looking for places to live. And I've told all of them they're welcome to pick up a shift or two at my shop. I've been showing them the ropes, just to give them an idea of what they'd have to do."

Hopefully that would explain why he'd been spending so much time at the shop despite having guests. Nasha hadn't asked. Maybe because she'd gone back to work herself.

"I think that's awesome of you. And I'm happy to have Marissa stay with me for as long as she wants. It's nice to have the company."

He smiled. "It's only been two days. You might feel differently in a month."

"Maybe. But right now, we're having a lot of fun. We're doing a lot of girl stuff that no one wanted to do with me in high school."

"So watching rom-coms, eating the chocolate I've been bringing you, and talking about boys?"

She laughed hard. "How do you know that?"

"I have two sisters, remember?" Sisters who'd unexpectedly reached out to him via text. It wasn't much, but it was a start, and he was optimistic things would get better. At least with them.

The doorbell rang and the pit in his stomach opened up again, erasing his smile and reminding him that he was about to meet an incredibly powerful man. Who might someday soon become his father-in-law. If all went well.

"That must be him." Nasha went to the door and opened it. "Hi, Dad."

"Hi." He held out a bottle of wine. "I hope this goes with dinner."

"I'm sure it'll be great." She stood back to let him in.

Her First Taste Of Fire

"Dad, this is Charlie. Charlie, this is my father, Harold Black."

"Hello, Mr. Black." The man was tall and slim to the point of boniness. An air of darkness clung to him that made Nasha seem like a bright and shining light. Charlie knew the kind of magic the man possessed, but he hadn't expected Nasha's father to look like the embodiment of that murkiness.

"Call me Hal." He stuck out his hand.

"Hal, then." Charlie had a split-second of hesitation before he quickly shook the man's hand. It didn't feel bony. It felt like shaking the hand of just about anyone. Was the way Hal looked just an illusion? "It's good to meet you."

"You, too." Hal said. He smiled at Nasha and suddenly looked so much more human. "My daughter has said so many nice things about you I was beginning to think you weren't real. And your chocolates have been life changing. As I'm sure you well know."

"I do know and I'm very glad." Charlie grinned. "Also, I promise, I'm real. And I hope I can live up to all of those things she's said about me."

"Don't worry," Hal said. "I'll only hold you to a couple of them."

"Come on in," Nasha said. "I'll introduce you to the rest of my new friends."

While Nasha did that, Charlie watched the older man. Other than how he looked and the amount of power Charlie knew the man possessed, there wasn't anything else about him that seemed sinister or frightening.

Well. Besides the fact that he was Nasha's father and Charlie really wanted the man to approve of his intentions.

When they sat down to dinner, the conversation was lively and entertaining, mostly with them telling stories about their time at the census. Hal kept up, asking questions, laughing along with them, and showing how well he'd paid attention to everything Nasha had told him earlier.

They had a few laughs about Nasha and Charlie's fake engagement, too, something he and Nasha had only just confessed to Laz, Henry, and Marissa.

As the meal wound down to coffee and dessert, which was a cake that Nasha had provided from her bakery and a large tray of Charlie's chocolates, Charlie's nerves returned.

With good reason. He was about to make his intentions toward Nasha very clear. He stood up and smiled at her. "Be right back."

He went out to his car, thankful the cool weather meant his special gift for her was just fine in the back of his SUV, and got the crate.

He carried it in and brought it to her, setting it down on the edge of the table. "This is for you."

She got up from her seat, smiling. "What is it?"

"Open it and find out."

Her First Taste Of Fire

She bit her lip as she checked out the crate. "I'm not sure I can without a crowbar."

"The lid's not nailed down like most of them. You can lift it right off."

"Okay." Grinning, she took off the lid, pushed aside the shredded paper, and lifted out the egg by the top of the cellophane wrapper. The iridescent black coloring he'd used on it made it gleam like an exotic pearl under the dining room lights. Her smile widened. "I knew it was an egg. It's really beautiful."

"Filled with more chocolates in dark, intense flavors."

She ran her finger across the cellophane. "I can't wait to try them all. The color is very dragon-like. And you know how I love my black."

"I chose that black especially for you. It's not just any egg," he said. "It's a tribute to you."

"Really?" Her brows shot up.

He nodded. "Yes. I call it the Dragonslayer."

She laughed. "You think I'm a dragonslayer?"

"After what you did at the census? You're the most fearless woman I know. You changed my life, Nasha. And I don't ever want to be without you again."

He looked at Hal. "With your blessing, I would very much like to marry your daughter."

Hal stared back, then a slow smile spread across his face. "If Nasha is happy, which I have seen for myself that she is, that's all I need. You have my blessing. And anything else you both need to make your new life together complete."

"Thank you." Charlie dug into his pocket and pulled out the ring she'd once worn to fool everyone into believing they were a couple. He'd almost put it in the egg, but if Nasha's dad had disapproved of their relationship, that would have been awkward.

Holding the ring out, he got down on one knee. "What do you say, Nasha? Will you marry me? For real this time?"

She put her hand to mouth. "This shouldn't make me emotional. After all, we've been engaged before—"

That made everyone laugh, although Marissa looked just as happily tearful as Nasha.

His fiancée continued, "But I'm all weepy just the same. I love you, Charlie. I can't believe I found a man who loves all of me."

"I *adore* all of you." And he was so grateful that he'd found a woman who didn't care about his curse.

"Yes, I will marry you." Then she let out a little laugh. "I would have said yes even without the chocolate."

He got up, slipped the ring onto her finger, then pulled her into his arms. "Really? Even without the chocolate?"

She lifted one shoulder. "Well...I do like the sound of for better or worse and all the chocolate you can eat."

He started laughing. "Of course you do. And I wouldn't have it any other way."

PARANORMAL WOMEN'S FICTION

First Fangs Club Series:

Sucks To Be Me

Suck It Up Buttercup

Sucker Punch

The Suck Stops Here

COZY MYSTERY:

Jayne Frost Series:

Miss Frost Solves A Cold Case: A Nocturne Falls Mystery

Miss Frost Ices The Imp: A Nocturne Falls Mystery

Miss Frost Saves The Sandman: A Nocturne Falls Mystery

Miss Frost Cracks A Caper: A Nocturne Falls Mystery

When Birdie Babysat Spider: A Jayne Frost Short

Miss Frost Braves The Blizzard: A Nocturne Falls Mystery

Miss Frost Says I Do: A Nocturne Falls Mystery

HappilyEverlasting Series:

Witchful Thinking

PARANORMAL ROMANCE

Nocturne Falls Series:

The Vampire's Mail Order Bride

The Werewolf Meets His Match

The Gargoyle Gets His Girl

The Professor Woos The Witch

The Witch's Halloween Hero – short story

The Werewolf's Christmas Wish – short story

The Vampire's Fake Fiancée

The Vampire's Valentine Surprise – short story

The Shifter Romances The Writer

The Vampire's True Love Trials – short story

The Vampire's Accidental Wife

The Reaper Rescues The Genie

The Detective Wins The Witch

The Vampire's Priceless Treasure

The Werewolf Dates The Deputy

The Siren Saves The Billionaire

Shadowvale Series:

The Trouble With Witches

The Vampire's Cursed Kiss

The Forgettable Miss French

Moody And The Beast

Sin City Collectors Series

Queen Of Hearts

Dead Man's Hand

Double or Nothing

Standalone Paranormal Romance:

Dark Kiss of the Reaper

Heart of Fire

Recipe for Magic

Miss Bramble and the Leviathan

All Fired Up

URBAN FANTASY

The House of Comarré series:

Forbidden Blood

Blood Rights

Flesh and Blood

Bad Blood

Out For Blood

Last Blood

The Crescent City series:

House of the Rising Sun

City of Eternal Night

Garden of Dreams and Desires

Want to be up to date on all books & release dates by Kristen Painter? Sign-up for my newsletter on my website, www.kristenpainter.com. No spam, just news (sales, freebies, and releases.)

∽

If you loved the book and want to help the series grow, tell a friend about the book and take time to leave a review!

Nothing is completed without an amazing team.

Many thanks to:

Cover design: Cover design and composite cover art by Janet Holmes using images from Shutterstock.com & Depositphotos.com.
Interior formatting: Gem Promotions
Editor/Copyedits: Raina James

Made in United States
Orlando, FL
17 August 2024